DARK OBSESSION

CHARLI CROSS SERIES: BOOK SIX

MARY STONE

DONNA BERDEL

Copyright © 2022 by Mary Stone

All rights reserved.

No part of this book may be reproduced in any form or by any electronic or mechanical means, including information storage and retrieval systems, without written permission from the author, except for the use of brief quotations in a book review.

❦ Created with Vellum

DESCRIPTION

When love turns into obsession, the result is deadly.

Being sidelined after her last assignment has allowed Savannah Detective Charli Cross too much time to think. So when she's called to a new murder case, she's relieved to trade her preoccupation over the threatening letters she's received for a double homicide investigation.

Her relief doesn't last long.

Nothing could have prepared Charli for the gruesome scene she and her partner find at a local park. A teenage couple have been slain, their throats slit and their naked bodies posed on a blanket. The motive remains unclear...until they discover one of the victims had a stalker.

Case closed?

Maybe not.

When another couple—this one newly engaged—is brutally murdered, Charli knows that not all is as it seems. But if their suspect isn't their killer, then who is targeting young lovers? And why?

And more importantly, can she catch this maniac before they strike again?

Puzzling and engrossing, Dark Obsession is the sixth book in the Charli Cross Series from bestselling author Mary Stone—guaranteed to make you believe that happily ever after is only a fairytale.

This book is dedicated to those who have ever or still suffer the sometimes agonizing pain of a broken heart.

1

Nicole Schott sat on the narrow park bench as the sun slid below the horizon. The moment it disappeared, the air around her grew colder, as though all the warmth had been sucked from the world along with the light. With a shiver, she wrapped her arms around herself, wishing she'd opted to wear a sweater instead of the little black dress with the sweetheart neckline and cap sleeves she'd been so excited to show off.

Although it was her go-to dress for special occasions, she felt a little silly wearing it now. Was wanting to look good for Mason worth it? For him, she'd donned the black heels normally reserved for church. She'd also spritzed perfume on her pulse points and applied heavy makeup, something she didn't usually wear to church.

Nicole had spent half an hour trying to get the eyeshadow and liner just right. Something about Mason made her want to step out of the ordinary. He made her feel alive and sexy. Protected. Grown-up, even, since he was nearly eighteen years old.

Where was he?

She cast an anxious glance around, rubbing her goose-pimpled flesh. Meeting in the park wasn't her first choice, especially after dark, and she'd much rather be somewhere safe and warm, preferably having a nice spaghetti dinner. Maybe some garlic bread with—

A hand landed on her shoulder. With a throat-shredding shriek, Nicole whipped around, nearly falling off the bench. With a jolt of adrenaline, she was ready to bolt as fast and as far as her legs would take her.

"Whoa, there!"

The familiar voice didn't soothe her. And the light laugh that followed was like gasoline being thrown onto a flame.

Furious to her core, Nicole jumped to her feet, glared up into Mason's handsome eyes, and poked a finger into his chest. "You scared me to death! Don't ever sneak up on me again."

"I'll try to remember that." Mason's chuckle didn't hold the slightest bit of repentance.

Her heart still hammered in her chest. But as he pulled her back onto the bench beside him, it changed rhythm.

Does he know how much I love him?

He tucked a lock of her auburn hair behind her ear. "Why so jumpy, beautiful?"

She punched him in the shoulder and nearly cried out when her knuckles connected with the steel of his arm beneath his letterman jacket. As quarterback of their high school's football team, he had an amazing body.

Go, Lions.

She was too pissed to be distracted, though. "You're late. And you shouldn't terrify me like that."

Mason's handsome face turned serious as he leaned in closer. "I didn't mean to scare you."

Leaves rustled, and she jerked around to see what had

caused the noise. Her imagination, most likely. Or the wind. Still, she was chilled to her core.

"I don't like being here. Why can't you take me out to dinner for a normal date? It's getting late."

He linked their fingers together, shooting her a smile that showed his dimples. "Let me guess, you're daydreaming of Angelo's spaghetti."

She moaned just thinking about it. "And garlic bread. Don't forget the garlic bread."

All the butter and parmesan cheese the restaurant piled on every delectable slice was to die for. Her stomach gave a low rumble.

"How could I forget the best part of the meal?" He squeezed her hand. "I promise we'll go to Angelo's later, but I wanted a little alone time with my girl first."

Nicole's heart slammed against her ribs for a second time that night. This time, she didn't know what fueled the adrenaline coursing through her veins—her nerves or the anticipation of spending time alone with Mason. "Oh, really?" A slow grin spread across her face. "Who is she?"

He rolled his eyes. "What happened to the quiet, shy girl I knew?"

"I heard she got a totally hot boyfriend."

Mason smiled and moved closer. The warmth from his body radiated off his skin, and Nicole's cheeks flushed as her blood sang with liquid fire. He leaned in, his breath minty, as his lips moved toward hers.

She placed a hand on his chest. "And that he takes her out to dinner."

He sighed and sat back. "Do you want to go to dinner first and then come back here?"

It's not that I don't love being alone with you. This place just gives me the creeps.

"No. I don't want to come back here after we leave."

"Then just thirty minutes." His voice was pleading. "How about that?"

God. How could she ever tell him no? "Ten."

She loved kissing him. Truthfully, she could kiss him all night, spaghetti and garlic bread be damned. Only—

Her gaze probed the darkness around them. She didn't like being out like this, isolated after dark. Maybe it had something to do with all the people who'd been killed recently, because she didn't remember always feeling this way, even six months ago. Or maybe it was because of the cold she'd felt earlier, seeping into her bones as the sunset deepened.

In the distance, the bushes rustled, and she jumped again. It was just the wind, but she still didn't like the uneasiness that wrapped around her like an itchy wool blanket. Something was…not right.

Mason gave her a coaxing smile. "Twenty."

Nicole focused on him, accepting his counteroffer. Twenty minutes in the park. She was with her big, strong boyfriend. What could happen? It wasn't even that late.

Mason picked up a blanket he'd dropped on the bench and grabbed her hand. Together, they headed into the woods. Nicole took measured steps, struggling not to let her high heels sink into the ground. She didn't want to have to clean them later. And if her mom saw them, she'd ask a bunch of embarrassing questions.

"Where are you taking me?"

He lifted her fingers to his lips. "Somewhere private."

When they reached a small clearing, he unfurled the blanket, letting the soft material float onto the ground like a velvet dream. He sat down and raised his hand. She took it, allowing him to tug her on top of him.

He lowered her onto the blanket before stretching out by her side, and Nicole twisted so she could face him. As his body pressed against hers, her breath caught in her throat.

He pushed another stray lock of her hair back out of her eyes. "You are so beautiful." His voice was a whisper, his warm breath tickling her skin.

She stared into his bright blue eyes and lifted a hand to his short, curly blond hair, loving the feel of it twisting around her fingers. "So are you."

Mason lowered his head to kiss her, his lips soft and gentle.

She closed her eyes and kissed him back, letting the world wash away. This was where she wanted to be—in his arms—away from life and the pain that came from missing her father. Mason caressed her through the silky fabric of her dress, his hands gently massaging her breasts.

His kisses grew harder, more passionate. After another minute, he rolled on top of her. She reveled in the sensation of being pinned down by his body, all of him melting into her.

"I love you so much."

She smiled against his lips. "I love you too."

The skin on her knee tingled as his hand caressed it, and Mason eased his hand up her leg. She reached down and pinned his hand with hers when he reached mid-thigh.

He groaned, deep and sexy in his throat. "I know. I just want you so—"

Crunch.

Terror pulsed through Nicole as she pushed Mason off her and sat up like a jack-in-the-box. "There's something there!"

"It's just the wind."

He kissed her throat, trying to pull her back down onto the blanket.

She shook off his arm and stood. Peering into the darkness, she called out, her voice shaking. "Is there someone there?"

Mason's groan was less sexy this time. "Nicky, it's probably just a squirrel."

He was wrong. Deep in her gut, she knew that.

Taking a couple of steps away from Mason, Nicole swept the darkness, wishing there was more light in the area. In the few minutes she'd been distracted, the night had grown complete. "I don't care. I want to get out of here."

Mason grabbed her hand. "Come on. It hasn't been twenty minutes yet."

Did he seriously not comprehend the danger they were in? "Well, it's been long enough. Let's leave."

Something wasn't right. Nicole sensed it to the depths of her being.

A million tiny hairs prickled on the back of her neck, and the chill that had ceased while in Mason's arms came back with a vengeance. Nicole made up her mind that she was leaving, and she really, really wanted Mason to go with her.

She turned toward the edge of the park. She could see the street through the trees. He could catch up if she decided to go now. Maybe that would make him realize she was serious.

"Come on, five more minutes and we can go." Despite Mason's coaxing voice, which normally made her melt, Nicole refused to be swayed.

"No, I'm going."

Nicole started walking, less worried about the high heels sinking into the ground, until she almost tripped as one sank in too deep and wouldn't dislodge without a tug.

A muffled sound came from behind her. Nicole froze.

Don't look. Don't look. Don't look.

A bead of sweat rolled down her back as tears stung her eyes.

Keep moving!

A small cry from behind her forced her head around, like she was a puppet and someone was pulling her strings. "M-Mason?"

In the darkness, Nicole fumbled for her cell phone and turned on the flashlight, illuminating the scene.

Bile rose in her throat.

Mason was on his knees, an arm wrapped around his head as a hooded figure restrained him from behind. Something silver glinted in the light.

Was that a...knife?

The silvery object descended toward Mason.

Terror rose in Nicole's chest. She opened her mouth to scream but no sound could escape through the tightness of her throat. She stood there, rooted to the spot, as the hooded figure sliced the blade across Mason's throat.

A crimson river of blood gushed out.

"No!" The scream that had been stuck erupted as she regained the ability to move. She turned and ran, abandoning her shoes for the sake of speed.

Her bare toe jammed into something hard, and pain seared through her leg to her knee. She propelled herself forward despite the pain.

Must. Keep. Moving. Almost to safety.

If she could get out of the woods and onto the grass of the park, she could pick up speed and run to the road. Surely, someone would see her then.

Just as she reached the edge of the tree line, something hit her in the middle of her back. Nicole pitched forward. But, before she could catch herself, her face was buried in the grass, her wrists screaming in agony from the fall.

"Hel—"

Her cry was cut off when a body landed on top of her and hands clawed at her throat. She bucked, trying to throw her attacker off.

"Who do you think you are? Juliet to his Romeo?"

She twisted her head to the side so she could breathe. Tears flooded her eyes as she clawed at the grass, trying to get away. "Please...w-why? We did n-nothing...wrong!"

Nicole knew she was begging. Maybe it wouldn't work, but there had to be something she could say that would make her attacker let her go. She had to try.

"Yes, you did!" The voice was angry, and hot spittle hit her cheek.

"Juliet w-was innocent...l-like me." It was a stupid thing to say, but maybe it would make him see reason.

It didn't.

"Juliet deserved to die, and so do you."

Who could hate her like this? She tried to be nice to everyone.

"W-why?"

"You fell in love with him." He straddled her back, knees pinning her arms. "You weren't supposed to do that. Didn't you know it was doomed from the beginning?" His tone was angry, but seemed to have a heavy dose of sadness and fear mixed in.

"P-please, I don't understand."

"If I don't get a happy ending, no one does."

Trapped under his weight, Nicole struggled to take in a gasping breath. "B-but...you c-can. There's...always h-hope."

She was babbling, but she had to keep him talking as she fought to get away. Pinned as they were, her hands still searched for something, anything, to use for a weapon.

Where is the rock I tripped on?

Her attacker's foul breath assaulted her cheek. "So many people think they deserve a fairy tale, a romantic comedy. But if I don't, then why should all the rest of you be that lucky? You know what happened to Juliet, don't you?"

"What?" Of course she knew, but she was stalling for

time. She couldn't scream anymore, the weight of his body compressing her lungs, her voice coming out as little more than a whisper. Maybe someone would come by, see what was happening. Help.

Fighting for every breath, Nicole sucked in as much air as she could. But it wasn't enough. "Same thing…happened to Romeo."

With a growl, the man pushed to his feet. She'd barely taken a full breath before he grabbed her hair, yanking her up.

"What are you—?" White-hot fire seared her throat before she could finish the question. The words died in her mouth, as did the scream she attempted to force out.

She clutched at her neck, touching a warm substance. Blood. Her blood.

Frozen to the spot, she stared at her hands and attempted to inhale. A hiss filled the air as her attacker stepped around her and came into view. The hood had fallen, and his cold eyes glittered.

You? No. Why?

Despair flooded through her body. How could he, who constantly talked about love, have done this to her? Why? What had happened to all his powerful words, to everything he said he believed?

In slow motion, she sank to her knees, the ground rushing up to meet her. She landed on a blanket of dark, glistening green. Everything around her grew dim.

We should have gone to Angelo's.

Her vision faded altogether, and her mind drifted into a dream. *She and Mason were eating a wonderful spaghetti dinner. His face was serious and a little bit older. With no warning, he got down on one knee and presented her with a ring.*

"Will you marry me?"

"Yes, a thousand times, yes!"

Nicole's wedding day flashed through her mind. Her mother crying. Then there were children, a boy and a girl. She and Mason would name them Ashley and Jordan.

She'd always heard that, in death, a person's life flashed before their eyes, but she'd assumed it was their past. This was much better. The vision was happy and warm and light. A good future to make up for all the terrible events from her past. Mason smiled at her as he walked their daughter down the aisle on her big day. She was loved.

As all the images faded, Nicole exhaled one last time...*garlic bread.*

2

This is more like it.

Savannah Detective Charlotte Cross immediately felt bad for being excited about a new murder case, but the faint jolt of remorse did little to stop her enthusiasm about getting back to work.

She'd spent the past few days on administrative leave. Though she'd passed a bit of that time with friends, most of her hours were filled with endless reams of paperwork. And for what? She wasn't even sure that she was the one who pulled the trigger in what was officially classified as an officer-involved shooting. She'd been fighting their suspect for the gun, after all. But policy was policy, she supposed. She was just glad it was over, and earlier than she'd imagined.

Charli hadn't expected to return to official duty until Monday, but Sunday evening was good enough. Sure, that blew the last part of the weekend, but the self-proclaimed workaholic thought weekends were overrated anyway.

And they allowed her too much time to think.

Not working these last few days had been hell. Diving

straight back into work would take her mind off everything else going on. With all the back-to-back cases and the haunting letters—which she assumed were from her best friend's killer or maybe the mafia—she'd spent too much time alone with her own thoughts. She needed an outside distraction, and this double homicide was it.

"Two teenagers were found in a local park," Sergeant Ruth Morris had told her only moments before. "I've already got Matthew on his way there. When can you leave?"

As glad as Charli was to be back on the job, the brief description Ruth had given her was somewhat disturbing. Savannah, Georgia had seen its share of weird occurrences in the past few weeks, and Charli would have put money on many of its citizens being on edge. She didn't imagine these new murders would help that any.

Her partner was getting out of his shiny black, extended-cab truck as Charli pulled into a parking space at Fountain Park.

Please don't ask me a thousand questions.

She'd had lunch with Matthew a couple days ago, and they'd managed to keep the conversation light, steering clear of discussing the letters she'd received. The terrible messages flashed through her mind.

Ten years and you still haven't found me. Do you give up?

No. She would never stop searching for Madeline's killer.

And to think...if we'd gotten you that day, along with your friend, you wouldn't be worrying about all this. What a heavy burden it must be.

Yes. It *was* a heavy burden. One she would never put down until she caught the bastard who'd killed her friend.

"Dead naked couple in the park. There's never a dull moment."

Matthew's grumble pulled Charli back from the two

notes she'd received about Madeline. As sick as it was, she'd rather talk about murders than think about her friend.

She forced a grin, not wanting him to clue in on what she'd been thinking. "Beats sitting on my butt like I've done the past few days."

He grinned. "Only you would prefer a crime scene to a little vacation."

Matthew knew very well that she hadn't been on vacation.

Officer-involved shootings meant paperwork, investigations, and mandatory counseling. Of course, after all that was out of the way, she'd met Matthew for lunch and had another lunch date with Preston Powell—her GBI agent friend—the day before. And her friend, Rebecca Lawson, had come over two evenings after work. While it hadn't exactly been a vacation, at least she'd managed to relax a bit.

"Well, you know, a few days of not looking at your ugly mug was kind of like a vacation."

"Nice one." He paused, and his expression changed when he spoke again. It was softer, more fatherly. "Seriously, you okay, Charli?"

There was nothing quite as annoying as when Matthew went all big brother protector on her. Charli didn't need it, and they'd had more than one talk about his frustrating tendency. Sure, she had bright blue eyes, a black pixie cut that accentuated them, and she stood all of five feet tall with a petite build. She looked younger than her almost twenty-seven years. This made some people, particularly older males, decide that she needed protecting.

But Matthew knew better. There was nothing helpless about her, and Charli wished he'd stop worrying already. She did enough of that for the both of them.

"I'll live." She winced. That hadn't come out as strong and

self-assured as she'd intended. Instead, it sounded pathetic, at least to her.

Matthew nodded, though. Apparently, her response was good enough. She took the win.

Charli shut her car door and locked it. "What do we know about the victims?"

Matthew shrugged. "To be honest, not much. I was helping Janice with running down partials on a license plate for an investigation."

"Oh, so you were *working* with Janice." Charli made the comment as suggestive as she possibly could, adding a bobbing eyebrow for emphasis.

For a while now, it had been clear to Charli that Detective Janice Piper wanted to be more than just Matthew's fellow detective and drinking buddy. Matthew seemed to be just recently figuring out that their colleague had designs on him, which had made things more than a little awkward at work, and hilarious for Charli.

"Knock it off, Smalls." His voice was a low growl, but his preferred nickname for her belied the gruffness. He did, however, flush at the implication.

Charli rolled her eyes. "Only when you do, Biggs."

Like her, Matthew had more than earned his nickname. He was a tall man with a stalwart build. Ever since his divorce, though, he'd been starting to gain a little around the middle.

As they approached the crime scene, she was glad to see that the entire section of the park had been taped off to preserve evidence and keep spectators out. There were several lookie-loos and reporters on site, curiosity seekers hoping to get a glimpse of a dead body. Charli's mind wandered to all the dead bodies she wished she could unsee.

She could tell from the faces as they passed through the small crowd huddled in the parking lot that many of the onlookers were more afraid than curious. It would take a long time for people to forget the recent spree of seemingly random murders. In the end, it didn't matter if the shootings had been connected. All everyone knew was that a murderer was, once again, walking the streets of Savannah.

She understood their fear all too well. For months after her best friend had been kidnapped right in front of her, Charli hadn't been able to sleep, let alone go for a walk.

"Good afternoon, Detectives." A young officer who looked like he could be in a Cuban boy band waved them over to a bench. He handed Charli the crime scene logbook.

She glanced at his name badge and committed *G. Acosta* to memory. After she and Matthew had signed in, Acosta let them under the tape and pointed them toward the trees where the bodies were discovered.

"We have a young couple. Preliminary identification is that they are likely Nicole Schott and Mason Ballinger, though no IDs were found on either body. Both were reported missing this afternoon by their parents. These two fit the descriptions. Their bodies were discovered an hour ago by a landscaper, Albert Foutley, who is employed by the city. He's over there." The officer motioned to a fifty-something man sitting on another park bench about twenty yards away.

Charli nodded toward Foutley. "Has he been interviewed yet?"

Officer Acosta nodded. "Yes, ma'am. He states that he was picking up some fallen limbs from the tree line when he spotted what appeared to be blood on the grass. He followed the path of the blood and discovered the victims. He immediately left the scene and called 9-1-1."

"Did he touch anything?" Matthew asked.

The young officer's black hair swayed as he shook his head. "He said he didn't. Do you want to interview him too?"

Charli nodded. "After we review the crime scene."

Officer Acosta gave a little salute. "Yes, ma'am."

Charli smiled at the young officer's enthusiasm and remembered the days when she had so much energy. She still loved her job, but the grind had certainly tarnished the shine.

Stepping into the path marked as safe to use by the crime scene techs, she examined the blood the landscaper must have stumbled on.

Matthew pressed a hand to his stomach. "Geesh. That's a ton of blood."

Charli nodded. "It sure is, and it covers such a large section of ground."

Images of how the blood got there flashed through her mind, and she closed them down. She wanted to examine only the facts, not the nightmares her imagination conjured up.

They'd gone about fifteen yards into the woods before coming to the small clearing.

"Christ," Matthew murmured, and Charli didn't need to look at him to know he'd paled. He hated this part of the job.

A young man and woman lay on a blanket, both of their throats slit. They were naked, and their hands were on each other's genitals.

Matthew made a weird gurgling sound in his throat and turned his head. "No way they were just lying like that when they got killed."

Charli was inclined to agree. Fortunately, they didn't need to rely on their opinions. Dr. Randal Soames, the medical examiner with the Georgia Bureau of Investigation, was crouched over the bodies, examining the injuries. Charli was glad to see him. He was the best there was, and she also enjoyed his dry sense of humor.

Soames lifted his head as they approached. "There's the queen of crime scenes. How is your majesty today?"

Queen? Your majesty? What was with the M.E.'s extra cheerful attitude today?

"Fine, and you?"

"I, your humble court doctor, was well until about an hour ago." The smile disappeared as he glanced back at the bodies. "I've seen enough dead kids lately to last me a lifetime."

Matthew took a half-step back. "Tell me about it."

"Since I knew you'd ask, I did a liver temp. Based on my initial calculations, death appears to have been between seven p.m. last night and midnight. The state of rigor mortis confirms this."

Charli knew that kids had a tendency to use places like this as make-out spots. "I'll never understand why anyone would choose a public outdoor location to get down and dirty."

Soames just shrugged. "What can you do?"

"Any signs of sexual assault or contact?" Matthew had his back to the teenagers.

Charli felt sorry for him. She knew that just as teen victims made her flash back to her best friend Madeline's kidnapping and murder, every dead girl made Matthew think of his daughter. Chelsea was living with her mother all the way out in California, far from his watchful eye.

"Not at this time." Soames glanced back at the bodies. "I'll know more after I get them on my table." His phone dinged, and he stripped off his gloves before pulling it from his pocket. "Well, looks like we can confirm that this young man is definitely Mason Ballinger."

Charli peeked at the screen. "How do you know?"

"We ran the victims' fingerprints through the system. It appears Ballinger's parents had completed one of those school programs that urged parents to provide the prints and other relative information in case their child ever went missing."

Or is killed.

"What about the girl?"

Soames shook his head. "She's not in the system, but based on the missing persons report, I'd bet my next paycheck that it's Nicole Schott."

Charli forced herself to walk closer to the bodies. "What else can you tell us now?"

"Cause of death seems obvious, but, again, I'll know with more certainty following the autopsy. As far as I've heard, their clothes haven't shown up."

"What do you mean?" Matthew kept his focus on the medical examiner.

Soames rubbed the back of his neck. "I mean that someone seems to have stolen their clothes."

Why would the killer do that? Was he destroying evidence?

Charli hadn't seen anyone go to that kind of extreme before.

"Why?"

Soames chuckled at her question. "The 'why' is your job. The 'how' is mine. Let me get back to work, and hopefully, I'll come up with something that helps you two."

She squeezed Soames's shoulder. "Thanks."

Soames nodded before returning to his work. Sweat had beaded on Matthew's forehead, which was unnaturally pale. He didn't bother saying anything as they walked away.

That's odd.

Officer Acosta, still present, though a respectful distance away, was shifting his weight from foot to foot like a child who needed to use the bathroom.

Or he has something to say but doesn't want to interrupt us.

Charli nodded at him. "Officer B…Acosta." She'd very

nearly called him "Officer Boy Band," which would have been disrespectful. She was more unsettled by the murders than she wanted to admit. "What else do you have for us?"

Acosta stepped forward and whipped a small notebook out of his pocket, pulling out a page with a flourish and handing it to her. "I have the parents' names and addresses. They've already been informed that we suspect one of the victims is their child."

Matthew closed his eyes. "Thank God."

He'd whispered under his breath, but Charli still caught the words and agreed wholeheartedly with the sentiment. Telling someone that a loved one was dead was hard enough. Even worse was telling them a loved one was murdered. When that loved one was a child…

It wasn't a job she wished on anyone.

The officer also carried a large envelope under his arm. He handed it to Charli. "Copies of the missing persons reports."

"Thank you." Charli gave the young man a small smile before examining the contents.

Acosta rubbed his neatly trimmed mustache. "Is there anything else I can do to help?"

"Yes, we're going to need to widen the search perimeter." Matthew took a step forward. "We need to see if we can find the missing clothes."

The officer flashed them a smile, revealing brilliantly white teeth. "I'll see that it's taken care of."

Charli thanked him and glanced back down at the paper. "Which family do you want to visit first?"

Matthew didn't hesitate. "The boy's."

That suits me just fine. Talking to the mothers of butchered daughters hits too close to home.

Matthew strode toward his pickup. "I'll drive. I'll drop you at your car later."

Charli almost refused—she enjoyed being the one in control of a vehicle—but Matthew was already climbing into his truck.

He was dreading this.

I don't blame him at all.

3

Charli had just finished reading through the missing persons reports and was steeling herself for their interview ith Mason's parents when they stopped in front of a quaint, well-kept gray house with white shutters.

Matthew let out a long breath. "This is going to be ugly."

Even if they didn't know that Mason's parents had already been notified about the discovery, the display on the front porch would have told its own sad story.

A woman, who Charli assumed was Mason's mother, sat on an old-fashioned swing, wailing at the top of her lungs. The presence of the man sitting next to her, arms wrapped around her trembling frame, didn't appear to be comforting her in the least.

His eyes were red and puffy, but it was clear that his own grieving process was put on hold while he attempted to comfort his wife.

"You're right." Charli opened the truck door slowly, giving her a few precious seconds to brace herself. "This is not a good time."

Matthew shot her a sympathetic look. "She was his mother. It'll never be a good time."

Charli hesitated a second longer before hopping from the seat and quietly closing the door. Closer to the house, she hesitated again, this time with her foot on the bottom step of the half dozen that led up to the porch. As the husband shifted his gaze on her, she forced her leaden feet to carry her up. She could tell by the rate at which he was moving that Matthew was as hesitant as she was.

"Hello, sir, I'm Detective Charli Cross, and this is my partner, Detective Matthew Church. We're with the Savannah Police Department."

The man rubbed a shaking hand over his bloodshot, swollen eyes. "I'm Richard Ballinger. This is my wife, Jane. We were told you found a body you all think is our son. Is it true?"

"Yes. We have fingerprint confirmation. We're very sorry for your loss." Charli glanced at Jane. "We know this is a difficult time, but we need to ask you both a few questions. We'll be out of your way as quickly as possible."

The distraught mother straightened her posture, dashing at her eyes with a wad of tissue. "The sooner we get through this, the sooner we'll know what happened and you can put that…monster…in jail."

Charli exchanged a look with Matthew, who gave an almost imperceptible nod. There was a wicker sofa on the porch at a right angle to the swing where they both sat. Charli took out her notebook and pen, ready to take down information she'd use later to refresh herself.

Pen at the ready, Charli began. "When did you discover that Mason was missing?"

Jane sucked in a sharp breath at her son's name. "It was this morning. Mason had gone out last night with Nicole, and he was supposed to spend the night with friends afterward. He was going to come home this morning in time for church."

"But he never came home." Tears welled in Richard's eyes. "We just figured he'd overslept and didn't think too much of it."

"I texted him before church, and when he hadn't responded when we got back home, we started calling his friends and their parents...everyone we could think of." Jane's lower lip trembled. "Mason never made it to his friend's house..."

These poor parents.

"What's the friend's name?"

"Rogan Ortega."

"How long had Mason and Nicole been dating?"

Jane swiped at a tear running down her cheek. "It's been...several months."

"Did Mason tell you his plans for the night?"

Jane dabbed her eyes with a wad of tissues. "Just that they were planning to eat dinner out before heading to Rogan's house. Well, he was dropping Nicole off at home, then meeting Sawyer at Rogan's for a sleepover."

Richard put an arm around his teary wife. "I spoke to Sawyer, and Mason never texted or called him about any change of plans so he didn't go to Rogan's either." Richard choked on tears as he tried to get his last sentence out. "But we spoke to his mom, and he's okay..."

Charli leaned forward. "Has anything like this ever happened before? I mean, did Mason ever change his plans last minute and not tell anyone?"

Matthew seemed more than content to let her take lead on this. That was fine. She could tell that he was watching both parents like a hawk. When something happened to a kid, the parents were always persons of interest until they could be ruled out. Looking at this couple, though, she had a hard time picturing either of them being responsible for what she'd seen at the park.

"No. Mason always let us know his plans when he went out. If something changed, he texted us. He was good like that." Jane's chin quivered. "He knew we didn't mind him going out as long as we knew where he would be in case something happened. And when we hadn't heard from him after church today, I called Nicole's mother. She worked all night and was asleep. When she couldn't find Nicole, that's when we called the police."

Jane leaned back into her husband as a fresh surge of tears rolled down her face.

Richard patted her shoulder several times before squeezing it. He bit his lip, the muscles in his throat working overtime as he struggled to compose himself.

"What is it?" Charli sensed he had something he wanted to say.

"We, uh, we didn't even think to try to use that app to track his phone until the police asked us if we had. I, uh, I keep thinking that if I had just remembered that this morning that…that our baby boy…would still be alive."

Jane began sobbing again, her slender shoulders shaking uncontrollably. "We c-could have saved him."

Richard wrapped both his arms around his wife and wept.

Matthew leaned forward far enough that he could touch Richard on the shoulder. "We don't have all the information yet, but I can tell you, it almost certainly wouldn't have made a difference if you had tried to track him this morning."

Richard grabbed his hand, the muscles in his arm cording. "Thank you. Thank you for telling me that."

For a second, Charli was sure the grieving father was going to come off the swing and wrap her partner in a bear hug.

Matthew gave the man an awkward pat on the shoulder with his free hand.

All the tension left Richard's shoulders for a brief moment, then he leaned into his wife.

He's relieved to know that there wasn't anything he could have done, but he'll still always blame himself.

Charli gave them a few moments to process and recover, vowing to wrap up with them as soon as possible. She could tell by the way their shoulders were slumped that they were both utterly spent. "When was the last time you saw Mason?"

"Breakfast yesterday morning. We were showing houses yesterday. Jane and I own a real estate company. We got home at five and Mason wasn't here. I figured he was with Nicole or playing basketball with his friend, Sawyer, before he met up with her." Richard swiped at his eyes with his sleeve. "We had a business dinner with other real estate agents. We got back at nearly ten and went to bed."

"Where'd you go for dinner?"

Charli relaxed, grateful that Matthew had managed to make the question sound casual.

Richard scrubbed a hand across his face. "The Olde Pink House."

"If you have a receipt for dinner, we'd appreciate it."

Richard nodded and then reached into his pocket and took out his wallet. He pulled out a receipt and handed it to Charli. "I always keep receipts, since it's a business expense."

Matthew flashed the man a sympathetic smile. "We'll be sure to get it back to you when we can."

He shook his head. "It doesn't matter. I mean, really."

Charli flipped to a new page in her notebook. "You mentioned a friend...Sawyer?"

Richard nodded. "Sawyer Liu. They were best friends."

Matthew leaned back on the sofa. "What about other friends?"

Richard shifted uncomfortably. "Not as many as he used to have. He's on the football team…" He swallowed hard. "Was…on the football team. He was very popular. After he and Nicole met, though, he didn't have much time for anyone else. Except Sawyer and Rogan."

"If you could get us Sawyer and Rogan's contact info before we leave, we would appreciate it."

Richard focused his attention back on Charli. "Of course."

She paused a moment before asking the big question. "Can you think of anyone who would have wanted to hurt your son?"

Both parents shook their heads, and Jane twisted her hands in her lap. "He was such a good boy. Everyone liked him."

The answer didn't surprise Charli at all. While friends and family of adult homicide victims could sometimes come up with a list of adversaries who held grudges, most people couldn't conceive of someone wanting to hurt a kid. And if the child did have enemies, the parents didn't always know, or want to know.

Charli made a note before capping her pen. "Do you mind if we take a look at his room?"

Richard didn't even flinch. "Of course you can."

His wife was a different story. She bristled, her entire body going rigid. "Just don't move anything. I want it just like he left it."

Richard recoiled, his eyes widening at his wife's sudden ferocity. "Jane, honey, be reasonable." When Jane turned her glare on her husband, he held up both hands. "Please be careful with his things, Detectives."

Charli nodded as she and Matthew stood. "We certainly will."

Richard seemed like he wanted to stand as well, but his

wife was clinging to him again. "Top of the stairs, second door on the right."

Charli put her notebook in her pocket. "Thank you. We'll see ourselves out when we're finished."

After walking past walls of pictures featuring Mason at every age, Charli peered at the clutter filling the young man's room. Clothes were strewn across a dresser. Papers and books littered a desk in the corner. A nightstand next to the unmade bed held a tiny reading lamp and a giant framed picture of Nicole. Since the frame was covered in pink and purple glitter hearts, Charli guessed it was a gift from her.

"What a mess. Reminds me of my bedroom when I was a kid."

Charli wrinkled her nose. "Your poor mother."

He snorted. "The poor mother of *any* guy *anywhere*."

She doubted that was entirely true, but she didn't bother to contradict him. "Remember, we have to put everything back where we found it."

Matthew let out a long sigh. "This sucks."

She wholeheartedly agreed, wishing she could assign a team to handle it for them. "If there's something in here that can help us in the least way, I want to find it."

"Of course you do, but I draw the line at gym socks and jockstraps."

Charli tried to hide her smile. Matthew was all talk. She knew he was one of the most thorough detectives on the force.

"I'll start with the desk." She pulled on a pair of gloves and steeled herself for whatever she might encounter.

Her search turned up more books, more papers, and a host of pens, pencils, protractors, and other school supplies. In the last drawer she opened, she found a small bottle.

"Look."

Matthew whipped around. "Please tell me you found a note that says *find my killer here*."

Charli wished that was the case but held up the bottle instead. "Nope, but I did find some CBD oil."

"At least it isn't joints."

"Right."

Charli didn't see how it could be connected to the murders, but she resolved to ask the parents about it anyway.

Once finished with the desk, she moved to the closet, surprised at how many clothes were actually on hangers, given the amount already scattered around the room. There were several pairs of sneakers and two pairs of dress shoes. A bin held a variety of balls and other sports equipment, including a battered old catcher's mitt. She checked inside, but there was nothing stashed in it. With great care, Charli replaced everything after having completely emptied the bin.

"Closet's clean. How are you doing?"

"Dresser, bed, and assorted clothes are clean. Just going through the nightstand."

She stood on the desk chair so she could check the top shelf of the closet. There were a few more books with a thick coating of dust. An umbrella and an assortment of hats took up the rest of the space.

Her partner gave a low whistle. "Check this out."

When she stepped down off the chair, Matthew was next to the open drawer of the nightstand, holding a small ring box.

Charli walked over to get a better look. Nestled inside the purple velvet was a silver ring featuring a red, heart-shaped stone topped by a silver crown. The heart was held by two hands.

She recognized it instantly. "It's an Irish Claddagh ring."

Matthew frowned. "Aren't these supposed to mean something special?"

Charli's throat constricted. She tried to keep her face and voice neutral as she replied. "I believe they're given as tokens of love."

Matthew studied the jewelry. "You mean like an engagement ring?"

"More like a promise ring."

Charli turned away as she fought back a wave of emotion. Madeline had a Claddagh ring she'd gotten from a grandparent. She'd always said that she was going to give it to a guy one day, but she'd never gotten the chance.

Memories came flooding back of one of the last days they'd spent at Bonaventure Cemetery, laughing, talking about boys, and what they envisioned their lives would look like when they grew up. Madeline had been crushing on a guy in their class named Donny, who had been a total nerd but also super adorable.

He was one of those guys who had no idea how cute he was. Donny had been too into computers and coding to realize that Madeline—or any other girl—had the hots for him. Madeline had schemed up ways to get his attention. She'd even daydreamed about giving him the Claddagh ring someday, as she'd confided in Charli.

"Charli, you with me?"

Charli gave herself a mental shake. "What?"

"You think he planned on giving this to Nicole?"

Charli didn't answer but turned toward the door as footsteps came down the hall. Moments later, Mason's father was in the doorway. His skin had taken on a sort of grayish tone that Charli associated with the dead.

Richard rubbed his eyes. "I gave Jane some tea, and she fell asleep on the swing. We've had a long day, and she's worn out. I figured I'd let her sleep. I'm feeling pretty useless at the moment, so I came up to see if there's anything I can do to help."

Charli was about to tell him there wasn't, but Matthew held out the ring box. "Can you tell me about this?"

Richard gave a slow nod. "Mason bought that for Nicole. Their six-month anniversary is next week, and he was planning on giving it to her. He said it was a promise ring, that he was promising to marry her someday."

Matthew's eyebrows shot up as he glanced at Charli before turning back to the father. "What were your feelings on the topic?"

She wasn't convinced the ring had any bearing on anything. Clearly, though, Matthew wanted to go somewhere with this. He was probably having another one of his famous oh-so-wrong hunches.

"I'll be honest. They were mixed. Seventeen is awfully young to start making decisions and promises like that. I didn't want to see my son or Nicole get hurt. They were both such good kids."

"Were you aware he had CBD oil in his desk?" Charli had seen a lot worse in rooms she'd searched, but she was curious how the father would react.

Richard nodded. "He had migraines, terrible ones. Sometimes, they'd come on unexpectedly. We didn't like to advertise."

There was one thing that Charli hadn't seen in the room, and that was any kind of computer. "Did Mason have a computer, laptop, or maybe a tablet?"

"He had a school tablet that stayed at school. Other than that, he did everything on his iPhone."

"Okay. Getting back to the ring." Matthew lifted the box in the air to reacquire their attention. He had to be working a hunch like crazy over that thing.

"Yes, well. For me, I had half a dozen different high school and college girlfriends before I met Jane." Richard thrust his hands into his pants pockets. "And I thought every single one of them was 'the one.' Mason is...was... always more like his uncle, my brother. Tommy and his wife have been together since they were fourteen. They never dated anyone else and got married in college. So yeah, I had mixed feelings about the ring, but never about Nicole. She was such a shy girl when Mason first started bringing her to church. It's been wonderful to see how she came out of her shell. I always believed they made a sweet couple."

Charli shifted her feet, trying to get the images of that "sweet" couple lying naked and holding each other's genitalia out of her head.

They finished up a few minutes later, and when they were ready to leave, Richard supplied them with Sawyer and Rogan's addresses, as well as the name and address of the school that both Mason and Nicole attended.

Charli took the paper, thanked him, and went outside. Jane was still on the porch swing with her eyes closed, but a tiny sob escaped her every few seconds. The noises sent a chill down Charli's spine. Was she making those sounds in her sleep, or was she just too exhausted to open her eyes?

As Charli started down the steps, the sensation of being watched made the hairs on the back of her neck stand up. She peered to the left. Two houses down, a tall, gangly boy peeked over a fence. Normally, she wouldn't have paid much attention. She was sure half the neighborhood had been listening to Jane cry.

The boy tilted his head, and she got a better look at his face. His expression gave her pause. There was definitely something odd about him. She finished descending the steps and then turned toward him, but when the boy saw Charli heading his way, he disappeared.

Matthew's hand descended on her shoulder, and she jumped.

With a look of surprise, he surveyed the street as though looking for signs of trouble. "What's wrong?"

Charli stared at the place where she had last seen the boy. "Probably nothing."

So why did her sixth sense tell her otherwise?

4

Charli took a sip from the cup of tea Millie Schott had handed her.

"Are you sure I can't offer you something stronger?"

"No, thank you, ma'am. We're on duty."

Although Charli hadn't wanted the tea, it was clear that Nicole's mother needed to do something, so accepting the beverage seemed like a small kindness.

They were sitting in the cramped apartment that, up until last night, she'd shared with her daughter, Nicole. She was much calmer than Mason's mother had been, but her red, puffy eyes revealed how many tears she'd already shed.

"Detective Church, would you care for some tea?"

"Thank you, ma'am." Matthew accepted the drink, shifting his bulk on a tiny Victorian chair with spindly legs that looked like they might break at any moment.

Charli was reminded of her own unfriendly sofa at home that kept collapsing when she sat on it. Her grandmother had loved that monstrosity, dubbed Priscilla, so she hadn't been able to bring herself to part with the antique…yet. She just hoped that Matthew didn't kill the poor woman's chair. Or vice versa.

Millie sat, her fingers wrapped around a steaming cup. "I suppose you're here to ask me more questions about my Nicole."

"Yes, ma'am." Matthew's voice was respectful.

"Grief is a strange thing. When my husband died, I felt like I was in denial for the longest time. I just couldn't believe it had happened, and I had to keep reminding myself that it was true." She tucked an auburn wave behind her ear. "Now, I honestly feel just sort of in shock. Numb. It's similar in some ways, but this time I know my little girl is dead. But it's like I'm holding it all back. Like there's a dam in my heart, and I'm afraid that when it bursts, I'll be swept away. That must sound strange."

Charli understood. Losing her mom and her best friend had torn her apart but in different ways. She didn't grieve more for one than the other, she supposed, but the grief unfolded itself at separate speeds and intensities. "Everyone experiences grief in a variety of ways, and it can vary from incident to incident. Nothing is strange about how you're feeling."

Millie smiled at them with eyes more vacant than sad. Charli had seen the effects of shock often enough to know this was what the other woman was experiencing. In a way, that shock was so much easier for Matthew and her, making the woman more capable of talking, more lucid than Jane had been. Just because she was coherent, though, didn't mean she'd have more information or clarity than Mason's parents had.

Still, as Millie sipped her tea with shaking hands, Charli felt sorry for the grieving mother.

"Is there someone you can call to be with you?"

"I have a sister down in Fort Lauderdale. I suppose I

should call her." Millie's eyes were glassy as her gaze darted to her phone lying on the coffee table. "I'm not sure why I haven't already."

When the shock wore off, she'd be in bad shape, probably worse than Mrs. Ballinger. "When we finish talking, it would be good if you called her."

"Of course." Millie's response was perfunctory, almost robotic.

Charli took out her notebook. "Now, I know it's going to be hard, but can you think of anyone who might have wanted to hurt your daughter?"

"I've been going over and over it for hours, and I'm quite sure there's no one who would want to hurt my Nicole. She was a good girl. Sweet. My husband died five years ago, and she withdrew into herself. For a long time, I didn't think she'd ever really come out of her shell and face the world again."

Millie took a sip of tea before continuing, her hands still trembling.

"Frankly, I couldn't blame her. The world hadn't exactly been kind to her. To either of us." The widow scanned the tiny apartment. "After the life insurance money ran out, this was all I could afford. We had to give away or sell most of our things. There still isn't room enough in here to hold what little we have. I'm sorry it's so cluttered."

The woman's eyes sparkled with unshed tears.

"It's a very nice home filled with love and memories." Charli did her best to sound reassuring.

Mrs. Schott's lips turned up in the faintest smile. "I work the graveyard shift at the grocery store, stocking shelves. Between my work and her school, my baby and I didn't get to see nearly enough of each other, but we were close. I always wanted something better for her. When Mason Ballinger came around, it was like an answer to that prayer."

Matthew took a slow sip of his tea, his face masking any emotions that swirled inside his head. "How so?"

"He made Nicole laugh. He got her to go to church with him. He took her places. I could tell he genuinely cared about her." Millie gave a soft smile as she reminisced. "And slowly, little by little, she came out of her shell. No, that's not quite right. She came to life. It was like she had been half dead for so long and suddenly she was so lively, so joyful."

Images of Madeline leaped unbidden to Charli's mind, and she struggled to put them aside so she could focus on Nicole, a girl she actually had a shot at getting justice for.

"We're going to need a list of friends, family, anyone she might have known at the church. We'll also need the name and number of your supervisor at work."

Millie frowned, the confusion on her face apparent. "Why do you need this information?" She stared at the two detectives, horror creeping over her face. "Do you think I could have harmed her? My only child?"

Before going into their "it's routine" spiel, Matthew set down the teacup he'd been holding with great care, as if afraid it might break.

Or maybe he's just afraid Mrs. Schott will break.

❋

WHILE MILLIE SCHOTT worked to get the list together for them, Charli and Matthew searched Nicole's room. The bedroom was pristinely clean and organized, in stark contrast to Mason's room. There was, however, a prominent picture of him on her bedside table, just as there had been one of her on his nightstand. Neat rows of books lined cherrywood bookshelves, and photos of Nicole's dad were hung on the walls.

They saved her closet for last. A deep ache had settled in

Charli's bones that had nothing to do with the time of day. A glance at Matthew revealed that he was moving a little more slowly than he should be, indicating that he, too, was battling fatigue. Searching one victim's room was one thing, but two in a single day could take the wind out of anyone's sails.

Fortunately, the work progressed quickly, because there was little to search. Nicole had a limited wardrobe and only four pairs of shoes on a rack. One pair was clearly missing from the middle, and Charli surmised it could be what she was wearing when she was killed...the shoes they hadn't been able to find. They had called in on the drive to the Schott apartment to discover the clothes were still missing and the medical examiner didn't have anything new for them yet.

Charli fished two gloved fingers into the last pocket of a pair of black skinny jeans, the last article of clothing in the closet.

"I don't even know why they bother pretending to give girls pockets when they're not deep enough to do anything with."

Matthew gave a half smile. "My daughter used to complain about that."

"Her and every other woman."

"With girls, it's all about form."

Charli rolled her eyes. "Many of us would choose function first. It must be so much easier to be a guy."

Matthew chuckled. "Tell that to any guy who's ever been hit in the balls with anything harder than a feather."

Charli put a finger to her lips but chuckled in spite of her own warning. The last thing she wanted was for Mrs. Schott to hear them laughing during such a somber time. "What's with that, anyway? I swear, it's like they're magnets for flying balls, any kind of sporting bat or stick, and—"

"Women's feet. Or knees, although I like to think my

couple of encounters with those were purely on accident." Matthew winked.

Charli smirked, enjoying their banter. "That's what your ex-wife let you think."

"Yeah, every time I'm in bed, and don't get kneed in the crotch, I miss that woman." Matthew moved over to glance in the closet. "You're right, not much here, particularly for a teenage girl."

"Given how few clothes she had, her mother might be able to tell what she was wearing last night."

Matthew grimaced in response. "Maybe, but I'm not going to be the one to ask her to paw through her dead daughter's clothes."

The only thing left in the closet was a backpack up on the shelf, out of Charli's reach. It seemed a bit out of place, given that they had already searched a backpack full of books next to Nicole's desk.

"Hey, Smalls, you want to grab it, or should I?"

"Very funny."

Matthew gave her a small, tired smile before reaching up and pulling the backpack down. From the way he maneuvered the bag, it didn't seem to be too heavy.

He set it on the floor and unzipped it. Reaching in, he pulled out a stack of letters. Little hearts decorated one of the envelopes.

Notes from Mason? "Love letters? I thought that was a lost art."

"Me too. Plus, I've yet to meet a football player who could spell well enough to try."

Charli rolled her eyes. "Remind me again what you played in high school?"

"Football. That's why I'm always trying to get you to write all the reports. I'm illiterate."

She punched his shoulder. "Sure."

Matthew held one of the letters, a frown forming on his face.

"What's wrong?"

"This isn't from Mason." He handed it to her as he opened another one. "Neither is this." He wet his lips before reading aloud. "'I stay awake at night and imagine touching you, stroking your hair and your skin. I kiss you in my dreams and then I take you in my arms, sighing as we become one.'"

Charli rubbed her temple. "Shakespeare, he's not."

"No, but he did sign his name. 'Your love forever and always, Jeremiah.'"

She took a second letter. "Who the hell is Jeremiah? Was she dating two guys at the same time? Because this letter is dated two weeks ago."

Getting love letters from a guy other than the one Nicole was supposedly in love with was odd. Although, who was Charli to judge?

She glanced around the room. Nicole wasn't the showy or flamboyant type. In fact, the pristine condition of the room indicated an owner who was concerned with order, logic, and keeping things simple. A three-way love affair was none of those things.

Charli handed the letters back to Matthew. "She didn't seem the type. Plus, it sounds like she and Mason went to school together and spent as much of their free time together as possible. When would she have time to be seeing another guy, even if she had the inclination?"

But still...this was evidence that needed to be followed.

"Fair point."

"How many letters are in there?"

He stuck a hand down inside the bag. "I'd say upward of a hundred."

Charli whistled. Even in college, her super popular roommate hadn't gotten that many letters from all her admirers combined. That many letters from one person could only mean one of two things. Either they were deeply in love, or…

"Nicole might have had a stalker."

"Yeah, but why keep the letters?"

Charli shrugged. "Evidence?"

"You seriously telling me a seventeen-year-old girl thinks that way? Because I'm telling you, a seventeen-year-old boy would keep them as a trophy."

"You were one weird kid, weren't you?"

Matthew grinned. "You have no idea."

It explained so much, actually. They'd take all the letters to the precinct and get help combing through them. They also needed to find out who Jeremiah was.

Matthew returned his letters to the backpack and zipped it up before finishing in Nicole's room. Once they had searched every inch, they headed back to the living room to talk to her mother again.

Millie was drinking some more tea. This time, Charli was certain she detected the smell of rum when she got close. There was a picture of Nicole on the table that hadn't been there before. Charli guessed the grieving mother had been staring at it right before she and Matthew entered the room.

Millie glanced up with tear-stained cheeks. She nodded to a piece of paper on the table next to the picture. "I wrote down as many names and addresses as I could."

"Thank you for your help." Charli scanned the list.

"Did you find anything in her room that was helpful?"

Matthew nodded. "Actually, we found some letters from a person named Jeremiah. Can you tell us who that is?"

Mrs. Schott swiped at a stray tear on her cheek. "Jeremiah Dunn. I haven't heard his name in a long time. He and my Nicole used to be friends. They went to the same elementary school together. They were in different classes, but they saw each other at recess. I took her to quite a few parties at his house. He was always an awkward boy, and they drifted apart when he went to middle school. Honestly, I didn't even know they were still in contact."

Charli handed the list of names to her partner. "It seems he's written her a number of love letters."

Shock passed across Millie's features. "Love letters? Jeremiah? That's ridiculous."

Matthew rubbed the back of his neck. "Nevertheless, it's true."

"Why didn't she tell me? We were so close. She could tell me anything."

"Some things feel more private than others, things we want to keep to ourselves." Charli couldn't stand seeing the pain in Millie's eyes.

Charli didn't understand parents and wished she knew what to say to help. She didn't even see eye to eye with her own father most of the time. Fortunately, Matthew came through.

"Oh, you know how it is. Kids always feel important when they have a secret or two. It doesn't have anything to do with how close you were or how much she loved you."

Millie wiped her eyes with the back of her hand. "Thank you. That's kind of you to say."

Matthew flashed her a sympathetic smile. "It's true."

"Is there anything else I can do to help?"

Millie seemed so lost that Charli couldn't help but be reminded of how Madeline's mom had looked after the shock of her daughter being kidnapped had worn off. And then later…Charli shook herself mentally. She had to stay focused on the case at hand.

"We didn't see any computers or tablets in Nicole's room."

"No. We had a family computer, but it died last year. I haven't been able to afford a new one."

"Okay. Do you happen to know what Nicole was wearing when she met with Mason?"

Millie frowned. "No, I don't, but I can look in her closet. Give me just a minute, please."

"Of course."

When Mrs. Schott returned, she shook her head. "Her black pumps are missing, but none of her other clothes. She sometimes borrows things from my closet. It'll take me a bit longer to go through my stuff." She pressed her fingertips to her temples. "I'm sorry. Everything's foggy right now."

Charli's heart went out to the woman. "That's understandable, Mrs. Schott. Please let us know if you discover what's missing. Thank you for your time. We'll be in touch. And if you think of anything else that might help, no matter how small or seemingly insignificant, please don't hesitate to call."

They'd both given her cards at the beginning of the visit, so there was nothing left to do but mutter a few more sympathetic words and go.

Charli and Matthew had no sooner gotten in the truck than their sergeant called on Matthew's phone. He put Ruth on speaker.

"Where are you?"

"We're just leaving the girl's house. We've already visited the boy's parents. We're going to drop off some letters we found at Nicole's before we head out to see Mason's friend, Sawyer Liu. We're still tracking down his friend Rogan Ortega. He apparently went on a hike this morning and his cell phone is out of service."

"Is the missing kid a suspect?"

Was he? Charli had no idea. "We haven't ruled anyone out yet. We have park rangers searching for him."

"And there's nothing on who might have wanted either of these kids dead?"

Matthew started the truck. "So far, they're good kids, great students, model citizens, yada."

"All that crap parents always think about their kids."

"Basically."

"So what are these letters?"

Charli piped up. "Love letters that a boy named Jeremiah Dunn wrote to Nicole. She had them hidden in her closet."

"Was she seeing him on the side?"

Charli buckled her seat belt. "That's something we'll need to determine."

"All right, get them over here and then get on with that next interview. We need answers fast."

Ruth was clearly in a worse mood than she had been earlier. What was setting her off? Charli just hoped the press wasn't already running with the story. That was the last thing this town needed.

5

As I dragged myself out of bed, my head was killing me, and the sheets were soaked from sweat. I wasn't sure why I'd taken such a long nap. After getting home this afternoon, I was exhausted, physically and mentally, and I did something I almost never did. I'd climbed into bed and slept the day away. My mouth tasted coppery, and I got up, determined to get my teeth brushed to get the horrible taste out of it.

My brain was foggy as I tried to piece the last twenty-four hours together. I recalled spending time on my computer, like always. When I'd gotten up this morning, I'd showered and gotten ready in the guest bathroom. But why?

I squinted as I flipped on the light in the master bath. A quick glance in the mirror showed me what a mess I was.

In the corner of my bathroom mirror was the smiling picture of my girl, the love of my life. She was winking at the camera and laughing. I kept it there to remind me to always take time to look my best. She'd want it that way. I had more pictures in the bedroom, even some in the closet, so I'd remember to be thoughtful when picking out my clothes.

After all, she was always watching, and she would know if I didn't make an effort.

Everything I do is for her. She's my whole world.

The first time I saw her, she was on the playground, swinging on a swing, her hair hanging loose and free around her shoulders. Her laugh was like the sound of little bells. I'd gone up and asked if I could push her to help her go higher.

She'd said yes, and it felt like my whole world both expanded and shrank in that moment. It expanded to encompass love and light and a future where I saw us together, forever. At the same time, it shrank so that only she was important. She was my sole focus. Every action, every breath, every thought was for her and her alone. We were only five at the time, but I knew then that I would always protect her and never, ever let anyone hurt her. She was my girl, and I would never let her go.

Having finished brushing my teeth, I turned, ready to leave the bathroom and return to my bedroom, where I would pick out something to wear for the evening. It was tempting to stay in my pajamas, but my mom had always told me that pajamas during the day were for sick people. I wasn't sick, even though I was very tired.

A red hue caught my attention out of the corner of my eye, and my gaze fell on the combination shower and tub. There was something wrong.

I took a step forward, focusing on a dark streak above the soap holder.

Was it…blood? No, it couldn't be. Goose bumps raced up my arms, and something sick twisted inside my stomach. I must have had a bloody nose, but I couldn't remember. That was strange. With that much blood, wouldn't I have noticed?

I grabbed a sponge and some cleaner from under the sink, since I couldn't just leave the bloody smear there. It would haunt me if I did.

After spraying the tile with the cleaner, I wet the sponge and started scrubbing. Moments later, the stain was gone. The blood was erased, just like my memory of how it came to be.

Unsettled, I glanced at the picture of my girl. It was as though the photo had changed, like she was no longer smiling and waving but was, instead, frowning and pointing. I blinked twice, and the picture returned to normal. I heaved a deep sigh.

"I think I've been working too hard."

Shaking my head, I stumbled out of the bathroom, trying to put the awkwardness behind me. I needed to get dressed, and then it was back to my computer.

I had work to do.

6

Was Charli shutting him out?

Matthew didn't understand her thinking. She'd be fine for a while, and then she'd be giving him the cold shoulder again, treating him like a stranger. It was confusing as hell. He knew from experience, though, that confronting her would get him nowhere.

As he drove them to Sawyer Liu's house, he was trying not to push his partner, no matter how much he wanted her to confide in him. They worked well together and were closer than family. Usually. Right now, he was doing his best to act like he hadn't a care in the world, aside from the two murdered kids, but it was exhausting.

"So who sends a hundred love letters to someone they're not in a relationship with?" Matthew wasn't really curious about Charli's answer. He just wanted her to talk.

She frowned. "I don't know, someone obsessive who wishes they were in a relationship?"

"These love triangles are strange. It's often the other lover who goes nuts and starts killing people."

Charli snorted. "You've been watching too many soap operas."

He worried the steering wheel with his thumb. "Do soaps even exist anymore?"

"How would I know?"

"I'm telling you, I think this Jeremiah is our guy."

"Let me guess. You have a hunch." The sarcasm was thick in her voice.

"Well, what do you know? It's like you actually know me, which is weird." Had he been too snarky with that comment? At a red light, he sneaked a glance at Charli, but she stared straight ahead.

She drummed her fingertips against the dash. "Call Janice Piper."

He almost told her to call Janice herself but caught himself just in time. Janice would answer a call from him faster than she would from Charli.

Janice's voice came on over the truck speakers. "Matthew, what can I do for you?"

"Can you run a name? Jeremiah Dunn. D-U-N-N."

"Of course."

"Thanks. I appreciate it."

Matthew disconnected the call before she could say anything else. Janice had a tendency to ignore his partner when she was around, which might be awkward. Plus, he wasn't in the mood for any teasing.

Charli's stomach growled. "Would you mind going through a drive-through? It's been a long time since I've eaten."

"Sure. Now that you mention it, food sounds amazing."

He wanted to ask her if she was still being watched. During a previous case, he and Charli discovered the mafia had contracted local funeral home employees to help them dispose of the bodies of the people they'd killed.

Once their operation was shut down—at that location, anyway—the mob hadn't been too happy. They threatened the detectives and started following Charli and sending her menacing letters about her friend, Madeline's, death. Matthew had a hunch the notes were from the mafia, at least.

Charli had asked Matthew to back off—he'd been keeping an eye on her—and he had. The problem was, he didn't know if whoever was stalking her had done so as well. But the topic was one Charli really hadn't wanted to discuss.

After picking up some burgers and shakes, they continued on their way. Matthew had long ago mastered the art of eating with one hand while driving with the other. As long as they didn't end up in some sort of high-speed chase, he'd be just fine.

He glanced at Charli, who was cramming fries into her mouth. "I think we should go straight to Jeremiah's. I'm going to call Janice back and see if she's got the address yet. If not, I can call Mrs. Schott. She said she took Nicole to all his birthday parties when they were younger."

Charli swallowed. "No offense to your hunches, but I think we need to stick with the plan and go visit Mason's friends next."

He grumbled under his breath but accepted that.

Matthew sipped on his chocolate shake and glanced at Charli again. She was scowling even as she was chewing.

"Okay, Charli, out with it. What's eating you?"

She swallowed her bite and cut her eyes at him. "Nothing. I'm fine."

"Don't lie to me. I'm a detective, remember?"

Charli huffed. "And I don't need help. I'm a big girl, remember that?"

Why did she have to be so stubborn? "Everybody needs someone to talk to. Lately, you've been playing things close to the vest, and I want to know why."

"This conversation's over."

Seriously, Charli? Just open up, already. "Is it because of the mafia case? Are you still being harassed? Getting letters?"

Charli's shoulders tensed. "I'm fine. I really am."

Looks like I struck a nerve.

"If this is fine, I'd hate to see what your 'not so fine' looks like."

She heaved a big sigh. "Sometimes when you talk about stuff, it makes it more real."

Matthew got that. He gave her shoulder a squeeze. "When you want or need to make it more real, I'm here for you."

"I appreciate that." Charli pointed to a house at the end of the street. "We're here."

Matthew parked in the driveway, and Charli practically bolted from the truck. He caught up with her on the porch a moment before a slim woman with long, dark hair and red-rimmed eyes opened the door.

"Can I help you?"

Matthew made the introductions. "Are you Sawyer Liu's mother?"

The woman smoothed the front of her blouse. "Yes, I am."

Charli gave the woman a sympathetic smile. "We'd like to ask him some questions regarding his friend, Mason."

Tears welled in the woman's eyes. "We heard the awful news. Sawyer was distraught. He and Mason have been best friends all their lives."

In her grief, maybe this woman needed some gentle prodding. "Ma'am, is your son here?"

Mrs. Liu cleared her throat. "No, he went to the gym to shoot some baskets. He does that when he's upset. He doesn't normally go there this late, but it's his way of processing everything. Please, I'd rather you didn't disturb him right now."

The tears in her eyes spilled over, streaming down her cheeks. She made no effort to brush them away.

"We need to speak with him, see if he might know something that could be helpful." Matthew kept his voice as gentle as possible while maintaining an air of authority. "Since Sawyer is a minor, do we have your permission to speak with him?"

"Why?"

"He might be able to tell us something that will help us catch Mason's killer." Charli paused. "We need to catch this person before they can hurt anyone else."

Easy there. We don't know if that's the case.

She had just subtly implied that other kids, that maybe even Sawyer, could be in danger from the killer. They had no way of knowing that at this point. *The murders could be an isolated incident or just the opening salvo in something greater.* Hopefully, talking to Sawyer would help them figure that out.

Mrs. Liu wrapped her arms tightly about herself and hunched her shoulders. "Oh. Oh, I see. Yes, yes. He's at the rec center three blocks away on Grove. It's next to the mini-mart."

Charli scribbled the directions in her notebook before shutting it and flashing the woman a grim smile. "Thank you for your time, Mrs. Liu. We're so sorry for the loss of your son's friend."

※

THE DRIVE to the rec center was filled with heavy silence.

When they arrived, they found that Sawyer was alone, playing basketball at one of the indoor courts. Matthew studied him as the kid took a shot from mid-court that went completely wide.

Matthew strode forward, prepared to take the lead. It was going to be important not to scare the kid or upset him more than he already was, so Matthew planned to try a gentler, more buddy-buddy approach.

"Hey, your name is Sawyer, right?"

The young man turned around. His eyes were glossy, and it was clear that he'd been crying. "Yeah?"

"Your mom said we'd find you here. My name is Matthew Church. I'm a detective. This is my partner, Charli Cross. We're with the Savannah Police Department, and we're working on Mason's case."

Hope blossomed on the young man's face. "You are? How can I help?"

"That's why we're here. We want to ask you some questions."

"Anything you need to know. He was my best friend." Tears rolled down Sawyer's cheeks, and he gave a hasty swipe with his hand. "I just want to find whoever did this and kill them."

Careful what you say, kid.

Matthew gestured toward the bench on the side of the court, and the three of them retreated to it. Sawyer sat on the edge. Matthew understood all too well. The young man was probably on the verge of collapse but still vibrating with rage. It was totally understandable.

Unless that rage was pointed at his best friend for some reason?

It was too early to eliminate any possibility.

If Matthew had been in Sawyer's shoes when he was his age, he would have gone crazy. He would have wanted to rip the perpetrator limb from limb. He couldn't imagine how devastated and helpless the young man must be feeling.

Of course, Charli could. He hazarded a glance at his partner, who was staring at Sawyer, pupils dilated. If he had to guess, Charli was reliving what the teenager was going through now.

He was surrounded by grief and its never-dying echoes, giving the air about them an oppressive quality, thick and smothering.

Stop being ridiculous. It's just the Savannah humidity that's smothering you.

After spending a few minutes putting the young man at ease, Charli got straight to the point. "Where were you last night?"

To Sawyer's credit, he didn't hesitate or look affronted. "I was home with my parents all night. We had pizza and watched some movies. I was supposed to spend the night with a friend. Mason was going to text me when he was on his way to Rogan's after he had dinner with Nicole, but he never did. And he didn't reply to any of my messages. I just figured he was with Nicole and decided to stay home for the night."

That tracked with what Mason's parents had said.

Matthew's heart clenched. He was watching movies, oblivious to his best friend being murdered. *Kid's going to carry that for a while.*

"Did Mason have any enemies?"

Sawyer swiped at a stray tear on his cheek. "Not that I know of. He was a good guy, you know? Just a really good guy."

Matthew peeked at Charli, who was taking notes. "And what about Nicole?"

"He loved her. Like for real." Sawyer gave a wistful smile. "We were out shopping, and he bought her this ring he was going to give her."

The Claddagh ring he'd found in the nightstand.

Matthew exchanged a glance with Charli. "What did Mason's friends think of Nicole?"

"Some guys were a little frustrated that Mason wasn't free to hang all the time, but they still all hung with us at school and after games and stuff."

Matthew nodded. "What about Nicole's friends?"

"I don't think she had any." Sawyer shrugged. "At least, I never met anyone who seemed to really know her before she and Mason met."

Matthew gave Sawyer an encouraging smile. The boy was doing well. "How did they meet?"

"Ms. Greer partnered them together on a history project. By the time they turned it in, they were dating. Nicky was super shy back then. She never used to speak up in class." Sawyer ran a hand through his short, black hair. "Even if you said 'hi' to her, she'd just sort of duck her head and not look at you. She was in my class in elementary school, and she wasn't like that back then. Losing her dad really messed her up, though."

Matthew cast a glance at his partner again. He was thankful she was such a copious notetaker, a task he wasn't too fond of. "Do you know a Jeremiah Dunn?"

Sawyer's face hardened. "That freak? Why?"

Charli looked as startled by Sawyer's vehement response as Matthew felt. "Were Nicole and Jeremiah friends?"

He scoffed, his hands tightening into fists. "Never."

He was that certain?

"Never?"

Sawyer deflated a little, though his face didn't lose its scowl. "Well, yeah, maybe back in elementary school." Sawyer folded his arms against his chest. "But not since then. She wasn't mean to him, but she didn't do anything to encourage him. Still, he'd follow her around like a puppy. At first, I thought it was super pathetic, but then it just got creepy. He was real obsessive and didn't understand anything about boundaries. He'd wait for her sometimes outside the girls' locker room during gym. I mean, who does that?"

Who, indeed?

"Was there any chance they were friends?"

"No, and if he said otherwise, he's a liar!" Sawyer's voice echoed off the rec center walls. "He just wouldn't leave her alone, and he would talk trash about Mason. He was always following them everywhere, taking pictures. Mason kept telling him to stop, and then he finally had to kick his ass. He backed off a bit after that."

Matthew did his best to keep his voice steady and soothing despite this new information. "What happened?"

Sawyer smiled, probably relishing the memory. "We were at the movies. We were in the parking lot, walking to the car, when Jeremiah showed up. He was trying to ask Nicole what she thought of the movie. Mason just turned around and popped him one, right on the nose. Loser dropped. End of story."

Or the beginning of the end for Mason and Nicole.

"When was this?"

The young man paused. "About three weeks ago."

"Do you think Jeremiah could have wanted revenge?"

"I don't know." Sawyer scratched his chin, his eyes widening. "Wait. Do you think *he* did this?"

Matthew gave a nonchalant shrug. "We're just exploring every possibility. Do you know anyone else who might have gotten into a fight or a disagreement with Mason or Nicole recently?"

Sawyer shook his head. "Not that I know of." Tears pooled in his eyes, and he balled his hands into fists.

Matthew felt for the kid, but he just needed him to hang in there a little longer. "Is there anything else you can think of that might help us?"

"No." Sawyer blotted at his eyes with the sleeve of his t-shirt. "I just can't believe he's gone, you know?"

"I know it's hard, but if you think of anything else, please don't hesitate to call."

Matthew handed Sawyer his card, and the boy wrapped his fist tight around it, crushing it into a ball. "I'm going to kill the bastard who did this!" He glanced between Matthew and Charli. "It's not supposed to be like this."

"I know." Charli's soft voice oozed pain and sympathy. The two of them were in a club that Matthew couldn't join. Not that he would ever want to, but it just made it feel like there was even more distance between him and his partner.

"Mason and I had a lot of plans. This was our senior year. Next year, we were going to go to the same college. After college, we were going to go into business together. Now what am I supposed to do?"

The question hung in the air. There was no answer that Matthew could give him, and he raised an eyebrow at Charli.

She cleared her throat. "You're going to live. It won't be easy. Some days, you'll have to take it minute by minute. Then some days, you'll forget, and you'll go to call to tell him something. Then you'll remember, and it will feel like losing him all over again. It's going to suck, no matter what anyone says. But eventually, it will get better. You just have to keep fighting to get there. Mason wouldn't have wanted you to spend your whole life grieving. He'd want you to live, to have a long, good, full life. It'll be hard, but try doing that for yourself and for him."

Leaving the kid in this state was difficult, but they needed to keep moving.

They were almost at the door when Charli spun around. "One more quick question."

Sawyer lifted his head. "Yeah?"

"What movie did you all go see?"

"Our English teacher suggested we go. It was an old

movie they were reshowing."

Charli reached in her pocket for her notebook. "Which one?"

"*Romeo and Juliet.*"

※

TEN MINUTES LATER, they were getting back into Matthew's truck. What Charli had told the kid had been good advice. Matthew just wished Charli would take it herself.

His phone shrilled, and he winced as he checked it. "It's Ruth." He tapped his screen. "Hey, Boss, we're both here."

"What have you found out?"

If possible, Ruth sounded even more tense than she had earlier. That wasn't good. He briefly filled her in.

"Tell me more about this Dunn kid."

"He appeared to be stalking Nicole. In addition to the letters, Mason's friend, Sawyer Liu, said that Jeremiah was following Mason and Nicole around, taking her picture. Apparently, it got so invasive that he and Mason had an altercation."

"Sounds like a potential motive to me."

"That's what I was thinking." Matthew shot Charli a triumphant glance. She just rolled her eyes in return. "We had Janice run his name."

"It came up clean." Ruth seemed disappointed. "He's eighteen. Lives with his dad. His mom died a few years back. Janice got an address, which I'll have her send you."

Matthew frowned. "Why didn't she call me when she knew that?"

"I've been keeping her hopping."

He wasn't sure what that meant, but it just made the tension in Ruth's voice seem all the more ominous. "Okay. We'll go question Jeremiah."

"It's past ten, so you better save it for the morning. I'll have an officer watch his house while you two go home. I want you both rested and ready to go bright and early."

It definitely had been a long day. "Anything we should know?"

"Just that this thing is a powder keg."

Charli snorted. "What hasn't been lately?"

"My point."

Ruth ended the call before Matthew could respond.

He chanced an uneasy glance at Charli. "Is Ruth scaring you a bit today too?"

"I guess." She dug her thumb into her neck muscle. "You were right. There does seem to be more reason to investigate Jeremiah. Letters are one thing, but it sounds like he was stalking her too. And that fight…"

"Thank you. I'm telling you, there's something there."

Charli rolled her head, grimacing as her neck popped. "From what we've learned so far, Jeremiah lost his mom, and Nicole lost her dad. It's possible the shared trauma bonded him to her in some weird way. Maybe that's why he thinks he understands her or that she would want to reciprocate his feelings."

"That would make sense, I guess. He could have just wanted revenge on Mason or to get him out of the way, but then things got out of hand."

Charli snorted. "Stripping them both naked after killing them goes a tad beyond 'out of hand.'"

She wasn't wrong.

"You know what I mean."

"I do." She ran a hand through her pixie cut, causing chunks to stand up straight. "And you're right, there's definitely something up with Ruth. Let's wrap this case before she explodes."

7

Charli hadn't slept well. After tossing and turning for half the night, she finally gave up, got up, showered, made herself an early breakfast, and started going over her notes.

The conversation with Sawyer Liu the day before had rattled her. She understood his pain. Hell, she'd lived his pain. Unlike her, though, he wouldn't have to endure months of waiting and wondering if his friend was alive or dead. The loss happened all at once for him, like ripping off a bandage. Charli envied him that.

When Matthew picked her up and they headed to grab some breakfast, she didn't bother telling him she'd already eaten. Fortunately, he didn't seem in a talkative mood either.

And, as much as I enjoy driving, I have to say that it's nice to have a break.

It was eight on the dot when they showed up at the Dunn house. Phil Dunn, Jeremiah's father, opened their door. After they made their introductions, he gave them a weary look. "What do you want?"

"We're investigating an incident involving one of your son's friends, a girl named Nicole Schott." Matthew's tone was mild.

"Oh, her." Phil shrugged. "Yeah. They're friends."

Most parents would ask a follow-up question at this point —*What happened? Is she okay?*—but Phil Dunn simply shifted from one foot to another, his expression impatient.

When he added nothing else, Charli asked, "Is Jeremiah here?"

Phil snorted. "Of course. He spends most of the time locked in his room, ever since his mother died. Anyway, I'm on my way to work. Feel free to go talk to him."

Charli smiled, hoping it might soften the gruff man. "If we could just ask you two or three quick questions, we would appreciate it."

Phil glanced at his watch, the lines on his face growing deeper. "Okay, I guess."

"Where were you Saturday evening?"

Phil frowned, squinting at some unseen mental calendar. "I was on a date out of town. Went to the Carnation Café on Tybee Island."

Charli pulled out her notebook and jotted that down. "Can anyone confirm that?"

Phil rolled his eyes. "Probably an entire restaurant full of people. I was having dinner with a woman named Grace. Our server was Jacques. He should remember us. Anyway, I'm sorry, I don't know what this is about, but I have to go."

Charli stepped into his path. "I'm sorry. I know you're in a hurry, but we have just a couple more questions. Do you know what Jeremiah was doing at that time?"

"I imagine the same thing he does every night. Sit in his bedroom and work on that damn computer. I should never have let his mother talk me into getting him one of those things so young. Maybe he'd have been playing sports, chasing girls, you know, doing normal stuff. Look, if you want to talk to him, he's in his room. I have to go."

He pushed past them and out the door, leaving it open for them to enter.

"He won't win Father of the Year." Matthew's tone was flat, and it was obvious he wasn't impressed.

"It's funny you should say that. That thought crossed my mind as soon as we started talking to him." Charli brushed her hands together, ready to move on. "Let's go speak to Jeremiah. He's eighteen, so we don't need his dad here anyway."

In the small apartment, the door to the second bedroom was a quarter of an inch ajar, and Charli pushed it open. She recognized the young man immediately.

That's the kid who was staring at me over the fence at the Ballinger house.

The young man was hunched over a computer, his fingers dancing over the keyboard. *Porn or coding?* With most kids, it could be either. Or both.

Charli knocked as she stepped into the room. "Jeremiah Dunn?"

He didn't even look up. The giant headset covering his ears was a good indicator as to why.

Before she could get his attention, her gaze was drawn past him. He had an entire wall dedicated to pictures of Nicole. Some were school pictures, posed and awkward. Others were candids, kids hanging out being kids. The most disturbing ones, though, were those taken from the side or behind where it was clear the subject had no idea she was being photographed. Surrounding the pictures were letters and some of the doodles she had seen on his love letters.

Charli drifted toward it, a bit mesmerized, struggling not to show her intense interest. At a bare minimum, Jeremiah was a stalker. One glance at her partner told her that Matthew was willing to bet that this guy had graduated from stalker to killer.

She tore her gaze away from the photos and walked over to Jeremiah. She wiggled his chair.

His head snapped up and his eyes went wide. He slammed his laptop shut before tugging his headphones off. "Who are you and what are you doing here?"

"What? You don't recognize me?" Charli attempted to look mock offended as she pulled out her badge and introduced them. "You watched us over the Ballingers' fence. What were you doing there?"

His face reddened, and he picked at a pimple on his chin. "I dunno. Just seeing what was going on, I guess."

He was on the offensive, so Charli decided to circle back to that question later, if needed. She smiled. "We heard you and Nicole are friends."

He smiled in return. Good. "Yeah. She's the best."

"How long have you been friends?"

"Forever."

Matthew cleared his throat. "And what about her boyfriend, Mason?"

Uh-huh. Too early for that line of questioning, but Charli kept the smile plastered on her lips.

"That asshole is all wrong for her." A scowl twisted his lips. "One of these days, she's going to figure it out too. He's a bully and a jerk. She's too good for him. She deserves someone better, someone who loves her."

Tell us how you really feel.

"Like you?"

Jeremiah blinked several times. "Yeah."

Charli fixed her gaze on Jeremiah. "What were you doing Saturday night?"

"Saturday?"

"Yes."

Jeremiah opened his mouth and closed it several times before answering the question. "I, uh…I guess I was here."

Matthew took a step forward, his bulk filling the space. "You guess?"

"Sometimes the days all blur together, you know?" The young man thought for a moment. "Yeah, I was definitely here. I was working on my computer."

Charli smiled and tried to keep her voice friendly. "You want to show us what you were working on?"

Jeremiah put a protective hand on his closed laptop. "No, and I think you should leave."

Matthew narrowed his eyes, giving him the stare that had more than once gotten a criminal to crack. "Tell me, Jeremiah, is stalking Nicole a full-time job or just a really intense hobby?"

"I am not a stalker! Nicole is my friend."

"Not for several years, the way we hear it." With his large stature and intense gaze, Matthew could be intimidating, to say the least. If Charli were a criminal, she'd hate to be on his bad side.

"I don't care what stupid people say." Jeremiah crossed his arms over his chest. "They don't know anything."

Matthew had Jeremiah on the defensive now, and Charli let him do his thing as she moved toward the wall, another possibility forming in her mind.

Given how closely Jeremiah seemed to have been watching Nicole, he might know or at least have a clue as to who killed her. That was assuming, of course, he was innocent of the crime.

Still, many people who killed spontaneously didn't clean up a crime scene that well or pose the bodies of their victims.

Charli slid her phone out of her pocket to take a discreet picture of the wall of photos. If nothing else, it could help them get a search warrant.

"Hey, stop! What are you doing? You can't do that!"

"Actually, if we are invited into a home or have a legal right to be there, then we can take pictures of whatever's within our sight."

"You have no right!" Jeremiah jumped up and took a step toward Charli. "It's a violation of my privacy!"

"Yeah, like you violated *her* privacy?" Matthew strode forward, jabbing a finger first toward Jeremiah and then toward the wall of photos.

"I didn't do anything wrong!" Fury was written all over the young man's face. "I have a First Amendment right to take pictures of anyone or anything. And all those pictures were taken in public."

"Oh! Look who amendments up when the shoe is on the other foot." The sarcasm dripped from Matthew's voice.

Jeremiah's face fell. "Wait, is that actually a thing?"

Matthew nodded. "Sure, and since you brought up freedom of speech, why don't you feel free to speak to us about Nicole?"

Charli bit her lip to keep from smiling. "I'm a little bit thirsty. Why don't we go into the living room and maybe get something to drink and speak about this calmly?"

She wasn't really thirsty, but she had a feeling this kid was going to clam up fast if they didn't start to set him at ease. Towering over him in his room because there was no good place to sit was good for scare tactics, but not necessarily for getting someone to open up and share. And, unlike her partner, she wasn't convinced Jeremiah was their killer. She was starting to think he might be able to help them, though.

"Oh, okay."

Given how fast Jeremiah darted to the door, she could tell he was relieved to have them out of his room. He clearly didn't like them near his wall of photographs. And he also didn't want them looking at his computer.

What is this guy hiding?

She'd call Ruth to get a warrant. They had permission to be in the room but that limited their search to anything in plain sight. She wanted to open drawers and peer in closets. Not that she believed she'd find anything that screamed this socially awkward kid had committed the murders.

Matthew, however, was on edge. If he knew this kid had been spying over a fence by Mason Ballinger's yesterday—nowhere near this apartment complex—he'd have cuffed him by now.

They took their seats in the living room while Jeremiah went into the kitchen. Matthew was tracking the kid's every movement, probably waiting for him to grab a knife or make a run for it.

She shook her head.

Jeremiah came back into the room with three sodas and a bowl of chips. At least he knew something about hospitality. He set it all on the coffee table and then hunkered down in the chair closest to the chips. When he grabbed a few, his hand had a slight tremble to it.

"What can you tell us about Nicole?" Charli figured a nice, easy, open-ended question might get him started talking.

"She's super nice." A grin spread across Jeremiah's face. "We've been friends since we were kids."

He's talking about her in the present tense. Doesn't he watch the news? Isn't that why he was spying on the Ballingers?

"How often do you hang out?"

"Often."

"Often, as in once a month, or several times a week?"

Jeremiah shrugged and grabbed some chips before rapid-fire funneling them into his mouth, one after another.

"When was the last time you saw her?"

Jeremiah kept his silence.

She decided to try a different approach. "Can you tell me more about her boyfriend, Mason?"

Jeremiah's face turned bright red, and he spit bits of chips out when he snarled, "He's no good for her! That guy's the worst, just like all those other stupid jocks. One of these days, she's going to see that. I don't know who he thinks he is, trying to date my soulmate."

Charli struggled to control her expression. "Nicole's your soulmate?" She shot a glance at Matthew.

Thankfully, Jeremiah wasn't looking at her partner's scathing expression. "Yes. One day, we're going to get married, and she'll forget all about that stupid jock and other guys like him. He doesn't really love her, you know. He doesn't understand her, but I do. I've loved her since kindergarten, and I'll always keep loving her. We're the ones who deserve to be together. We deserve happiness, don't we?"

From the look on Jeremiah's face, the question wasn't meant to be rhetorical, but Charli had to tread with caution. "I think most people deserve happiness."

Jeremiah narrowed his eyes. "Most people. Sheep. Mason is just one of the crowd. He goes along with whatever his buddies on the football team are doing. He doesn't care who they hurt."

Charli couldn't help but feel a little bit sorry for him. "Have they ever hurt you, Jeremiah?"

He clenched his free hand into a fist and pounded it on the arm of the chair. "Of course they have! That's what bullies do. But Nicole's better than them. Better than all of them. She makes me a better person."

He was still talking about Nicole and Mason in the present tense, as though they were still alive. That either meant he wasn't the killer, or he was clever enough to watch what he said. Given the way he'd nearly spit potato chips all over the coffee table when she mentioned Mason's name, she very much doubted it was the latter.

Jeremiah lurched forward, picked up the bowl of chips, and cradled it against his chest. He took a ragged breath. "I think you need to leave now. I'm not going to ever say anything bad about my Nicole. And if you want to know more about Mason, just look at the company he keeps."

"We need to ask you a few more questions."

He shook his head. "No, no more questions. I'm done talking."

She glanced over at Matthew, who gave her a brief nod. It was time to let Jeremiah know the truth.

Charli spoke in her most soothing tone. "Jeremiah, we need to ask you more about Nicole and Mason."

"No."

Please cooperate. I don't have time for this.

"It's important."

"Why?" Jeremiah slammed the bowl of chips on the coffee table and glared at Charli. "What has he done?"

She held his gaze. "I think you know why."

"No, but I think *you* know why."

"What's that supposed to mean?" Matthew scoffed.

Charli knew what it meant. They'd made eye contact back at Mason's yesterday, however briefly. But Jeremiah's puzzled look told her what she wanted to know. He was anxious, and he didn't like them being there, but she was sure he had no idea why they were.

"Do you enjoy social media? Watch the news?"

Jeremiah wrinkled his nose. "Not really. The first is nothing but people trying to be someone they're not, and the second just causes stress. I code and watch movies and do things I like."

If he was telling the truth, that explained why he hadn't heard of the murders. News of this type of tragedy traveled fast and hard.

Rip the bandage off.

Charli drew in a deep breath. "Nicole and Mason were murdered Saturday night."

Jeremiah stared at her for a full minute. "What?"

"They're dead, Jeremiah."

"What?" Jeremiah tugged at his collar. "What are you saying?"

Matthew leaned forward. "Nicole was killed, and we're trying to figure out who would have wanted her dead."

Charli had never witnessed anyone fold in on themselves so completely as Jeremiah did.

His wail pierced the air, and he rocked back and forth, once again clutching the bowl of chips. The harder he rocked, the more chips spilled over the sides, landing on him and the floor.

Charli put a hand on his shoulder. "Jeremiah, what do you need?"

She didn't ask him if he was okay. She knew the answer to that. Once, not too many years ago, she found out her best friend had been murdered. The only difference was that her and Madeline's friendship had been real. Jeremiah's friendship with Nicole had been in his head. Still, it clearly didn't make the pain less intense.

When Jeremiah didn't answer, she glanced at her partner, in distress.

Matthew stepped out of the room and came back a minute later. "Found his dad's number on the fridge. He isn't answering. I left a message. Hopefully, he'll call back or get himself home as fast as possible."

As detached as the man had been earlier, Charli wasn't sure that he would. She didn't know what made a person so distant. Her own father tried so hard to connect with her, even though they had their differences. Tears sprang to her eyes unbidden, and she knuckled them away.

Jeremiah's grief was raw and primal, and with no one there to act as a buffer, it was overwhelming. At this rate, he'd soon be in shock, if he wasn't already.

"We have to do something."

Matthew called for an ambulance. When he hung up, she threw him a questioning look.

"They're on their way."

"We can't leave him alone in this state." Charli massaged the back of Jeremiah's neck. "I have a feeling he might hurt himself, by accident or on purpose."

Matthew cursed under his breath. "The paramedics can sedate him and take him to the hospital until his father...or someone...can be with him."

Charli flashed a wan smile, knowing her partner had made a good call. She gritted her teeth and tried to keep it together. It was clear there was no way they were going to get any more information out of Jeremiah. All they could do now was watch him until help arrived.

All the chips had been shaken out of the bowl, and Jeremiah peered at the container. "Empty."

Charli nodded, encouraged that he was speaking. "Yes, it is."

"Everything is empty!"

Jeremiah lurched forward out of the chair and slammed his face on the coffee table. He lifted his head up and did it again, his expression a mixture of rage and pain. Before he could do it a third time, Matthew pulled him back away from the table and eased him onto the floor.

Charli went to the kitchen for a towel, relieved Matthew

had called for an ambulance. She could hear the sirens ringing out in the distance.

A minute later, Matthew opened the door and escorted two paramedics inside.

Charli stepped back so they could get to Jeremiah.

Why the hell am I shaking?

She bit the inside of her lip, frustrated that she was letting herself relive her own loss all over again. That, combined with the sinister notes…

"It's okay, Detective. We'll take it from here."

The paramedic who was speaking to her was about Matthew's age. He was tall and muscular and exuded an air of authority that was only accentuated by the dusting of silver in his black hair. His eyes were kind.

She nodded, not trusting her voice.

He regarded her, then Matthew. "Take your partner out of here. We've got this. I'll call after we get him safely to the hospital."

"I appreciate that." Matthew shook the man's hand before grabbing Charli by the elbow and steering her outside. "He's a person of interest in a double homicide case. I'll get someone out to guard him."

The cool, fresh air hit her, and she drew in deep, steadying breaths, which helped to clear her head of the nightmares that had been filling it for the last ten minutes.

Matthew dropped her elbow, and they headed to his truck together. Once inside, he leaned his head back against the headrest.

"Son-of-a…he just went batshit crazy on us."

Charli had seen it before, but she didn't want to talk about it. Not now. Not ever. "You still think he's the killer?"

Matthew was quiet for a solid minute. "I don't know. On one hand, surely nobody's that good an actor. But on the other, that little scene could have been all about guilt."

She knew Matthew had a point, but she didn't think the kid they'd just seen could have taken a knife to the girl he was so crazy about.

But, then again, she'd been wrong before.

8

When they left Jeremiah's house and arrived back at the precinct, Charli could swear she was stepping into a whirlwind. Like magic, Ruth appeared at the top of the stairs, as though she'd been waiting for them.

"You two, with me," she barked.

Charli and Matthew shared a trepidatious glance. The boss had her murder face on, and she meant business.

They followed the sergeant into a conference room. On one end, someone had set up a murder board with information about the victims and what little they had on potential suspects. So far, the only name up there was Jeremiah Dunn.

Even more surprising, his letters to Nicole were scattered all over the table, and half a dozen detectives, including Janice, were combing through them.

Charli gestured at the piles. "Find anything?"

Clark, an older man with graying hair, grunted in disgust. "This is one obsessed kid. Seriously. He should seek help."

Mindy put a hand on her hip. She was a stocky woman with shoulder-length waves and dark brown eyes. "For stalking Nicole Schott or for writing epically bad poetry?"

"Both. And not necessarily in that order."

Janice gave a dramatic sigh. "I was up reading this crap half the night. And now I'm back at it."

Better you than me.

"Thanks for your help, guys. Seriously." As much as Janice irritated her nerves, Charli thanked her lucky stars that she and their colleagues were combing through these letters, freeing her and Matthew to be out in the field.

Ruth stepped across the room. "We're working on getting a formal warrant to search the Dunn residence."

Charli shared a look with Matthew. After what they'd just witnessed, she was pretty sure neither of them believed he was the killer. "I don't think he did it."

The sergeant picked up a handful of the letters, waved them in the air in front of Charli, and then slapped them back on the table. "Excuse me?"

Charli gritted her teeth. "I don't think Jeremiah Dunn should be a suspect, ma'am. At least I'm not to the point where I believe our focus should only be on him."

Ruth's face turned frigid, and she lifted an eyebrow. "One hundred and twenty-seven letters say otherwise."

"Love letters."

"These, plus the pictures at his house," Ruth took a step toward Charli, "and the fact that he was stalking her in public say otherwise. It all adds up to stalker, which is a huge red flag. It's a slippery slope from stalker to killer."

True. But not this kid.

"I know that."

"And it wouldn't take much to send the young man who wrote these over the edge."

"That's true, and normally I would agree with you, but he was devastated when he learned she was dead. I don't think he could have brought himself to hurt her."

"Maybe not, but that doesn't mean we can rule him out.

This whole mess has jealousy written all over it, and this kid is the textbook case for jealousy. People can fake grief when they've got something to hide."

Matthew cleared his throat. "Respectfully, ma'am, you weren't there. You didn't see this kid."

Charli didn't know if Matthew was defending Jeremiah or her, but either way, she was grateful. Ruth was just doing her job and exploring every possible angle. But sometimes, the sergeant had tunnel vision. If Charli didn't know her so well, she'd be intimidated, but in this line of work, thick skin was a requirement. She knew better than to wear her feelings on her sleeve.

Her phone rang, and she glanced down at the screen. Soames. Though ready to accept the call, Charli hesitated. She preferred to speak with him away from the others.

Ruth didn't seem to notice the trill of Charli's phone and kept right on going. "Jeremiah Dunn is a sick young man." She walked over to the murder board and tapped a nail on Jeremiah's name for emphasis. "For now, he is our only serious person of interest. I want you ready to roll as soon as the warrant comes in."

"Yes, ma'am." Matthew moved with Charli toward the door. "Let's get out of here," he whispered.

Charli agreed wholeheartedly and followed him to their office, where she sank into her chair with a sigh. "That didn't go well."

"True. Sarge is wound tight."

Her phone trilled again. There was a text from the medical examiner.

Call me.

"It looks like Soames has something."

Matthew grabbed her arm before she could tap the call button. "Let's get out of here first. I'm hungry. Let's grab some lunch."

"Sure, yeah, I could eat."

Charli slipped her phone inside her pocket. If Matthew didn't want them to call the medical examiner back until they could be sure they were alone, maybe her paranoia was rubbing off on him. Whatever it was, the walls of the room were closing in on her. Getting out and away from everything for a while was probably a good idea.

She was still shaken from witnessing Jeremiah Dunn's violent form of grieving this morning, on top of having to watch Sawyer Liu go through the same thing the night before. It all hit too close to home. Charli just hoped Ruth didn't realize that and try to take her off the case. That would be worse. Kids were dead, and she wanted—needed—to solve their murders for herself and for Madeline. That was how she honored her friend.

Charli made it to the truck half a step before Matthew and slid into the passenger seat, eager to hear what Soames's autopsy had turned up. She waited for Matthew to get in. As soon as her partner started the engine, he nodded. He pulled out of the parking space as she tapped the medical examiner's name, making sure to put the phone on speaker.

Soames picked up, his voice full of mock relief. "And here I thought you weren't taking my calls anymore. It was like being in high school. It felt terrible."

Charli couldn't help but smile. "Come on, Doc, you know you dated the homecoming queen."

"Yeah, but only after she was stripped of her crown for conduct unbecoming a human being."

She laughed out loud, surprising herself. Matthew shot her a quick glance before returning his eyes to the road.

Charli was eager to get down to business. "As much as I hate to ruin the mood, I have a feeling this is more than just a social call."

Soames sighed. "You'd be right."

Charli's heart sank at the M.E.'s words. She closed her eyes. "I'm braced for impact."

"Good." He sighed again. "First off, the victim wasn't sexually assaulted. Rather, I should say, neither victim was."

A small sense of relief washed over Charli. "That's good news."

Nicole and Mason were dead. Whatever happened to them was over...done...but Charli was still glad that they hadn't been harmed and humiliated in that way.

Matthew seemed troubled. "You sure about that?"

"Positive. A lack of DNA evidence precludes any sexual activity involving any orifice. Additionally, there was no penetration of the vagina by the killer...or anyone else ever."

"She was a virgin?"

"Yes."

Charli didn't know why that surprised her so much. Maybe she'd made assumptions and judgments based on the way the bodies were naked and positioned holding each other's genitals. Whatever the cause, she shouldn't have jumped to conclusions so quickly. Letting assumptions get in the way made it easier to see only the evidence that backed a theory and ignore the evidence that didn't.

This was one of the reasons why she didn't always like Matthew's hunches. They gave him tunnel vision. None of them could afford to have that. Not now. Not ever.

"They both died from blood loss caused by their throats being slashed. Their attacker was standing behind each of them and made a sharp cut across the throat. Death would have followed quickly after. I'd say the girl, at least, struggled. There was a clump of hair pulled out."

Charli closed her eyes and imagined how the scene might have unfolded, attempting to understand the sequence of events better. "What conclusions can you draw from that?"

"I believe that Mason was surprised by their attacker and killed first. Nicole struggled and was killed second."

Matthew nodded. "Makes sense."

"The majority of the blood pooled beneath both bodies was Mason's. Nicole's blood was found on the edge of the woods."

That was how Charli had pictured things in her mind.

"You think she was running away?" Sorrow flooded Charli as she pictured the scene in her mind.

"Running to safety. Yes." Soames's voice had gotten soft and serious. "There was an impression in the grass left by a body, but it was too deep to have been from Nicole's weight alone. I believe she saw what happened to Mason, turned to run, and was tackled by her murderer."

Charli could swear she could hear Nicole's frantic cries echoing in her mind.

How must she have felt, watching her boyfriend murdered? Knowing she was next?

Charli shuddered.

"You find anything else?" Matthew's tone was gruff.

"Punctures in the grass that looked like they were from high heels, with one in particular being twice as deep as the rest. The ground was still damp from the rain earlier on Saturday, so it was easy to follow her footsteps. Well, until her pattern changed."

Charli frowned. "What do you mean?"

"Based on the footprints, it's likely that one shoe lodged in the soft ground, so she kicked both off and kept running. That would explain the only other problem I discovered with the body." A tantalizing pause ensued after that announcement.

Charli glanced at Matthew, who just shook his head. "Don't hold out on us."

"Before her death, Nicole had very recently broken the big toe on her right foot."

So the killer came up behind Mason and slashed his throat. Nicole saw, turned, and ran. She lost her high heels, broke her toe on something, then got tackled to the ground by the killer, who then proceeded to yank her up by her hair and slash her throat.

The images unfolded so clearly that Charli could have been watching it play out on a screen.

She cleared her throat. "What happened after he killed her?"

"She was moved and posed next to Mason."

Matthew scowled. "What about their clothes?"

"My money is on the killer removing them postmortem because the victims had streaks of blood on their bodies."

"Was there anything else on the bodies? Fingerprints?" Charli was pretty sure she knew what the answer was. If there had been, Soames would have probably led with that.

"Clean as a whistle. Only thing we found was some clothing fibers on the girl. Nothing distinctive about them on first examination. I'm waiting on analysis to come back. It's possible they could have come from a bulky sweater."

It's too bad Nicole's mom wasn't sure which clothes were missing from her daughter's closet. Although, I'd be willing to guess a bulky sweater wouldn't be top of the list. That's not the kind of thing you wear when sneaking off to make out with your boyfriend while wearing heels.

Of course...what did she know about dating?

Charli let out a long breath. "Thank you, Doc. Anything else?"

"No, but if something else comes up, you'll be the first to know."

9

It felt wrong for Charli to be enjoying something so much when they still had a killer to find and put away. Her eyelashes fluttered as she bit into another piece of buttery, cheesy garlic bread.

"Was I not right?"

Charli chuckled as her partner shoveled a forkful of spaghetti into his mouth.

"Oh, you were right." She paused a second before amending her statement. "About this. You were right about this."

Matthew closed his eyes and groaned as he chewed his mouthful of pasta. "I swear Angelo's has saved my life."

She had no idea how Matthew could still be intelligible with his mouth stuffed full and a spaghetti noodle dangling out of it, but somehow, he was managing. "Do I even want to know?"

"When I was going through my divorce, I ate dinner here many nights. Took the leftovers home for breakfast or lunch. I would have starved to death if it wasn't for this place."

He gave a contented sigh as he finished swallowing and reached for a piece of the cheesy garlic bread.

Although Charli considered swatting his hand away, she decided against it. He had, after all, offered to pay. She could be a big girl and share. "So how come you never told me about this place?"

Matthew twirled another forkful of spaghetti. "Great food. Bad memories."

"Oh."

"Besides, we're usually having to grab something and go."

She had to give him that one. As it was, she felt guilty about taking a break now, but the sergeant had made it clear that she wanted them to be ready to roll as soon as she got the warrant for the Dunn residence. Getting the warrant signed could take several hours, but Ruth was highly motivated, so she might get a judge to sign off on one sooner.

The last thing Charli and Matthew needed was to be in the middle of questioning teachers and school officials at Nicole and Mason's school when they got the order to head out immediately. So they could take a bit longer for lunch today than they normally would. Still, there was no reason why it couldn't be a working lunch.

"Statistically speaking, while knives are used in about ten percent of all homicides nationwide, they're only used for four percent of all the homicides in Georgia."

Matthew tore his gaze away from his plate and raised an eyebrow. "And…?"

"Death by knife is pretty uncommon here."

"Maybe our perp didn't have a gun or didn't want to attract attention by firing it off. It wouldn't have given him enough time to pose them, steal their clothes, and all that."

She shook her head. "Knives are used in a few types of circumstances. These murders didn't take place in a home where a kitchen knife would make a handy weapon. A sociopathic serial killer...someone with no empathy...likes the power play and precision of using a knife."

Matthew took a swig of his soda. "So you think we're looking for Dexter?"

"Very funny."

He leaned forward, lowering his voice. "I thought so. In all seriousness, you think we're looking at another serial killer? I mean, what are the odds?"

"At any given time, they say there're twenty-five to fifty serial killers operating in America, but there's probably more." She didn't tell him that she thought there were probably more considering that serial killings comprised about one percent of all murders.

"We've met our quota."

"I hope you're right." She snatched up the last piece of garlic bread as Matthew was also eyeing it. "That leaves us with a crime of passion."

"Like a jealous rage."

"Yes, but not necessarily."

Matthew rolled his eyes. "The victims were seventeen and may have been killed while making out, which would explain the blanket. What other crime of passion could we be talking about other than jealousy?"

"You think Jeremiah did it?" *Seriously? Ruth and you too?*

He hesitated, swirling his spaghetti around on his fork. "I wasn't sure after his breakdown when we were questioning him, but you know what they say. If the shoe fits..."

Charli sighed. "I get it. He fits the profile, stalker turned killer, jealous rage, blah, blah, blah."

"You don't believe it."

She thought hard. Something was bugging her about the whole idea, and she was struggling to put it into words.

"I don't think he intentionally...maybe not even knowingly...killed Nicole and Mason."

Matthew frowned and waved to the server. The man came over right away. "Could we get some cannoli, please?"

"Of course. I'll have it right out."

As the server left, Matthew turned back to her. "Maybe he followed Nicole, like he always did, saw them getting hot and heavy, freaked out, and killed them? Then what, he blocked it from his mind?"

Charli sighed, knowing she needed to follow every possibility. "It's possible. The mind can do funny things when it's trying to protect a person from trauma."

Matthew narrowed his eyes. "That ever happen to you?"

Shit. She so didn't want to have this conversation.

"What?"

"You ever block something?"

Charli's stomach twisted into a knot, and she drummed her fingers on the table. Of all the things she could talk about, she didn't know why this one upset her so much.

"The day after Madeline was kidnapped."

"What about it?"

"I lost the whole day. People have told me what I did, how I acted, about the extra rounds of interviews with police and even talking to reporters, hoping to get information about Madeline out. I've seen a video of myself doing that. But I don't remember any of it."

Matthew whistled low and gazed at her, his eyes full of sympathy. "That's rough. I'm so sorry, Charli."

"It's okay. It's just...why that day?" Charli released the breath she'd been holding. "Why not the day she was actually kidnapped? I mean, seeing her being taken like that had to have been worse."

Matthew reached out and wrapped his hand around hers, stilling the fingers that had started drumming faster. "Maybe that day, it became more real."

She had never thought about it that way, but he could be

right. After all, the kidnapping itself had always seemed surreal, like something that couldn't have really happened. The day after, she might not have been able to deal with just how real it all was. "My theory doesn't explain the knife, though."

"Why the killer had it with him." Matthew finished her thought. "True, but it's still an interesting one."

"Here we go, two cannoli."

As the server set down the pastries stuffed with creamy filling, Charli's phone chimed. A moment later, so did Matthew's.

He got his phone out faster, frowning down at the device. "Could we get those to go?" Matthew turned toward Charli. "Ruth got the warrant. Uniforms are heading to Dunn's place, and she wants us there when they go in."

❇

Charli wasn't sure exactly what they'd find at the Dunn residence. She didn't know if Jeremiah was still at the hospital or not. And she also wasn't sure if his father would be home yet. Searching someone's house was easier without them there. And it didn't require extra law enforcement to watch the residents as they remained outside.

Two squad cars were parked across the street from the apartment complex when Charli and Matthew arrived. Officer Acosta strode up with a proud smile on his face, and he presented the search warrant to Charli as if it were a sacred scroll.

"Thank you, Officer Acosta."

She glanced down at the warrant and was pleased to note that it had been written broadly, giving them access to not only the apartment but also any vehicles Jeremiah had access to and all computers on the premises.

Charli handed the document to Matthew and strode toward the front door. Best to get things started. The complex was made up of just eight units, with Jeremiah and his father's being the one on the southeast corner on the first floor. As she approached, her stomach tightened in anticipation.

Matthew pounded on the door.

Moments later, Phil Dunn answered.

The man took one look at them and flushed. "What the hell did you do to my son? I had to leave work to pick him up from the hospital. The hospital! They had to give him sedatives. Now I'm supposed to stay here and watch him."

Shit.

"When did Jeremiah last take a sedative?"

Phil frowned. "I'm not sure. Why?"

Because we can't interview him if he's on meds.

Charli handed him the warrant. "Mr. Dunn, we have a warrant to search the premises and any vehicles you have access to."

"What?" The man snatched the paper from her hand and started reading. "I...I need to call an attorney."

He may not be the world's greatest dad, but his concern for his son seems genuine...this time.

"You're free to do so while you and your son wait outside."

A vein in the man's head began to pulsate, and his eyes dilated. "Is this a joke?"

Fear and anger dominated his expression. Although his reaction to the situation was a natural one, Charli didn't want things to escalate.

Matthew took a step forward, drawing himself up to his full height. "No, it's not, sir. We're going to need you to step outside."

Mr. Dunn did as Matthew said, taking several steps out onto his porch and then onto the walkway.

Matthew continued in the same authoritative tone. "Where is your son, presently?"

"In…in his room, sleeping. I mean, he should be, I think."

Charli signaled to Acosta and then stepped inside the apartment. The eager officer followed her in, and she led the way to Jeremiah's room. As she opened the door and stepped inside, Jeremiah was sitting on the edge of his bed, staring into space. He turned his head in slow motion, like it was on a swivel, his gaze wide-eyed.

"You're back." His voice was slurred.

"Yes. Now, I want you to go with this officer. He's going to take you outside to wait for a while."

Charli half-expected Jeremiah to resist that idea, but he stood robotically, allowing Acosta to help him, before taking a jerky step forward. Holding Jeremiah by the elbow to steady him, Acosta led him out of the room. He talked to Jeremiah the whole way out of the apartment.

Maybe he'll put Jeremiah at ease with his chatter.

Charli put on gloves and readied some evidence bags to collect anything they might find, scooping Jeremiah's laptop off the desk and depositing it into a bag. Next, she pulled out his desk drawer and began to rifle through the papers and odds and ends haphazardly crammed inside.

From the other room, there came an assortment of noises as officers spread out in their search.

Matthew strode into the room a minute later, pulling on a pair of gloves. "We have Jeremiah in the back of a squad car. His dad's still trying to wrap his head around what's going on."

"Good. I grabbed the laptop already."

"Great." Matthew flashed her a too-cheerful smile. "I'll check the closet."

"We need extensive photographs of his Nicole wall unless we decide to take the whole thing down and take it with us." After a moment's thought, she made a decision. "You know what? Let's just take the whole thing. One of those photos might show us something of interest, in case Jeremiah's not our guy."

Matthew was wrestling with the jammed closet door. "I'll get O'Malley in here after we're done with the room to take some pictures before disassembling and bagging it."

"He's going to love you for that." Charli let the sarcasm drip from her tongue as she moved on to the next drawer in the desk.

"Sure. I can just guess what he's going to get me for Christmas to thank me." He grunted. "I hate these sliding doors. They get dislodged from their tracks."

"You need help?"

"The day I need your help muscling something like this is the day I quit the force."

Charli smirked. "You should have told me earlier, and I would have planned a retirement party for you."

"Har har, very funny." With another grunt, Matthew managed to force the door back into place. "There. Now let's see what skeletons young Mr. Dunn has in his closet."

Charli had busied herself with the third and final drawer in the desk. Matthew sucked in his breath, and she turned to see what he was looking at. His body was blocking her view, so she moved forward to see around him.

There, in the middle of the closet, was a small box that looked like a treasure chest. On top was a framed photograph of Nicole, perhaps a school picture. The frame was covered in glittery pink and purple hearts.

Charli nudged her partner. "You recognize the frame?"

He scowled, giving a slow nod. "I'm trying to remember—"

"Mason had the same frame with a picture of Nicole on his nightstand. The picture was different, but the frame is identical."

"Any chance that's a coincidence?"

"No way. It's not the kind of frame most teen boys would pick out. At least, I don't think so."

"Definitely not." Matthew eyed her. "I didn't even bother framing the picture of my high school girlfriend. I just pinned it to the wall."

"Good to know. I think Nicole gave the picture and the frame to Mason."

Matthew crouched down and got closer to the picture. "And one to Jeremiah too?"

Charli wasn't sure. "Maybe. Or maybe stalker Jeremiah saw the frame she bought and purchased the same one so he could pretend that she gave him a framed picture too." *Creepy much?* "We should make sure to ask him."

Matthew pointed to the objects around the picture. "Look at the rest of this stuff."

There was a candle, several more pictures scattered and lying flat, and a dried wrist corsage, the kind guys usually gave girls when they took them to a formal dance. There was a note written in orange crayon in what looked to be a child's handwriting as well, and next to it on the shrine was a heart-shaped drop earring.

Charli also crouched down to get a better view. "Was Nicole wearing earrings when her body was found?"

Matthew shrugged. "I didn't get a close enough look at the body to tell you."

Her partner had avoided looking at the naked bodies of the two kids as much as possible when they were at the crime scene the day before. She would have to call Soames later and ask him.

Charli continued her perusal of the chest.

What the hell?

Bile rose in her throat, and she turned to Matthew, the horror on his face mirroring her own emotions.

On top of the chest in the back right corner was a lock of auburn hair.

Matthew straightened and stumbled backward. "Soames said the girl had some hair pulled out. Isn't her hair auburn?"

Charli nodded. "Yes." She was trying to be objective, not jump to conclusions or make what she saw fit the facts of the case. "It doesn't look like something ripped out of someone's head, though. It's neater, like it was cut."

"So either he cut a piece of her hair when she wasn't looking, managed to steal it from a salon, or he just came back here after killing her and cut off the ragged parts to pretty it up."

She couldn't deny that it was a possibility. Charli rose and perused the room. "Let's have O'Malley take pictures of this, too, before we disassemble and bag it."

Matthew strode out of the closet. "He's got a lot of snapping, tagging, and bagging to do. I'm going to go grab him to get started."

"Good idea. We can continue with the rest of the closet once we've got that taken care of. The desk is clean, so I'll start on the rest of the room."

As Matthew left to get the other officer, Charli walked over to the bed. She crouched down and searched under it, shining a penlight from her pocket to help her see under there. Toward the head of the bed, she spotted a small box. She pulled it out, opened the lid, and discovered half a dozen love letters that Jeremiah apparently hadn't mailed to Nicole yet. She placed them in an evidence bag.

Matthew returned with O'Malley in tow, and Charli held up the box. "Found more love letters under the bed."

It was Matthew's turn to smirk. "You're going to be

popular with those who've been reading through the last batch."

"Well, at least it's only six this time."

As Charli glanced up, O'Malley was staring slack-jawed at the Nicole wall with all the pictures and drawings.

"You okay, Officer O'Malley?"

"What the hell is wrong with kids today?" The officer scrubbed a hand across his face. "When I was his age, I was collecting baseball cards and comic books."

She'd heard similar sentiments before from many of the older officers on the force. It served to remind Charli just how much younger she was than most of her peers. Of course, she and Madeline had never done anything like this, but she understood how kids could mistake infatuation for love. To a degree, she even got how an obsession like Jeremiah's started.

"Could you start with the shrine in the closet? We need to get it out of there so we can keep searching."

While O'Malley worked on documenting the shrine, Charli and Matthew made short work of the room. As soon as the officer was done with the closet, he started on the wall of photos, taking pictures before bagging the items.

After several more minutes of checking out the closet, Matthew closed the door. "For a messed-up kid, the closet is pretty boring. When the skeleton is front and center, there's not much else to see, apparently."

Charli picked up last year's yearbook, which was on Jeremiah's lone small bookshelf. She thumbed through it and found Nicole's picture. Predictably, Jeremiah had drawn a heart around it. The guy was more romantic and cheesier than Madeline had been when she was crushing on Donny.

She flipped through a couple more pages, stopping when something caught her eye. Jeremiah had taken a black marker and completely scribbled out one of the student's faces.

Surprise, surprise.

The name underneath the marked-out photo was Mason's. She bagged the yearbook as evidence too.

10

When Charli finally walked out of the Dunn house, she found Jeremiah's father outside, still in a state of anger and shock.

As she approached, the man leapt forward. "Can you tell me what's going on?"

Although Phil Dunn probably meant to sound demanding, his tone came out as whining. Underneath the anger, there was a lot of fear, and Charli couldn't blame him for that.

"We had to search your house as part of our ongoing investigation into the murder of Nicole Schott."

"Murder?" The man's eyes blinked in rapid succession. "On the way home from the hospital, Jeremiah kept saying she was dead, but he didn't say anything about murder."

Murder is a ripple effect. It's crazy how many people someone's death can affect. "I'm afraid it was murder."

The man passed a hand over his eyes. "Wait. Is my son a suspect?"

"We're investigating many possibilities, and hopefully, we can clear Jeremiah's name."

Phil's knees started to buckle, and he leaned back against a police cruiser. "Oh."

His reaction spoke volumes, not only about Mr. Dunn as a parent, but also about his opinion of his son. From most parents, Charli would have expected a longer outburst, a protestation of their child's innocence.

Her mind wandered again to her own father and how hard he had tried to be there for her after Madeline's kidnapping and murder and, again, after her mom's death. He would never have shut her out or given up on her.

"What do you think about Jeremiah's picture wall?"

Phil looked confused. "What picture wall?"

Seriously?

"The shrine your son has on his bedroom wall." When Phil only blinked, Charli prodded. "Of Nicole Schott."

He scratched his temple. "My son is an adult. I don't go into his room, and he doesn't go into mine."

The truth was, Charli believed him. This man was more roommate than father to his son.

"What now?" Phil's voice was resigned as he remained leaning against the car for support.

"We're going to take Jeremiah down to the precinct and ask him some more questions about Nicole. Hopefully, something he tells us will help us find her killer."

"I see."

And we'll be checking out the alibi you gave us this morning too.

Charli waited for the man to act like a normal parent and offer to come along or at least call an attorney to be with his son. He did neither.

With a slight shake of her head, Charli walked over to the other cruiser.

Jeremiah was sitting in the back, his eyes and face puffy and red from crying. But he appeared more awake and lucid.

He lowered his face in his hands. "I loved Nicole."

"I know you did." Charli kept her voice gentle. Pushing him now wouldn't do anyone any good. "We're just going to go down to the office so you can help us figure out what really happened to her. We need your cooperation. Do you understand?"

Jeremiah nodded.

He wasn't under arrest, so she didn't need to read him his Miranda Rights. By couching it in terms of helping them to help Nicole, maybe he'd be more willing to talk by the time they got to the precinct.

Jeremiah raised his head and met Charli's gaze, tears streaming down his face. "I want to help Nicole."

"You're going to get a chance to, real soon."

Matthew was a few feet away and had clearly watched the exchange. "Crocodile tears," he said, fortunately keeping his voice down.

"I don't think so."

Still, there were lots of people who killed in the heat of the moment and deeply regretted it later. For now, nothing excluded Jeremiah from being the killer and genuinely mourning the girl he'd loved. Hopefully, soon, they'd know the truth.

❆

Charli and Matthew sat across the interrogation table from Jeremiah, whose head was down, his cheek resting on the cold metal table. The young man had finally stopped crying, although Charli figured he was a ticking clock where that was concerned. He'd be crying again as soon as a new wave of grief—and guilt, perhaps—overtook him. She understood that, just as she understood that now was their best chance to get him to confess.

If he really did kill Nicole and Mason. And that was a really big *if*.

Although she still had serious doubts about that, she couldn't contravene any of the evidence they'd collected so far. Whether or not he was a murderer, he was most certainly a disturbed young man in need of help.

"Where were you on Saturday evening, between six p.m. and midnight?"

Jeremiah had told them that morning that he was probably at home.

He lifted his head off the table and gazed at her through teary eyes. "Saturday night?"

Come on, Jeremiah. Keep it together.

"Yes, Saturday night."

"I told you I was at ho…wait." His voice was raw, fading in and out. "I was at The Gaming Den."

Charli folded her hands on the table between them. "What's that?"

"It's a gaming store." Jeremiah rubbed his face with his hands and took a deep breath. "You know, tabletop games, roleplaying. I was checking out some of their new stuff and picking up some Magic cards."

Charli tried to look interested. "Magic? Like tricks or something?"

"What?" Jeremiah gaped at her, seemingly as confused by her question as she was about his statement. "It's Magic the Gathering."

Matthew sighed. "It's a trading card game."

Charli gave Matthew a look. She'd ask him about his interest in magic later.

"Yeah, it's one of the ways I make money. I buy and sell Magic cards."

It amazed Charli how the internet had made it possible for anyone to make a living selling pretty much anything.

She scribbled some notes in her notebook. "When were you at the shop?"

"I got there about six. I stayed until just before closing at ten."

That covered some of the window that Soames had given them for time of death. As Jeremiah dropped his head back down on the table, Charli pulled up the store location on her phone and slid it toward her partner. It was about five miles away from the park where Nicole and Mason were killed.

Matthew glanced at her phone and nodded. "Can anyone confirm that, Jeremiah?"

"I don't know. There was a gaming tournament that night, so everyone who was there was pretty much focused on the game."

Triumph lit Matthew's face. "Then the tournament should be logged on your DCI card."

As she picked up her pen, Charli froze, shooting Matthew a *speak English* look.

Without raising his head from the table, Jeremiah flipped his hand dismissively. "They discontinued DCI accounts for Magic in 2020."

Matthew's shoulders slumped. "Aw, man. I had mine since college."

Shaking her head, Charli wrote *check for security cameras* and *verify DCI?* in her notebook. She'd make Matthew follow up on that second one.

"What did you do after the gaming store?" Charli waited for the answer, pen hovering over her notebook.

"I went home."

Matthew leaned forward. "By way of Fountain Park?"

Jeremiah sat up in his seat in a slouch, shaking his head from side to side. "No."

"Tell us about your collection." Charli's tone was gentle, nonjudgmental. "We've spoken about the pictures on your wall, but I'm more interested in some of the other items you kept. Did you know the picture frame in your bedroom is the exact same one Mason had on his nightstand? The picture of Nicole inside the frame was different from yours, but it's the same."

He frowned. "What frame?"

Charli flipped through their folder of evidence and pulled out a picture. "This one. We found it in your closet."

Jeremiah reeled back as if he'd been punched. "I-I made Nicole that frame. Made one for me too. It couldn't be in Mason's bedroom. You're lying."

Oh boy. Hundred bucks says Nicole regifted the present.

Charli found another image and pulled it from the folder. It was a picture of Mason's bedroom. She placed it in front of the young man. "Is this the frame you made for Nicole?"

Jeremiah's chin trembled. "She wouldn't do that. I made it for *her*."

Time to change the subject before the kid falls apart.

"What about the lock of Nicole's hair in your collection?"

Jeremiah swiped at his eyes. "What?"

She pulled a picture. "This lock of Nicole's hair. Where did you get it?"

He reddened and sank into his seat, but at least he'd stopped crying. "I don't remember."

Liar.

"I think you do, and it's okay. Did Nicole give it to you?"

A full minute passed before he shook his head. "Not really."

"Then how did you get it?"

"Off her back porch, okay?" He sounded like a petulant child. "Her mom was cutting her hair and some of it blew into the yard."

Matthew made a disgusted sound, but Charli shot him a

warning look before he could explode. "So you took it as, what, a souvenir?"

He shrugged. "I guess. It's a pretty color. I just—"

"Just what?" Matthew slammed his palms on the table, and Jeremiah jumped, yelping like a scared hyena. Charli almost did too. "Jacked off to it? Is that what you did?"

Jeremiah reddened even more, and Charli gaped at him. Matthew had called it right.

"No."

"Liar." Matthew's fists landed on the table this time. "Tell us the truth! You wanted Nicole for yourself, didn't you? You fantasized about her? Followed her? You couldn't stand her being with someone else, could you? How jealous were you that Mason had swooped in on your girl?"

Hand trembling, Jeremiah ran his fingers through his hair. "Of course I was jealous, but that doesn't mean I could do anything to hurt her. I couldn't even hurt him, even if I wanted to."

Again, Matthew leaned forward, jabbing a finger at Jeremiah. "You expect me to believe that you didn't want to hurt him?"

"Not physically, dude. I'm not into that kind of violence." Jeremiah fidgeted in his seat, his face drained of color. "Besides, if you really want to hurt someone these days, you don't need to hit them. Only morons like Mason think that."

A flicker of hope ignited in Charli's chest. "What do you mean?" Their guy was on the verge of admitting to something. She just knew it.

Jeremiah's shoulders slumped. "Look, everything these days is about image, reputation. It doesn't matter what's true or not. It just matters what people *think* is true."

Charli softened her voice and asked again. "What does that mean?"

He bowed his head, and a single tear rolled down his face.

"With Nicole, what you saw was what you got. She was the kindest, sweetest, most beautiful girl. She never did anything wrong or said a mean word to anyone, even after that walking asshole tried to corrupt her and make her more like him and the people he hung out with. She was still such a pure soul."

Charli struggled to keep her voice neutral. "And Mason? How was his soul?"

Jeremiah's head snapped up. "Black as his heart." He pounded his fist in his hand to punctuate his words.

That struck a nerve. "Can you elaborate?"

Jeremiah threw his arms up in the air in a gesture of despair and surrender. The tears were streaming down his cheeks. "He was mean. He was a nasty little kid back in elementary, and nothing changed. He just got older and more devious."

Jeremiah leaned forward, and Charli mirrored him, trying to win his trust. "Why do you say that?"

"You have to believe me."

"I want to, Jeremiah. Help me."

He bit his lip and stared down at the table for almost a minute before nodding, his gaze filled with determination. "You saw me on my laptop this morning."

Charli nodded, not wanting to interrupt him now that he was talking.

"I was doing some coding. I was going to phish Mason's login information, so I could get into his TikTok account."

Matthew scowled. "Couldn't you just follow him?"

Charli glared at her partner for interrupting Jeremiah. He ignored her.

"No. His account is private." Jeremiah glanced between the detectives. "Only people he approves can see his vids."

Interesting how he's referring to Mason in the present tense again. I don't think it's an affectation.

Jeremiah leaned in even closer. "Nicole didn't know he had a TikTok account. I heard him deny it in front of her, but I overheard his buddies joking about it. He had one, and I know he had stuff on there he didn't want Nicole to see. I figured if I got into it, I could show Nicole who he really is, and then she'd drop his ass so fast his head would spin."

That explains how he managed to block out the news for twenty-four hours.

He sat back, nodding as if it had been a *fait accompli*. Except it wasn't. Instead, Mason and Nicole were dead, and Jeremiah was in a police interrogation room with his laptop downstairs in evidence.

Charli exchanged a glance with Matthew before focusing on Jeremiah. "What was in Mason's TikTok?"

In slow motion, Jeremiah's countenance crumbled. It was obvious he'd been so sure of his mission, sure that this was all he had to do to get his love to reject her current boyfriend. Charli could see the way he'd planned it all out. He'd be the strong, sympathetic shoulder Nicole would cry on until he became the strong, sympathetic guy that she called her own.

As plans went, she'd heard worse, but still, it depended on several big *ifs*.

"I, um...I don't know." Jeremiah's face turned a bright shade of red. "That is, I'm not exactly sure. I just know he had stuff he was hiding."

Charli jotted down another note. "And you assumed whatever it was would be enough to drive a wedge between Mason and Nicole?"

"Yeah, of course. Why else would I have gone to all the effort?"

Matthew shook his head and held up his hand. "What if you hacked into his TikTok and discovered that there was nothing there? How would that make you feel?"

"Angry, frustrated, I guess." Jeremiah squirmed in his seat, and Charli couldn't blame him. These chairs weren't meant to be comfortable. "I don't know, because it never happened."

"But what if it did?" Matthew put both palms on the table. "What if you discovered there was nothing you could use to drive the two apart? What would you have done next?"

Jeremiah arched his lower back and rubbed it. "I never thought about it. I mean, why would I have to? My plan was going to work. It had to. I couldn't stand another week seeing them together. It was driving me out of my mind."

"Must have been hard," Matthew propped an elbow on the table, resting his chin in his palm, "seeing her in the arms of another man, watching him kiss Nicole, wondering what he was doing to her when they were alone."

"Stop it."

"He was touching the woman you should have been touching. Doing things to her—"

Jeremiah's face contorted in rage. "Stop it!"

Matthew sat up straighter and put his hands in his lap. "I'll stop. Just tell me what happened Saturday night. Otherwise, I'll keep going."

"I told you! I was at the game store. I didn't hurt N-Nicole." Jeremiah's face crumpled. "I could n-never hurt her! She was my soulmate." He threw himself down on the table, sobs racking his body.

Genuine or acting? Charli still couldn't tell.

She stood and headed for the door, motioning for Matthew to come with her.

They exited and went into the observation room next door so they could keep an eye on Jeremiah while they talked.

Matthew peered through the two-way mirror. "What do you think?"

"I think it's time we start exploring other possibilities. Find other suspects."

He turned toward her. "Seriously? This guy has murderer written all over him."

"Except he doesn't." Charli drummed her fingers against her thigh. "Stalker, yes. Murderer...I'm not convinced."

"Ruth is. I agree with her too. Maybe he's lying to us, and maybe he's lying to himself, but all that rage, all that frustration?" Matthew gave her a pointed look. "You can't tell me he isn't a powder keg ready to explode."

Charli folded her arms and leaned against the wall. "Yeah, maybe. He's an obvious suspect, but I think we need to widen our net. We've had tunnel vision since his name first came up. I just want to make sure that while we're focusing on this kid, we're not letting the real killer get away."

Matthew ran both hands through his hair. "All right, what do you suggest?"

"How about we go check out the gaming store before it closes? If they have cameras or there are eyewitnesses that can place him there all evening, then it's over, and we need to look elsewhere."

Matthew stroked his chin as he peeked through the glass. "He's about to crack. I feel it in my gut. We give him that much time to pull himself together, we could lose this opportunity."

Charli stared hard at Matthew, willing him to turn and look at her. In the silence that stretched between them, her phone chirped, and she pulled it out of her pocket with a smile. Rebecca had texted.

Our movie night still on?

It was so not a good time. Then again, Charli needed the breather. Plus, given how wound up and frustrated she was, going straight home would prove to be counterproductive, and the last thing she needed was to sit around and stress all night. She glanced up at Matthew, wishing they could be on the same page.

With a sigh, she texted back.

Can we do dinner instead?
When?
Late. New murder case.
I can do nine.
Perfect.
I'll meet you at Clam Digger.
See you there.

Charli put her phone back in her pocket.

"Come on, Matt, work with me."

In the other room, Jeremiah was still sobbing uncontrollably. As she peered through the glass, he slid off his chair and onto the floor, curling into the fetal position.

Without making eye contact with her, Matthew cleared his throat. "I suppose you're going to want me to send him home so he can sleep in a nice comfy bed." The sarcasm was thick in his voice.

"Do we have enough to arrest him?" Charli narrowed her eyes, no longer caring that her partner wasn't looking at her.

Matthew cursed under his breath. "Nothing airtight."

She refrained from throwing her hands up in celebration. "Then let's work our asses off to either find what we need to make an arrest or find the person who did this terrible thing."

"Fine, we'll go to the store to check out his alibi." Matthew turned to face her. "After that, I'll make some calls and get his old man's alibi checked out too."

Charli flashed him her brightest smile. "Perfect. And while we're doing that, tech can check when Jeremiah started coding again. If there's a gap in the timing from when he left the store and accessed his computer, I'll read him his

Miranda Rights myself. But...if we can prove he didn't have time to kill two people..." She bobbed her eyebrows.

"Yeah, yeah." Matthew huffed. "We'll let him go."

Charli exhaled a long sigh of relief. "Thank you."

He flipped her a middle finger. "Don't thank me yet. You're the one who has to tell Ruth."

11

Matthew tapped his fingers on the steering wheel to the tune of "Tennessee Whiskey." His partner was lost in thought as he drove them to the gaming store. Or maybe Charli was just tired, stressed, and pushed to the max, like he was.

Jeremiah had just been picked up by his father, who'd assured them he'd keep a watch on the young man. Ruth wasn't thrilled about any of it, but she'd relented when Charli kept pushing. She did make it clear that if the alibi didn't check out, she'd be sending officers immediately back to Jeremiah's house to arrest him. Matthew figured that was perfectly reasonable. Hell, they didn't even have to let Jeremiah go. They could hold him for forty-eight hours without charging him with anything.

Truth was…no one at the precinct needed to hear the kid's wailing all night long.

We probably should have sent him back to the hospital instead of home.

They'd tried calling the store before they cut Jeremiah loose, but it just rang and rang. One way or another, they needed answers, and Matthew had his fingers crossed that they'd get the information they needed at the gaming store.

Matthew was familiar with The Gaming Den. He'd been there a handful of times in his days as a beat cop.

"So I take it you never gamed at all as a kid?"

"No." Charli didn't even turn away from staring out the window as she gave him that fantastic one-word-answer conversation killer.

"I know you think the kid is innocent, but I—"

"I'm not banking on his innocence." Charli shifted in her seat. "I just don't think we're exploring all our options."

Matthew waited several moments, but she didn't continue. Usually, Charli could explain and theorize all day long. "How you doing, Charli?"

"Tired and getting hungry."

Not quite the answer I was going for, but I'll take it. At least you gave me more than one word this time.

"Yeah, I get that. You worried about the mafia boss's trial?" The mafia leader in a recent case who was awaiting trial for having bodies cremated at a local funeral home had threatened the detectives, even going so far as to have Charli followed.

She gave a noncommittal shrug.

Come on, Charli. Give me something.

He couldn't make her talk if she didn't want to. Well, he could, but it wouldn't be moral or ethical. And it would definitely make him lose a partner.

Maybe if he opened up about what was going on with him, it would encourage her to do the same. It was a long shot, but he hated riding around with the silence stretching between them. "I'm still having trouble talking to Chelsea these days. Yeah, it's gotten a little better, but we still have a long way to go."

"Hmm."

He drew in a deep breath and then let it out in a steady stream. "Sometimes, she responds to my texts, but I've had better luck with memes and TikTok videos."

Pain stabbed through Matthew's heart, white-hot fury roiling just beneath its surface. How dare his ex-wife take his daughter all the way across the country like that? His perfect little girl now viewed him as little more than a stranger who was out of touch with her life and kept trying to intrude upon it anyway.

It wasn't right. He should have pushed for full custody when his ex announced she was moving. He hadn't thought that was fair to Chelsea, though. How could he deprive a young girl just entering adolescence of her mother? She was going to need that womanly advice and understanding. He couldn't give her that.

Matthew glanced at his partner. And Charli hadn't exactly had a normal teen experience, so she wouldn't have necessarily been a good one to give advice to Chelsea.

Or to me.

He'd also worried that all the hours he put in on the job would be unfair to Chelsea. She would have eaten a lot of dinners by herself and come home from school to an empty house. That was not how he wanted his daughter to live. She deserved a parent who was present and engaged. Not just once in a while, but consistently.

He cursed himself for slipping into obsessive worry about his daughter over trying to talk to Charli, which had been the whole point.

Great job, jackass.

He inhaled a breath and held it before exhaling slowly, trying to calm himself down.

Think of something positive to say.

"I'm still texting with your friend, Rebecca. She's actually given me some really good advice. And she's funny. She's sent me some hilarious memes that also make Chelsea laugh. You know, she might have her mom's looks, but she's got my sense of humor."

"Good."

He glanced over at Charli and shook his head. Was she really that lost in her own private world, or was she being a dick for a reason?

"Anyway, I was thinking maybe I should schedule an appointment to see Rebecca more formally. I mean, the texting advice has been great and everything, but I'm sure we could actually go deeper. Obviously, I've got a lot of issues about my divorce, losing my daughter to California, and all of that. I don't know, what do you think?"

Charli just kept staring out the window.

"Charli!"

"Hmm?" Charli shifted to face him. It was about time. "What?"

"I asked you what you think about me scheduling an appointment with Rebecca about Chelsea."

"You should just hang in there. I know it's hard, but… Chelsea…you'll, um, get through to her eventually."

Enough was enough.

Pulling to the side of the road, Matthew threw the truck into park before asking the next question. "You going to tell me what's eating you, or not?"

For a moment, he thought she wouldn't answer, but she finally melted back into her seat. "I'm sorry. I'm just…stressed."

Matthew was pretty sure they'd passed "stressed" weeks ago. Still, it wouldn't do him any good to point that out. "Want to talk about it?"

Were those tears in her eyes?

Hell, he hadn't wanted to make his partner cry. Though, maybe that was exactly what she needed.

"Charli?"

Scrubbing her face with her hands, Charli shot him a lifted eyebrow. "How about we talk about this case instead?"

Matthew sighed. This would get them nowhere. When he put the truck back in drive, the two remained silent until he pulled up outside The Gaming Den.

"Time to put your *game* face on." Matthew's small attempt at humor took a moment to sink in, but Charli finally cracked a faint smile.

He'd take victories where he could.

They got out of the car and headed into the store Matthew hadn't stepped foot inside since college. What always amazed him was how he viewed places that he used to frequent differently, now that he was a detective.

What he and his roommates had once seen as a place of safety now looked like a soft target to him. There were no visible security cameras, and he noted that the cash register was just a handful of steps from the front door. Most of the kids were buying stuff with cash, as were a few of the adults who were potentially trying to hide from others just how much they were spending.

Matthew's friend had done that, since his father had access to his credit and debit card information. He could come up with dozens of excuses as to what he needed cash for. As long as his dad didn't know he was paying a small fortune at the gaming store, everyone was happy.

Matthew shook his head at the memory as he perused the room and noted how poorly it was laid out.

Forget convenience stores. Crooks should be knocking this place over on a weekly basis.

A girl behind the counter with straight, bottle-black hair and a ring in her left nostril eyed the two of them with suspicion as they approached the counter.

She raised an eyebrow. "Can I help you?"

Matthew flashed his badge and made the introductions. "We're checking on one of your customers."

The girl's eyes widened as she regarded Charli. "Wow, you're that detective chick from the newspaper."

"She is, and I'm that detective dude from the newspaper." Amusement rippled through Matthew.

"You're so much younger than I thought you'd be." The clerk was still gawking at Charli. "And even hotter."

Matthew hid a smile behind his hand.

The look on Charli's face was priceless. "Thank you."

"Detective Cross, my name is Alice." The young woman stuck out her hand, and Charli shook it. Instead of letting go, Alice pulled Charli toward her, leaned forward, and gave her bedroom eyes. "And I am a wonderland."

Charli wriggled her hand free of Alice's grasp. "I bet you are."

This. Is. Freaking. Awesome.

Witnessing his partner get so flagrantly hit on like this was making Matthew's day. Hell, it made his whole week. He forced himself not to laugh out loud.

"Alice," Charli took a few steps back, an awkward smile plastered on her face, "I was wondering if we could get your help."

"Anything for you, Detective." Alice flashed her a wink. "Gotta support our gals in uniform."

Ignoring the comment, Charli held out her phone, displaying a picture of Jeremiah Dunn. "Do you know this man?"

Alice grabbed hold of the phone, wrapping her fingers around Charli's in the process as she pretended to take her time perusing the picture. When she let go, Charli snatched her hand away.

Don't laugh. Don't smile. Don't say anything.

This had to be killing his partner. She didn't like to be touched even casually, let alone in such a flagrant way.

"Sure." Alice ran her tongue across her bottom lip. "He's one of our regulars."

Charli's eyelid was starting to twitch. "Was he in here on Saturday night?"

"I wasn't working Saturday. You'd have to ask Riley. He's off the next few days, but he'll be back on Thursday."

Charli did a good job of masking her disappointment, but Matthew could tell just how frustrated she was to not have an answer that night.

She curled her fingers into her palms. "Maybe we can give Riley a call and ask him now."

"Sorry. Can't. Boss's orders." Alice shrugged. "No one calls employees at home."

"Well, then maybe we can call your boss and get him to make an exception."

The young woman scrunched up her face. "Yeah, no one's allowed to call the boss at home. Sorry."

Matthew could swear Charli's eye twitched even more. He had to bite the inside of his cheek to keep from guffawing.

Charli drummed her fingers on her thighs. "Who *are* we allowed to call?"

Seriously, Charli? You have to see what's coming.

"Well, *you* can always call *me* at home." Alice waggled her eyebrows as she reached into her pocket and pulled out a card, which she handed to Charli.

The look of consternation on his partner's face was priceless. Normally, it took a lot to flummox her, but it was the end of a very long day. Plus, Charli never usually even thought about the fact that someone might be flirting with her, and this time, there was no way she could remain oblivious.

Tears stung Matthew's eyes as he forced himself to hold in his laughter.

When he let out a snicker, Charli glared at him, and he debated how much longer to let this go on.

Charli's going to kill me if I don't step in and give her a hand.

"Alice?" He took a step forward. "Have you ever heard of obstruction of justice?"

She shifted to face him. "Sure."

"Good. Because that's what I'll be charging you with when I take you down to the station if you don't get me those phone numbers."

With her jaw gaping wide open, Alice put a hand on her hip.

"I wouldn't test him." Charli's lips were set in a hard line. "I've seen him do worse over less."

Alice sighed and rolled her eyes. "Fine." She grabbed a pen and ripped a piece of paper off a notepad. "Here's Riley's number." She handed the page to Charli with a flourish. "It won't do you any good, though."

"Why's that?"

"Riley's at New York Comic Con. When he's at one of those conventions, he doesn't answer the phone for anyone. So, honestly, your best bet at talking to him is here, on Thursday, like I already said."

Well, that was an unexpected snafu.

"Does the store have any surveillance cameras?" Matthew already knew the answer, but it didn't hurt to ask.

"Just in the storage room in the back." Alice glanced over at Charli before fixing her gaze on Matthew. "Only employees are allowed back there, so it's super lame."

Charli scribbled in her ever-present notebook. "Any chance the field of vision covers any of the public areas?"

"Nope." Alice tucked her stick-straight hair behind her

ears and thrust her hands into the back pockets of her skintight jeans. "None whatsoever."

Frustration coursed through Matthew. He glanced at Charli, the irritation on her face matching his own.

She turned back to Alice. "Thank you for your time, Alice. We appreciate it."

The young woman only nodded, but Matthew didn't miss the way she eyed his partner up and down as they started to leave.

"Hey, Detective Hot Stuff, how about you and I go grab a coffee?" A grin spread across the clerk's face. "I close up in a little while."

Charli half turned and smiled. "I'm sorry, but I have a boyfriend."

"Too bad. You ever dump him, you know where to find me."

Nearly tripping over her own feet, Charli nodded and hurried out the door.

Matthew followed her outside. "*Boyfriend?*"

"What was I supposed to say? I got the distinct impression she wasn't going to take 'no' for an answer."

"Whatever you say, Detective Hot Pants."

She poked him in the chest. "First off, don't you dare breathe a word of this to anyone at the precinct. And second, it's Detective Hot Stuff, not Hot Pants."

Matthew laughed all the way to the truck.

12

Charli did her best to shake off the day as she entered the restaurant, spotting a waving Rebecca at the bar. After Matthew had dropped her off at home, she'd gotten a quick shower before driving to Clam Digger to meet her friend.

She hurried over to join Rebecca, happy for the distraction after the long day.

Barstools were not made for people her height, and it always felt like she was mounting a horse to get on top of one. Once there, she perched, feet firmly planted on one of the wooden rungs, which made her feel even more like a jockey in some bizarre race to Tipsyville.

"Rough day?" Rebecca's eyes were full of concern as she pushed one of two glasses of red wine in front of her over to Charli.

With a wordless nod, Charli wrapped her hand around the glass. She knew she'd been drinking more than she normally did lately, and she'd also been missing some of her early morning runs. If she wasn't careful, the combination would be enough to lose muscle mass and stamina, which was the last thing she needed.

Still, Charli was in a whirlwind of crazy and was trying not to judge her own coping mechanisms too harshly. Once the mafia trial was done, hopefully, she could get back into a regimen.

But Madeline's killer will still be out there.

She shoved that thought to the side. That was the last thing she wanted to think about or deal with right then.

"Did you get another letter from Madeline's killer?" Rebecca was all wide-eyed curiosity, and her voice was gentle, sympathetic.

Great. Exactly what I didn't want to think about.

Charli downed half her glass. "No, just regular work stuff."

"How's your partner doing?"

"Matthew appreciates the memes you've been sending him. It's given him something to forward to his daughter. I think it's the main way they're communicating right now."

"I'm happy to hear that. He mentioned that it wasn't too long ago that Chelsea told him not to speak to her again when he texted her on her birthday. That was last month. I'd say they've come a long way since then. And speaking of birthdays," Rebecca leaned down and grabbed the handles of a sparkly red gift bag with crisp, white tissue paper sticking out, "I got something for you. I know your birthday isn't for a few weeks, but I just couldn't wait."

Charli gasped as she accepted the gift. "You didn't have to get me anything."

"Of course I did." A small smile crept onto Rebecca's face. "Go ahead and open it."

"Okay." The faint scent of leather wafted out of the bag as Charli pulled out layers of white tissue paper. A black messenger bag with black buckles appeared. "This is incredible! I've been wanting one of these forever. How in the world did you know?"

"Well, I could just say I'm that good, but to be honest, I had a little help. I texted Matthew to get some ideas, and he mentioned you'd said something about wanting to buy one." Rebecca took a sip of her drink. "I hope the color is okay. I figured it would go with pretty much any outfit."

Charli hopped off the barstool to embrace her friend. Although showing affection through physical contact used to be rare for her—no, almost unheard of—this was a situation that called for a hug.

A warm sensation fluttered in Charli's stomach. She may not have many friends, but the ones she did have were gold. "Black is perfect. I love it. Thank you so much."

The hostess approached them, flashing a wide smile that revealed her even white teeth. "Ladies, your table is ready."

After they got up and followed her to a small table, the conversation was shelved for a bit as they both perused their menus. When their server arrived a few minutes later with waters and bread, Charli had made up her mind.

"I'll have the filet mignon, rare, with mashed potatoes and a salad with ranch dressing."

"My favorite." The server flashed her a smile and a wink.

What the hell?

"I'd like the clams three ways with rice and a Caesar salad." Rebecca shut her menu and smiled at the server. "And bring a bottle of something nice, please."

The server quickly wrote down her order and then left.

Rebecca unfolded her napkin and put it into her lap. "He liked you."

"Who?"

"The server."

Charli picked up her wine and set it back down, frowning. *Did I really drink that whole glass already?* "I'm pretty sure all he wants from me is a big tip."

Rebecca brushed her strawberry blond hair back over her shoulders. "I think it's hilarious when detectives can't see things that are right under their noses."

"I think it's that we're trained to be suspicious and not take things at face value." Charli smiled, taking a sip of her water.

"Or maybe that you expect the worst from people. Therefore, how could a cute guy your age possibly be interested in your brains or your body? All you see is someone wanting money. You don't leave open the possibility that he might want *you*."

Charli glanced in the direction their server had gone, but he was already out of sight. Time to refocus the conversation. "Anyway, I was saying a couple of minutes ago that Matthew appreciates the help you've given him with his daughter."

"I'm happy to do it." Rebecca broke her roll in half, inhaling as the steam hit her nose. "He really is a good text communicator."

That was something outside of Charli's experience. The few texts they'd shared were usually perfunctory.

"You don't say?" Charli leaned forward, trying not to smirk.

Was it possible that her friend was text-crushing on Matthew?

"Absolutely." Rebecca took a bite of her roll, closing her eyes as she chewed. "Man, this bread is sinfully good. But tell me, what does Matthew look like?"

Charli drummed her fingers on the table, struggling harder to keep from grinning. "You mean the great communicator hasn't sent you a picture?"

She held in her amusement as her friend's cheeks turned decidedly pink.

Rebecca wiped her hands on her napkin and took a sip of her water. "No, and it hasn't exactly been professional to ask."

Charli chuckled. "He's not a paying client, right?"

"We've been dancing on that line, I'll admit. He's been talking to me casually, and obviously, I could never see anyone personally if I were seeing them professionally."

Charli leaned forward, no longer able to hide her grin. "You like him!"

Rebecca's blush deepened. "I find him…interesting."

Charli was enjoying someone else's discomfort for once. A little harmless teasing was fun and therapeutic. Still, she didn't want to steer either of her friends wrong. "Well, I know that he's been thinking of making an appointment to see you…professionally…if you want to know."

Rebecca frowned. "I was afraid of that."

"You want me to try to dissuade him?"

"No, it's fine." Rebecca sighed as she reached for the other half of her roll. "I've probably already crossed into counselor territory anyway."

"Occupational hazard?"

Rebecca leveled a stare at her. "How many times do you find people want to ask you questions because of what you do, that they specifically shouldn't ask you precisely because of what you do?"

I know just what she means.

"Like my second cousin, who wants to know how much weed he can carry around without it being a felony?"

"Exactly."

The server delivered their salads, and Charli took the opportunity to observe him more closely. She did note that his smile was fifty percent bigger when looking at her than when he was looking at Rebecca.

Interesting.

As soon as the server left, Charli picked up her fork and attacked her salad. Lunch had been a long time ago, and she hadn't realized until that moment just how hungry she was.

"What did you tell your second cousin?"

"I told him he could find out for himself firsthand and arrested him on the spot."

Rebecca set her fork down, her mouth gaping. "You didn't!"

Charli smiled at the memory. "I did. It made the rest of Thanksgiving dinner awkward, but what can you do?"

Rebecca laughed so hard that heads all over the restaurant turned toward them. Charli did her best to ignore everyone else and continued eating her salad.

"I wish I could have seen that. I deal with so many dysfunctional families who enable each other's bad behavior." Rebecca dabbed at her eyes with her napkin and took a sip of wine. "That would have been…refreshing."

"That wasn't the word my uncle used."

"I bet it wasn't!" Rebecca stabbed a few pieces of lettuce with her fork. She lifted it toward her lips, glancing at Charli. "So what about you and Matthew?"

Charli picked up her water glass. "What about us?"

"Have you ever considered a relationship with him?"

What the hell? He's my partner.

The absurdity of the surprise question nearly caused her to spit the water out. She choked down the cool liquid, sputtering and coughing.

When she could breathe again, she wrinkled her nose. "No, and eww."

The server appeared with their meals, and Charli thought the subject was over as she attacked her steak.

Rebecca didn't let it drop, though.

"Why eww?" Rebecca took a bite of her clams. "I mean, you guys have been partners for a while now. You've been through a lot together, and you've got to be close."

Charli took another sip of water, careful not to choke on it this time, and looked her friend in the eyes. "That would be like dating my brother."

Rebecca held her gaze. "So that's how you think of him? As a brother?"

"Yeah, I do. And you're right. We *are* close, and we *have* been through a lot, but we're partners and friends, and that's it. Why do you ask?"

Sudden worry shot through Charli. She had always assumed that Matthew thought of her like his kid sister. Heaven knew he treated her that way. She had spent months trying to train the overprotectiveness out of him, but it couldn't be eradicated altogether.

"I wouldn't want to step on any toes." Rebecca toyed with her napkin. "Plus, you guys seem quite...close."

Just spit it out already.

Charli scowled. "Of course there's a closeness there. We're homicide detectives, and we're partners. Some of the things we've seen, it's hard to describe, let alone share with other people. We've seen each other at our best as well as our worst. That kind of camaraderie forges a bond, even when, like in our case, it's a platonic one."

Rebecca smiled and raised her glass. "Good answer."

Silence ensued as they continued eating, and Charli was relieved when talk drifted to a new subject. Rebecca was having trouble with getting some repairs done on her house. It wasn't scintillating conversation, but Charli reveled in the sheer dull normalcy of it.

Her cell phone buzzed, and she reached for it. *Please don't be work. I just need a break right now.* She glanced at the screen, and a series of emotions washed over her as Preston Powell's name appeared.

Relief. Guilt. Happiness.

Hey, what are you up to?

She blinked in surprise. What was she supposed to say? She still felt awkward after their unfortunate hookup. With a sigh, she started to put the phone away.

Rebecca studied her with a curiosity she didn't attempt to conceal. "You need to take that?"

"No. He...I don't."

Rebecca's face brightened with interest. "Okay, who is 'he,' and what's wrong with him?"

Don't blush.

Too late. Heat crept into her face. "What do you mean?"

"Uh-huh, I thought so." Rebecca set her fork down and fixed Charli with a pointed stare. "You have feelings for this guy?"

Do I?

Charli barked out a laugh so loud, a few patrons turned to glance at her. Could her face get any hotter? "No, absolutely not. I mean, he's a nice guy. Great, even. He's smart, funny."

"Good-looking?"

Absolutely. "Yes, if you must know."

Rebecca leaned forward, her elbows on the table, and flashed a huge smile. "Oh, I absolutely must know."

Charli hesitated, but the truth was, it would be good to talk it through. Who else did she have to discuss this stuff with? Certainly not Matthew. He was her partner, probably her best friend, but this was definitely a topic she wanted to steer clear of with him.

"His name is Preston Powell." Charli reached for her wine glass and took a fortifying gulp. "I've worked with him on a few cases. He's nice. A lot of guys I meet are stereotypes, but he's not like that."

"Cops and criminals." Rebecca winked and took a sip of her own drink. "Yeah, I totally get it."

Charli rolled her eyes and took another bite of steak, chewing meticulously while she considered how to answer. "Yes, okay. Preston works for the GBI, but he's different from others I've met."

"What's wrong with him?"

As much as Charli didn't want to admit it out loud, how else was she going to work through what had happened?

"I drank too much one night, and we had sex."

The noise in the restaurant had lulled right as she said the last word. Charli cringed as several people at adjacent tables glanced over.

Rebecca put her hand over her mouth, but her laughter was obvious.

Charli took another gulp of wine. "It never fails. The one word you don't want people to hear is the only one they do hear."

"Every single time." Rebecca pressed her lips together, though her eyes still shone with suppressed laughter. "So then, what, he ghosted you?"

"More like the other way around. It was just so awkward. Mechanical." Charli's mind wandered to that night. "And it had been a long day, I'd had a couple drinks, and we were both exhausted. The...*act*...didn't go well at all."

Rebecca patted her arm. "It's okay. That happens to lots of couples the first time, particularly if alcohol is involved. And exhaustion."

Was she serious? "Really?"

"Yes. It's not a good reason to spend the rest of your life avoiding him."

"I don't plan on spending the rest of my life avoiding him." Charli chewed on the pad of her thumb. "I plan on waiting until he gets the hint and moves to another state."

She was trying to be funny, but Rebecca gave her a squinty-eyed look that said she wasn't amused. "You say he's smart, funny, not your Average Joe?"

"Yeah." Charli dropped her gaze to her plate. *Why do I feel like I've gotten called into the sergeant's office for a dressing down?*

"And there was obviously some attraction there." Rebecca smiled, sincerity radiating from her gaze. "I think you owe it to yourself to give him a chance. Just make it clear that you'd like to move forward slowly."

That sounded like more talking about the situation than Charli was comfortable with. Still, Rebecca had a good point. "Do I have to?"

Rebecca grinned. "No. You don't have to do anything, but I do have a question for you. May I ask it?"

Inhaling deeply, Charli nodded. "Sure."

Rebecca squeezed her hand. "Are you using that night as an excuse to push him away so he can't step far enough into your life to hurt you?"

Wow. That was a punch in the gut. To Charli's horror, tears burned the backs of her eyes, and she took another sip of wine. "That would be a childish thing to do."

Rebecca traded glasses with Charli, giving her the fuller cup. "Not childish at all. People who've been hurt badly will often do or think just about anything to protect themselves from being hurt again."

"Like push people away?"

Rebecca nodded. "Yes."

It was true. That was why she had so few friends. Lived alone. Heck, she didn't even have a pet, out of fear of losing it one day.

"What do I do?"

"Text him back. Tell him you're free to hang out and talk."

"But I'm already hanging out with you."

"Uh-uh, you're not allowed to use me as an excuse. I'll fix

this right now." Rebecca opened her purse, pulled out a handful of bills, and dropped them on the table. She gave Charli a bright smile. "Call me tomorrow and tell me how it went."

Charli gaped at Rebecca's back as she hurried from the restaurant.

The whole situation was ridiculous. Still, after a moment, Charli took a deep breath, retrieved her phone, and texted Preston back.

Just wrapping up dinner with a friend. Free in a couple of minutes.

Meet at your house?

Actually, can you pick me up at a restaurant?

Sure. Where?

Clam Digger.

Be there in ten.

Charli put down the phone. That would give her just enough time to finish her meal. Given how much she'd already had to drink, though, she would most certainly not be finishing Rebecca's glass of wine. That would only lead to trouble.

13

I loved Angelo's. The staff was always so nice, so warm and welcoming, and when I went there, I felt less alone, less empty. Besides, she'd loved that restaurant. She always talked about it.

What was it about comfort food? My day had been a long, hard one and a plate of pasta made it a little better. My medication had made my head feel a little bit fuzzy, so I ordered tea instead of a drink.

It was better that way.

In the middle of dessert, tragedy struck. Two tables over, a man in a suit stood and threw nervous glances over his shoulder. Why was his face so pale? Was he going to pass out? After a moment, he knelt on one knee, the emotion on his face so intense it made my stomach sour.

My fork slipped from my hand, striking the plate with a loud clatter.

"No, please, no." My voice was a whisper as my body filled with rage. Why did I have to witness this? Life was so unfair.

With a shudder, I balled my hands into fists and told

myself to look away. To just breathe. That's what a doctor had told me once.

I couldn't look away, though.

The woman gasped, pressing her hands to her face in shock. Were women ever really shocked by these things? Sometimes, I wondered.

The man on the floor began to speak, his voice shaking as he poured his heart and soul into every word. Around the restaurant, all conversation ceased as the voyeurs strove to be party to this moment that belonged only to the two people at its center.

And to me.

"Anna, the moment I saw you, it was like magic."

That first moment is always magic. Stop pretending like you're the only one who's ever felt that way.

"You were a goddess."

She's only a handmaiden. You never saw my goddess. She's gone now, so you never can.

"And I was speechless."

If only you could be struck mute now. I could do it for you.

I shook my head, my thoughts growing more violent. What was wrong with me? I wasn't normally an aggressive person. The longer I sat there, the hazier my mind became.

Squeezing my eyes shut, I forced myself to inhale and exhale. Maybe this was all a bad dream. But when I opened them, Anna was staring at the moron kneeling before her as though he were her knight in shining armor. She was a fool.

"I could barely bring myself to speak to you."

You shouldn't have spoken to her. If you knew anything about the way the universe works, you never would have.

"I was sure you could never love someone like me, and yet, you did. I still don't know how or why."

Because women love idiots and losers, even when they shouldn't.

"But I am forever grateful. I want you to know how much I love you. I want to cherish you for the rest of our lives."

That won't be long if you don't stop this right now.

"I want to spend each and every day proving my love to you. And I want to start my life with you. I can't wait any longer."

Please, wait longer. Wait a lifetime. It's not too much to ask.

With every passing moment, I grew more frantic, more desperate. They didn't know the mistake they were about to make.

"I admit, I don't deserve such happiness."

No, you don't. Stop while you're ahead.

"But now, there's nothing left to say, except—"

No! Don't say it.

"Anna Miller, will you marry me?"

Say no, say no, say no.

Over and over, I repeated the mantra in my head. Maybe if I believed hard enough, I could will it not to happen.

Anna paused, the ensuing silence stretching on for an eternity.

Finally, I've done it. She's going to say "no."

"Oh, Parker, yes! I will marry you."

What the hell?

Anger rolled off me in waves, and I slammed my fist on the table. Heads whipped around at my outburst, and I resisted the urge to snarl at the nosy bunch.

Why? Why did Anna have to be so stupid, so blind? Did she think she could make this moment last a lifetime? What a conniving little bitch.

Parker stood and put the ring on Anna's finger. Utterly helpless, I sat and stared.

Maybe something will happen to destroy their happiness. Maybe they won't go through with it.

But no, their blissful smiles morphed into a passionate

kiss. Anna put her hand on Parker's shoulder, and the light from the overhead chandelier reflected off the diamond. That was when the anger inside me morphed into blinding rage.

How dare that ring shine so brightly? How dare they look so happy? Don't they know that's not how the story goes? There is no happily-ever-after.

For a long time, I sat there, the seconds ticking by. I'd paid my bill and remained at my table, frozen. Waiting. Watching.

My server gave up coming over to me.

At long last, the euphoric couple left.

I followed them.

They were so wrapped up in each other that they didn't see me, couldn't fathom my pain. As I trailed them, my rage built until it had nowhere to go but out.

Should I tell them that everything is doomed to perish?

For a brief moment, I hesitated. No, if my love had died, then so would theirs.

The happy couple made their way toward a beach on the river. Romantic. Secluded. Absorbed in themselves and their hopeless romance, they were oblivious to the world around them.

Still, I followed.

In my hand was the steak knife from dinner. I'd cleaned it on my napkin, noting the way the light had gleamed off the razor-sharp teeth.

But not like the engagement ring on Anna's finger.

Anna sat on the sand, pulling Parker down after her. They began to kiss, the ardor of the engagement fresh in them, the future stretching in front of them, in their eyes, as shiny as the diamond that winked and blinked and blinded and lied and betrayed.

And killed.

Those fools were all over each other as I walked up. They only had eyes for each other as he took her there on the beach, no doubt thinking themselves the only people in the world.

Maybe they were. Maybe I was a ghost. I glided toward them, not bothering to tread lightly.

In their haze of lust, the couple was oblivious to their surroundings. To me.

Interesting. Maybe they wanted this as much as I did.

The darkness of the night cloaked me as I approached, concealing the knife in my hand. But I was ready. I knew what to do.

At the last moment, Parker sensed my presence. With a startled cry, he whipped his head around.

What a perfect opportunity. I slid the blade across the soft flesh of his throat, the blood seeping out as life drained out of him. The lustful bastard had brought death upon himself. In the restaurant, he'd sealed his fate.

Frozen in place, Anna stared up at me, mouth agape, as Parker's blood poured down on her.

Parker fell onto his side, blood spurting from his wound with every beat of his dying heart.

Clawing like a rabid animal, Anna let out a bloodcurdling scream, forgetting, perhaps, the very solitude that had driven them to this place. With primal fear in her gaze, she scrambled onto all fours and tried to crawl away, her pleas and sobs futile.

The ring flashed in the moonlight, mocking me. I followed her. When she finally had the nerve and the strength to stand, I stepped behind her, snaking my arm around her middle. This traitorous bitch would not get away.

If she'd just said "no," they both could have lived.

For one glorious moment, I stood behind her, knife poised in the air, and reveled in my power, the crimson blood of her lover dripping off the blade. It was time for her to join her lecherous partner.

In one swift motion, I brought the blade down, slitting her throat from ear to ear. Something released in me at that moment—a sense of peace.

Justice was served.

And if not justice...

Destiny.

I did that diamond's job for it. And yet, it still betrayed me. As Anna flopped around in my arms during her death throes, her hand came up, and the diamond scratched my throat.

How ironic.

14

Preston had texted after he pulled up to the restaurant. Charli walked outside and got into his car.

"Thanks. I had a couple of drinks. And though my dinner companion left, I wasn't ready to drive just yet."

Preston flashed a full-toothed smile. "Not a problem. I'm happy to chauffeur you wherever you need to go."

He really was quite attractive when Charli viewed him objectively. Maybe Rebecca was right, and she did need to give him more of a chance. Give *herself* another chance.

But it had been one hell of a day to be thinking about a relationship with Preston.

He lifted an eyebrow. "You okay?"

Am I?

She shrugged. "I'm...I don't know."

Her knee-jerk response had been to say she was fine, but she stopped herself. If she was going to give this guy any kind of honest chance, then she'd have to be honest with him. And the truth was, she wasn't fine, but things weren't spinning as out of control as they could be. Charli was stressed, and she felt attacked on multiple sides. Still, she had work that generally fulfilled her. She was having some stress with Matthew, but she knew it was because they were both going through a lot.

When Matthew talked about his struggles to communicate with his daughter, Charli's heart ached for her partner, but she had no idea how to help him. So she'd tried to listen without judging.

"That's okay. I'm pretty 'I don't know' myself."

His words were lighthearted, but his tone was not.

She tried to smile, but she had a feeling her expression was more of a grimace. "I'm sorry to hear that."

Charli couldn't help but wonder if she was partially to blame for his state of uncertainty.

"So how can I help you? What's going on?" His voice was kind and sincere, and she needed someone to talk to, bounce ideas off.

Open up a little, Charli. He's not going to bite.

"I'd love to talk about the case I'm working on."

"Shoot."

Charli leaned her head against the seat and closed her eyes. "Let's get to the house first. We're almost there, and I want to sit down and gather my thoughts."

Preston flashed her another genuine smile. "Sounds like a plan."

They rode in silence for the next few minutes, which was a breath of fresh air. This quiet was comfortable, and she let herself relax as they neared her house.

Rain began to beat down, and Preston turned on the wipers. Their rhythmic motion, combined with the patter of the drops falling on the car, was even more soothing.

Preston glanced at her. "I love rain. It makes everything else seem so peaceful."

"I agree. Somehow, a storm outside quiets the one inside."

"That's beautiful."

"My mom used to say that. When I was little, and it would storm, we'd sit in the bay window at home and watch it come down together." Charli swallowed the lump in her throat as she remembered those times with her mother and wished they had more moments like that again. "Everything would just get so quiet and calm in the house, and she would have the most peaceful look on her face."

"Your mother sounds like she was a very wise woman, and I agree with her completely."

Charli blew out a long breath. "I miss her."

Preston gave her hand a quick squeeze before releasing it. "I'm sorry."

They fell back into silence, but Charli didn't feel alone. After a while, she surreptitiously watched Preston. He drove with confidence, not overly cautious but not aggressive either. Just calm and steady, like someone who knew what he was doing and was unafraid to do it.

Man, I'm in a pensive mood. I've got to cut back on the alcohol.

As she continued to sneak glances at Preston, though, she wasn't sure the wine was entirely to blame. After all, she'd found this man attractive enough to lower her guard once.

Realization hit her full-on. Charli had found him attractive, but she hadn't actually lowered her guard, not really. She hadn't given him access to her mind or emotions, which was why all the physical stuff had been so awkward, so...

Meaningless.

She bit her lip and stared out the window. Had she sabotaged them even before they could really begin? And was he the only one she was constantly pushing away for fear that she would somehow get hurt?

Intuitively, Charli guessed that she had a lot of self-exploration to do before she got to the bottom of this. And she didn't want to do any of it that night.

She closed her eyes, focusing on the sound of the rain.

She let it wash over her and imagined it washing over him, over *them*. This was an opportunity for a fresh start, and she shouldn't waste it.

"Home sweet home."

Preston's words intruded on her thoughts. Charli opened her eyes and discovered that they had indeed arrived at her home. "Thanks for the ride."

He unbuckled his seat belt but didn't open the door. "Do you want to be alone?"

He was more intuitive than she had given him credit for. Part of her did want to be alone. But the other part still had a case nagging at her and would very much like help working through it. Plus, if she allowed herself to admit it, she didn't want him to leave.

"No. Let's get inside." She forced a smile. "I'll put on some coffee, and we can take a run at this case."

He reached for the door handle. "Sounds good."

They dashed to the front door. Once inside, Charli excused herself to change clothes. She donned a pair of comfy pants and a sweatshirt. There was no need to give him the wrong impression about where the evening was heading.

She made it back downstairs and found him in the kitchen, already brewing coffee.

"I see how it is. Give a guy an inch, and he takes over your whole kitchen."

"Sorry." His smile was sheepish. "As soon as you said 'coffee,' I couldn't think of anything else."

"It's fine, but don't ever tell another soul I let you touch my coffee maker. Some things are sacred."

His grin turned sly. "A gentleman never tells."

Charli enjoyed the banter. She ran a hand through her damp hair. "Do you need a towel or a dry shirt?"

"Nah, I'm a drip-dry sort of guy."

She giggled and clamped her lips together to stop the

girly sound. If she wasn't careful, she might start batting her lashes next.

As soon as the coffee was ready, they took their cups and adjourned to the living room. Charli grabbed a notebook and pen. She settled into one of the comfy chairs, tucking her feet underneath her, and sipped her drink.

Preston sat on the couch. "Okay, let me guess. You're working on the naked couple case."

"You've heard about that?"

Why am I surprised? Heat crept up her face as she imagined him on top of her.

He nodded, seemingly oblivious to her mental *faux pas*. "You always seem to catch the weird ones."

She chuckled. "You should know."

It just slipped out, but now it was out there.

He raised an eyebrow. "Are you implying that *I'm* a weird one?"

She winked. "Make of it what you will."

"Okay, filing that away. Tell me about your case."

Glad to be on more solid ground, she brought him up to speed, filling in all the pertinent details.

"So far, Jeremiah Dunn is your only suspect?"

"Yes, so far." The coffee mug kept her hands nice and warm, and she clutched it close.

Preston tapped the arm of his chair with his index finger. "It's a fairly rare occurrence for a minor to commit murder. Only about eight percent of murders involve a minor as the offender, and about half of those involve either a group of kids or a minor and an adult working together. And honestly, most murders involving minors are related to drugs or other criminal activities."

A surge of joy shot through Charli at Preston's revelation. Statistics were part of her marrow. And it was nice to know she wasn't the only one who found them informative.

"Of course, that isn't really what we're talking about here, since Jeremiah is eighteen."

She sighed. "Yes. Jeremiah is eighteen. Barely. But the mind of an eighteen-year-old is still far from developed."

Preston nodded, taking a sip from his mug. "And they struggle with impulse control, giving them more in common with young children than adults. I've read that research too. What other possibilities do you have?"

"Unfortunately, not a lot yet. There's been nothing in the databanks about similar killings locally or in other parts of the country."

"How far back did you look?"

Charli ran a hand through her damp hair. *I bet I look like a hot mess right now.*

"Fifteen years."

"Thorough. I like that." Preston set his cup down and leaned forward. "What else?"

"We haven't been able to rule out a random act of violence yet."

"Oh, let's hope it's not that." Preston scrunched up his nose as he shook his head. It was actually kind of adorable. "*Random* means without a pattern or an ability to predict anything, including targets or frequency. It would mean there's some guy tromping around out there so jacked up on rage that he could go off on someone, *anyone*, at any time. Nope, not good for public morale or for our chances at catching him, especially after the sniper case."

"Not a proponent of one and done?" As soon as the words left her mouth, she winced. *If I could crawl in a hole and die right now...*

Preston searched her face, a ghost of a smile playing at his lips. "No, not as a rule."

Time stood still as they sat there, with Preston finally

standing and breaking the silence. "I think I could use another cup of coffee. What about you?"

Charli nodded, surrendering her cup to him. While he was out of the room, she took the opportunity to take some deep breaths to clear her head.

Hold it together, Charli.

When he returned, she accepted the fresh cup with a smile. "Thank you."

"You are most welcome." He settled back into his chair. "Okay, let's look at this logically. Say you're right, and Jeremiah didn't kill Nicole and her boyfriend."

"Okay."

"Let's say it wasn't even a random act of violence."

"Sure." Charli sipped her coffee. *Where is he going with this?*

"Then someone, somewhere, wanted one or both of them dead for a very specific reason. Let's rule out serial killers for now, since you didn't find any evidence of something like this happening before."

Charli sat up straighter, almost sloshing the hot coffee onto her sweatshirt. "The question becomes, why would someone want a couple of seventeen-year-olds dead?" Several thoughts sprang to Charli's mind, and she was happy to bounce ideas off Preston. This was what she'd wanted to do earlier with Matthew, but he'd been too stuck on the Jeremiah-did-it train to focus any attention elsewhere.

"Jealousy." Preston took another sip. "Meaning, someone other than Jeremiah, since we're looking past him right now."

"It's a little far-fetched to believe that their relationship would have spawned such ferocious feelings in more than one person."

"Yeah, but it *is* high school." Preston shrugged. "You remember what it's like. All the petty jealousies, imagined slights, bullying."

"Jeremiah does contend that Mason was a bully." Charli's brain whirled with possibilities.

"Okay, good. Maybe Mason bullied someone else, the wrong kid. He found a way to get even."

"Or a parent or sibling did."

Preston chuckled and nodded. "My brother beat up more than one bully on my account when we were kids."

"Really?" *I would have thought the other way around.*

"I was scrawny for my age, read a lot, had asthma, you know, basically the whole package."

"So I see a lot hasn't changed." Charli smirked. "You're still the whole package."

"Thank you, I think." He flashed most of his teeth. "And if not, then screw you very much."

She laughed at that, harder than she'd laughed in a while, and Preston joined in. After a few seconds, Charli wiped her eyes on her sleeve. "That felt good."

"It sounded good. You have a beautiful laugh."

"I bray like a donkey, and you know it."

Preston winked. "If you say so."

She took a sip, needing the barrier between them. She needed to get the subject back on track. "Okay, we've got jealous kids and bullied kids or their families in the group. Tomorrow, we're going to Nicole and Mason's school, so hopefully, we can check out those theories."

"Good. Now, what other possibilities do we have?"

Charli set down her cup and flipped to a new page in her notebook. "I've got a potential motive. One or both of them saw something they shouldn't have."

"Nice one. Now, they're seventeen." Preston got up and started pacing. "Where are they likely to be going that they can overhear or see something worth getting killed over?"

"School." They answered in unison, giving Charli a warm sensation deep inside.

She began jotting down some notes to herself—questions to ask, leads to run down.

"Inappropriate conduct by a teacher, counselor, or parent." Preston was going down the list that she was coming up with. It was amazing how often they thought alike.

Her mind wandered to the gym teacher she'd interviewed a few cases back. He had to deal with the aftermath of allegations of an affair, forcing him to leave his job. Things like that could ruin not just careers but also lives.

"Drug dealers in schools can also be an issue." Charli yawned. She was getting a lot out of the conversation, but her body was demanding sleep.

"Too true, unfortunately. And if they're in cahoots with anyone, it just gets worse."

"Okay. Where else might they have heard or seen something they shouldn't have?"

"They could have stumbled on something at the park they weren't supposed to see."

She'd thought about that, but it fell into the random category. She drew a line on her page and added that theory there. "That would still be random, though. Let's circle back to that."

"Then how about they saw or heard something they weren't supposed to at home, his or hers?"

She shook her head. "I can't see Nicole's mom doing anything that could have gotten her daughter killed. And I don't believe she would have killed her either."

Preston continued to pace. "What about other family members?"

Charli barely suppressed another yawn. "I can check on grandparents, too. See if they're around, and if Nicole or Mason ever spent any time with them."

Preston sat back down and took another sip of his coffee.

"Did either of them have older siblings who might have been into something?"

"No. Both only children."

It was Preston's turn to yawn. "Sorry, long week."

Charli gave him a sympathetic smile. "It's okay. I totally get it. At any rate, this has been extremely helpful."

And she'd been having a good time, despite the grim subject matter they'd been discussing.

Preston glanced at his watch and grimaced. "It's late. I should probably get going."

Charli was immensely grateful that he was the one saying that. It would have ruined the evening if he'd asked to stay over.

"All right. Thanks for the ride and your time."

"Anytime. You know that." He searched her face, his gaze intense. "At least, I hope you know that."

She swallowed the emotion that wanted to surface. "I do, and I'm really happy you're here. You helped clear my mind."

His smile didn't hide the exhaustion all over his face. "I'm happy to help." Preston started toward the front door, and she followed him. When he reached it, he glanced at his watch again. "It's nearly midnight now, so I guess I'll see you in the morning?"

She frowned. "You're going to be at the office tomorrow? Are you working a local case?"

Preston grinned. "Would you be jealous if I were?"

She knew he was teasing, so she refrained from telling him the truth—that it would bother her a great deal if he were working a case in her precinct with someone other than her.

She shrugged. "I'm not the clingy type."

"Well, for your information, I'm not. I merely figured I'd play the part of the gentleman and pick you up so you can get your car at the restaurant."

Charli smacked her forehead with her palm. "Oh my gosh. I forgot all about my car."

"Ah, but lucky for you, I didn't. So see you at seven?"

"Yes, thank you." Warmth and tenderness rushed through her, which she covered by holding out her hand.

"Good." Preston gave her hand a squeeze. "Sleep well."

"You too."

Preston left. As she locked the door behind him, the whole house felt a bit empty. She leaned her head against the door and silently lectured herself.

You don't need a man in your life, Charli. If you're lonely, get a cat.

15

As she yawned for the third straight time while trying to eat some cereal, Charli regretted her choice to stay up late. She was chasing the little circles round and round the bowl with her spoon. Her phone rang, and she shoved her breakfast away.

"Good morning." She tried, and failed, to suppress another yawn.

Preston chuckled. "Well, the second word is accurate."

"You're tired too?"

"Fell asleep in the shower. What does that tell you?"

A picture of a very handsome—and very naked—Preston flashed into Charli's mind.

Get a grip.

She shook off the image, glad he wasn't in her kitchen to see her cheeks flush.

Charli cleared her throat. "Glad you didn't fall down and hurt yourself."

"You and me both. Anyway, I'm a few minutes early. Sorry about that."

She stood and carried her cereal bowl to the sink. "Never apologize for being early. I love that."

With a suppressed groan, she cringed. *What a dumb thing to say.*

"I'll be sure to remember that." He inhaled like he was going to say something else and cursed instead.

"What is it?"

"There's a truck parked out here. I think someone is watching your place." Preston's voice was terse, all hints of friendly flirtation gone.

Charli dropped the bowl. "It's probably just some more goons from my mafia case coming to intimidate me."

"Excuse me? Say that again."

She flipped the light switch off before leaving the kitchen. "You remember the cremated remains in the morgue?"

"Yeah."

Charli strode to the living room window. "Well, you were right. It was a mafia thing."

"I knew it!"

"The case goes to court soon, and they just want to rattle me."

"You need to put an end to that shit." Preston's voice was a deep growl, and she smiled in spite of herself.

"Been a bit busy."

Charli drew back the curtains and peeked outside. Sure enough, Preston's car was in her driveway. Across the street—certainly parked in a lurking, stalkery manner—was another vehicle. One that was even more familiar.

"False alarm." She sighed, irritation prickling her. "That's Matthew's truck."

"Your partner? Does he normally pick you up in the morning?"

"Usually only if we have an early morning call and it's his turn to drive. Not sure why he's here today." Charli took a deep breath and squeezed her eyes shut. *He's going to jump to conclusions about Preston.* She snapped her eyes open. "But since he is, I can get him to take me to my car. Thank you for coming all this way, though."

"No problem."

Charli detected a hint of disappointment in Preston's voice, but she didn't have time to deal with it right now. She was too busy wondering why Matthew was staking out her house.

"I really do appreciate it."

"You're welcome." Preston's tone was warmer now. "Whatever you need, I'm here."

She blinked at that. Something in Preston's tone told Charli he meant what he'd said.

"Okay." It was a lame way to answer, but it was all she had. "Well, I'll talk to you later. Bye."

"Bye."

Charli hung up before he had a chance to say anything else. She grabbed her new messenger bag and threw on her navy blazer before heading outside.

As she yanked open the door and got into Matthew's truck a minute later, she could tell he was just dying to ask questions, but she was determined to beat him to the punch.

"Why are you staking out my house?"

"I wasn't staking it out." His head fell back against the seat. "I was just doing a security drive-by."

Excuse me?

"Why?"

He twisted in the seat to face her, the *get over it* look on his face speaking volumes. "I know you've been getting threats, so I've been driving by occasionally, just to make sure no one is lurking around. Normally, I just cruise down the street. I stopped today because your car wasn't here, and a strange car was in the driveway."

"It was Preston Powell. He gave me a ride home last night from the bar where I met Rebecca."

Matthew smirked. "And he figured he'd help himself to some breakfast while he was at it."

"Actually, he didn't. He got here like a minute before you did, apparently."

Charli had been partners with Matthew long enough that she could tell he thought she was lying, and it frustrated the hell out of her.

I can't let him put me on trial for something I didn't do...well, that I didn't do last night.

"I appreciate that you're concerned for me, but you don't need to do this. I'm a big girl. I can take care of myself."

And it's an invasion of my privacy.

The argument was weak, even to her. Being detectives and partners who worked closely together on challenging cases made it difficult to have secrets from each other. Or privacy, for that matter. And it wasn't just emotionally inhibiting. It was also impractical. That was part of what made it awkward when she didn't feel like sharing completely with Matthew.

"I know you can take care of yourself." Matthew's tone was measured, which meant he was either super irritated or really struggling to make himself clear. "But when dealing with the mafia, it doesn't hurt to have someone watching your six."

While Matthew's logic was perfectly sound, it did nothing to make Charli feel better. She leaned her head back against the headrest and closed her eyes with a sigh.

Just change the subject. You're beating a dead horse here.

"What do we have on deck for this morning?"

Matthew put the truck in drive and eased away from the curb. "I figure, midmorning, we could head over to Nicole and Mason's school."

"Good idea. Maybe some of their teachers or friends can tell us more."

"I still think Jeremiah did it." Matthew glanced at her. "But it never hurts to gather as much information as possible."

Charli didn't want to waste energy disagreeing with him. "Maybe we should go back to Fountain Park now, look over the scene."

Matthew nodded. "Works for me. You want me to drive you to get your car?"

"Yes, but let's do that later. Right now, I just want to get to work."

16

Charli was still irritated with Matthew as they neared Fountain Park. She tried to reason with herself why she felt as strongly as she did. After all, Matthew was just trying to look out for her. Why did that upset her so much? Odds were, he would have done that for any partner and that it had nothing to do with her gender, age, or physical stature.

In the back of her mind, a niggling sensation demanded that there was something missing underneath the surface. She could sense it. Was she afraid that if she let Matthew be protective, he would somehow lose respect or treat her differently?

Maybe. Charli didn't have the luxury of trying to solve the mystery of her own complicated emotions right now, though. Not when there were more pressing mysteries to solve with more tangible, real-world consequences.

Once they arrived at the park, Matthew headed straight for the crime scene, which was still taped off. Charli got out of the truck much slower and wandered around, studying each detail with fresh eyes. Maybe something new would stand out.

Something had drawn Mason and Nicole to this particular park. What was it? Was it just youthful hormones and the need for some privacy? That would make sense. Was there anything special about this place to them? To their killer?

"Repent! Repent, all you sinners and whores of Babylon!"

The sudden shouting startled Charli, and she whipped around. The speaker was an older man with frizzy, white hair and an overgrown white beard. He was pacing back and forth on the sidewalk, not that far from where Mason and Nicole would have likely entered the park.

Charli walked forward, pulled by invisible strings. Something about the man drew her in. As she got closer, she could read the sign he was carrying—if she could call the piece of cardboard taped to a metal pole a sign. On the cardboard, a message had been scrawled in black marker. *The End of the World Is Night!*

She blinked and reread the words, approaching the man with caution. "Excuse me, sir?"

Giving her a stern glare, the elderly man turned one bright green eye on her, the other one covered with a cloudy gray film.

"Yes, ma'am?" His tone was more polite than she'd expected.

"I was curious about your sign." Charli flashed him a disarming smile. "It says *the end of the world is night?*"

"*Night?*" He barked the word, jabbing his finger at the sign. "No, *nigh*! As in imminent, present, coming to pass."

Charli bit her lip. "It says *night*."

The man frowned and lowered the sign. "Can you hold this a minute?"

He thrust the sign at her.

Surprised, Charli grabbed it before it could fall. The metal was surprisingly heavy and cold.

How the hell did he carry this thing for hours?

With gnarled fingers, he reached into his pocket and pulled out a pair of glasses, sliding them on his face. As he leaned in close, bright crimson splotches bloomed on his neck and cheeks.

"Damn idiot pup! Should have never trusted him to write it down for me." He glared at Charli, his good eye boring into hers. Underneath the anger, there was also something else. Was it sadness? Despair?

With shaking hands, he replaced the glasses in his pocket. "You ain't got a marker on you, do you?"

"No, I don't. I'm sorry."

Before Charli could hand him back the sign, Matthew strode up, pulling a marker out of his jacket pocket.

"Here you go, sir."

The older man started to reach for the marker and then shook his head with a sigh. "Would you mind doing the honors for me, young man?"

Matthew nodded, and while Charli continued to hold the sign, her partner carefully turned the *t* in *Night* into another exclamation mark.

"Thank you." The man took the sign back, shouldering it. He flashed them an affectionate smile. "What's a nice young couple like you doing out here?"

Before Charli could speak up and tell him they weren't a couple, Matthew answered. "Just enjoying the park. It really is beautiful here."

"I know. I come here all the time. It's restful, serene, peaceful. Nature has a way of making a body feel closer to God. 'Course, Him and me is already pretty close." The elderly man laughed and tapped a hand on his chest.

Charli smiled. "Have you noticed any others who like to come here a lot?"

He lifted a gnarled finger and pointed at a woman with a

brunette ponytail, wearing a black sports bra and turquoise shorts. She was jogging toward them.

"That one's always here." He cupped his hand around his mouth and shouted, "Put on some clothes, you whore of Babylon!"

The jogger flipped him off. From the look of hatred on the woman's face, Charli guessed this was not the first unpleasant encounter the two had shared.

Appalled by his words, Charli stepped between him and the woman. "Do you really think calling people names will change their behavior?"

The elderly man's eyes narrowed into slits, still focused on the jogger. "It should. The Bible says that—"

"Have you seen anyone else around here, especially anyone with not a lot of clothes on?" Charli had no desire to get into a religious discussion she'd most likely lose.

He swung his head back around to look at her. "Saw a couple just the other day, naked as jaybirds. God struck 'em down for their wickedness."

Charli's jaw dropped open. "Did you see them get struck down?"

"Nah. I missed the show." He ran gnarled fingers through his wizened beard. "I'm a mite glad I did, to be honest. It's a terrible thing when a sinner dies in his sin. He never gets a chance to make it right." Tears sprang to the old man's eyes.

"Sir, when did you see the couple?"

He frowned and scratched his temple. "After church, I suppose."

Today was Tuesday morning. Had this guy really seen the dead couple and said nothing?

"Church this past Sunday? Two days ago?"

He waved a hand, clearly annoyed. "Isn't that what I said?"

"Why didn't you call the police?" She worked hard to keep the annoyance from her voice.

He shrugged. "What could the police do? They were already dead."

This would get them nowhere. She decided to change course.

"Did you see anyone else near them before or after?"

The old man shook his head and wiped at his eyes. "What are you young folks so curious about that for?"

Charli flashed her badge. "Actually, we're detectives. I'm Detective Cross, and this is my partner, Detective Church. We're with the Savannah Police Department." She started to hand him a card.

"You mind putting it in my pocket with my glasses? Paper's hard to hold."

She stepped forward, gingerly placing her business card in the man's shirt pocket.

Matthew smiled at the man. "Do you have an ID we could see?"

"I do, but I left it in my other pants." He scratched his head, the frizzy hair sticking up in all directions. "I forget that sometimes. Name's Desmond Turner. I can give you my address, if that would help."

"It would, Mr. Turner. Thank you." Charli pulled out her notebook and jotted down the address. "Where were you on Saturday night?"

"I was having dinner with several people from church. Would you like their names?"

Charli nodded, adding the names and times to her notebook. "You have my number, so if you think of anything or see anyone strange around here, I'd very much like to know."

"You've got it, little lady. Say, why don't you come to church on Sunday? Nice girl like you probably has her own church, but I'd be honored to see you at mine." Mr. Turner glanced at Matthew. "And there's always time to be saved, young fella."

Matthew blinked. "How do you know that she's not the one who needs saving?"

Mr. Turner chuckled again and patted Matthew on the arm. "Service is at nine a.m. It's the prettiest church you ever seen, but it's what's on the inside that counts. Just like with a person."

He gave them the address for the church, too, and Charli scribbled it down.

He ambled away. "Repent, all you sinners! The Lord sees all that you do in darkness and will bring it into the light!"

Charli shook her head and turned to Matthew. "You thinking what I'm thinking?"

Matthew scrutinized the old man. "That I'm not sure if he really saw the dead bodies or made that shit up?"

"Well, there's that, but not exactly what I was thinking."

He waved his fingers in the air. "That there's no way those messed up fingers could hold a knife, let alone use it on a couple of teenagers?"

"True, but I was thinking this guy seems a little overzealous. He was so enraged when he yelled at the jogger."

"I don't know. He seemed a little off his rocker, but he didn't strike me as killer material. But if he did actually see the bodies before the landscaper found them, maybe he even saw the murderer at some point, or even knows him."

Charli rubbed the back of her neck. Talking with the elderly man had made her melancholy, and she couldn't exactly explain why.

"Crippled hands or not, we need to check him out. Him and people who think like him."

"Do me a favor."

She sighed. "What's that?"

"If I ever get that old or that crazy, just shoot me and put me out of my misery."

Normally, she would have thought Matthew was joking,

but one look at her partner's face revealed that he was experiencing some of the same feelings she was.

"Excuse me, are you guys cops?"

The jogger Mr. Turner had shouted at earlier had made a circuit of the park and returned. She was standing, jogging in place a few feet from them.

"Yes, I'm Detective Cross. Can we help you?"

"I hope so." Her face contorted in disgust. "Someone needs to put that nutjob away. I run here every morning, and half the time, he's here. He's threatened me and a lot of other people. Having him here is a safety issue, and I think the police should do something about it."

Matthew cleared his throat. "If he's harmed anyone, they can come down to the precinct and fill out a report. Then—"

The jogger cut him off with a wave of her hand. "Who has time for all of that? I wish you could just make him go away."

"It's a public place. Without any charges being brought against him—"

"Forget it." The jogger had grown impatient. "Hopefully, the old guy will just shrivel up and die soon." With that, she continued on her morning run.

Charli scowled at the woman's diminishing form. "There's so much hate in this world. And these days, everyone seems to have it in for someone else. What separates those who act on those feelings and those who don't?"

Matthew shook his head. "Sadly, not as much as you would think."

17

Charli and Matthew walked around Fountain Park for a few more minutes, but she couldn't get the encounter with Desmond Turner out of her head. Even though she believed the old man was physically incapable of committing the murders, he had given her some new angles to think about. What if Mason and Nicole's murderer didn't have a personal grudge against either one of them but was, instead, offended by them ideologically?

Matthew sat on a bench and stared at the crime scene. "I don't see anything new that's speaking to me. Do you?"

She shook her head, forcing herself to focus. "What did you say?"

"I don't see anything." He searched her face. "You okay?"

Charli played with a short lock of hair. "Yeah...just thinking, that's all."

"Care to share with the class?" There was a hint of sarcasm in his voice.

She turned to face him. "What if this had nothing to do with jealousy or grudges?"

"You mean, what if some whack job had a thing against young couples making out?"

"Yeah. I guess that's what I'm thinking."

"I don't know." Matthew put his palms on the bench and stretched his back. "I mean, it's not like we haven't seen puritan assholes trying to cleanse the world before. You think we have a killer who has the same issue?"

Charli studied the markers in the grass. "It seems like a lot, but what if?"

Matthew leaned forward, mirroring her posture. "What are we staring at?"

"The murder scene. The place where Nicole was killed, specifically."

"You and I both agree that the old geezer couldn't have done it, right?"

Charli took a deep breath, trying to clear her mind. What if Nicole and Mason had sat on this same bench before they were killed?

"You're right. I don't think he could have done it. That doesn't mean there isn't someone connected to him who could have."

"An accomplice?" Matt frowned, causing a garden of lines to appear on his forehead.

Charli remembered the old man's sign. Who misspelled *nigh* on it? It wasn't the old man. She drummed her fingers on the arm of the bench. "Or an acolyte."

※

THEY TOOK a quick loop around the park, but Mr. Turner and his sign appeared to have moved on.

Matthew finally threw up his hands in defeat. "We can check his home later. Now it's time to get over to the school."

Charli wasn't happy with the solution, but she didn't have any better ideas.

When they arrived at Midtown High School, Charli was pleased to see that one safety modification had been put in place since their last visit. A video camera was prominent, recording people entering the front door.

The secretary behind the desk hadn't had any upgrades, though. She was just as inattentive as the last time.

When they walked into the principal's office, Charli was surprised to find a different person in the room.

A tall woman wearing an impeccably pressed navy pantsuit stepped out from around her desk and held out her hand. A diamond the size of a quarter gleamed from her left ring finger. "I'm Ms. Aletha Lopez, interim principal here."

Charli shook the woman's hand. "Ms. Lopez, I'm Detective Cross."

Matthew handed her a business card. "Detective Church."

Ms. Lopez returned to her chair and folded her hands on the desk. "A couple of weeks ago, when I was asked to step in on an emergency basis, I was told this school was going through some challenges. Needless to say, this is not the sort of challenge I'd expected."

Charli didn't know if the previous principal had resigned or been forced to step down, and she didn't really care. What she did care about was finding out who killed two of Midtown High's students.

"I'm sure all of this has been a challenge." Charli nodded to indicate Matthew. "We'll try to be out of your hair as quickly as possible."

Ms. Lopez frowned. "We have grief counseling presentations and sessions going on today. You can speak to whichever teachers you like, but I'd ask that you not disturb any of the students until school is over."

Charli didn't like the idea of waiting. And by the way

Matthew scowled and straightened to his full height, it was clear he didn't either.

Ms. Lopez held up a hand. "This is my decision, and I take full responsibility for it." She picked up a couple of files from her desk and handed them to Charli. "These are Nicole's and Mason's files. The list of teachers and classrooms is on top for each. Just let my assistant know who you want to see, and they'll get them to the conference room."

"We'd like to see all of them." Matthew's voice was tight as he took the files from Charli and began flipping pages.

"Very well. I'll have the first one sent to you in a couple of minutes." Clearly, from her bearing and the level looks she gave them both, Ms. Lopez was used to being in charge.

"We can split up the list and visit the teachers to make the whole process faster." Charli figured that made sense since they'd done something similar the last time they were at this school questioning teachers.

Ms. Lopez shook her head. "Absolutely not. That will cause too much disruption. We'll send them to you. Good day."

She sat, ending the conversation as she picked up a piece of paper and started to peruse it. Charli didn't appreciate being dismissed like an unruly student.

Matthew balled his hands into fists and narrowed his eyes. "Please don't plan on leaving campus today until we've interviewed *everyone*."

That got the principal's attention, and she jerked her head, clearly startled. "You can't possibly think I'm a suspect."

Matthew gave her a cherubic smile. "Just need to be thorough, *ma'am*."

Charli turned to leave before Ms. Lopez could catch her smiling.

When she and Matthew had taken their seats in the

conference room a minute later, Charli finally let out a small snicker.

Matthew was shaking his head. "Did you catch that?"

"A bit hard to miss."

"I mean, kids are dead, and she thinks now's the time to have a pissing contest with us."

Charli took the files back from him. "Just so long as you didn't let her win."

Matthew glared at her. "Is that your way of telling me it takes two?"

"Does it?" She was only teasing him a little. Charli hadn't enjoyed the woman's attitude either. "Hey, there are three files here."

"I noticed that back when I grabbed them."

The top file was Nicole's. The second one was Mason's. That meant the third one belonged to...

Charli snapped her head up and locked in on her partner's gaze. "She gave us Jeremiah Dunn's file."

"You get the feeling she thinks Jeremiah did it?" Matt's tone was mocking now.

Charli scowled and looked back down at the file.

"Hello, I was told you wanted to speak with me?" An older woman with gray hair pulled into a severe bun appeared in the doorway. She wore a prim blouse and a full-length skirt and had a pair of horn-rimmed glasses perched on the end of her nose.

After Matthew stood up and introduced the two of them, he gestured toward a chair. "Please, take a seat."

Once the woman settled in the chair, Matthew resumed his seat.

"I'm Ms. Grant. I'm an English language arts teacher. Are you here to ask about Nicole and Mason?"

The *Romeo and Juliet* teacher?

Charli wondered if Ms. Grant knew her recommendation for the kids to see that movie had led to blows.

"Yes, we'd like to know anything you can tell us."

"They were both excellent students. Never caused me a lick of trouble."

"Do you know anyone who might want to hurt either of them?"

Ms. Grant straightened in her chair and looked Charli square in the eyes. "No, I do not." Her answer was forceful, her chin thrust out.

The response was a little odd, and Charli glanced at Matthew. He returned her stare, seeming just as puzzled.

Matthew leaned toward Ms. Grant. "You seem very certain."

"I am, and I won't say otherwise." Defiance gleamed in the teacher's gaze. "I don't care if she fires me."

Wait, what's going on here?

"Ms. Grant, who would fire you? And what is this person trying to get you to say?"

"There was a meeting yesterday after school. Ms. Lopez warned us that the police were coming, and she told us to be sure we told you everything we knew about a certain student." Ms. Grant smoothed a wrinkle in her skirt. "All the others agreed. He's not well-liked because he's different. But he couldn't harm a fly."

Charli glanced down at Jeremiah's file on the table, unease settling in her stomach. "What's his name?"

"Jeremiah Dunn. And let me tell you, he's not a killer." The teacher's expression softened. "He's a poet. Tortured, as so many great artists are. I've been teaching for forty years, and I've only seen half a dozen kids in all that time with talent like his."

Charli found herself touched by the older woman's fierce

defense of her student, but they still had unanswered questions. "Were you aware of his feelings for Nicole?"

"Of course. The poor boy needed to learn how to move on, but children don't understand that first loves almost never last. I just know that when he gets out of this place, filled with all these judgmental, small-minded people, he's going to thrive. He'll find others who truly care for and encourage him."

Matthew raised an eyebrow. "It sounds like you really... care...for him."

Ms. Grant narrowed her eyes. "Don't be crass, young man."

"Yes, ma'am." Unlike with the principal, Matthew's tone with this teacher was respectful. "I didn't mean it like that."

"The boy has nobody in his corner." The teacher peered between Matthew and Charli. "It breaks my heart to see a talented child having their spirit broken."

Charli tried to ease into her next question gently. "Did you find Jeremiah's behavior at any time...inappropriate?"

"You're asking if he was stalking her." Ms. Grant pushed her horn-rimmed glasses up over the bridge of her nose. "Yes, I suppose he was. But he meant no malice."

Matthew rubbed his chin. "You really think he couldn't have hurt anyone?"

"I don't. I do, however, have serious concerns that, with the object of his affection gone, he might try to hurt himself."

I do too.

Before Charli could respond, her phone rang.

It was Ruth.

"Thank you, Ms. Grant. If we have more questions, we'll let you know." Charli handed the woman her card. "If you think of anything else that we should be aware of, please give us a call."

The teacher stood, nodded at each of them, and then left.

"Detective Cross speaking."

"I need you and Matthew to get to River Street Beach right away. Two new bodies have turned up. I'm texting you the coordinates."

The sergeant ended the call abruptly, and Charli's stomach flip-flopped as she stood. "We've got to go."

"Another body?"

"Two."

18

When I woke up this morning, there was a bad taste in my mouth. Coppery. I discovered I must have bitten the inside of my cheek sometime in the middle of the night. Funny that it didn't wake me. The night before was a blur. All I could remember was being at *her* favorite restaurant and seeing a man propose to his girlfriend. Then...

The rest was...nothing. *Gone.*

When I went into the bathroom, though, there were traces of blood in the shower. Again. It terrified me, but also excited me in a way I didn't like. Not one bit.

After I'd cleaned it up, I let the hot water flow down over my head and body, renewing me. Life had been so hard without her, and I never in a million years could have imagined it would be like this. I always thought it would be her and me, together forever. Sometimes, I forgot that she was...

I couldn't even bring myself to say the word. All the euphemisms people used about death didn't describe the final sleep for what it really was. Empty. Dark. The absence of light and warmth and love. Hopeless. Reeking of despair. Wrought with rage.

Sometimes, I swore that the next time a person said something like "gone on to a better place," I would kill them. They didn't understand. Why couldn't I go with her to this "better place"? How could any place be good where we were apart?

I got dressed even though I didn't want to. I couldn't find the belt I'd worn the night before, so I had to go without one. My pants were loose. Food hadn't appealed to me that much the last several days, though last night's pasta had been pretty tasty.

At least, I think it was? Why couldn't I remember?

When I entered the kitchen, I stood in front of the stove, wondering when it had last been turned on. Instead of bacon and eggs, I settled for cold cereal each morning.

I walked to the cabinet, trying to decide what to do. My brain was foggy, and I didn't have the energy to lift spoon to mouth. *Maybe I'll skip breakfast.*

My gaze settled on an object on the counter.

I froze. The only part of me that moved was my heart, which had started hammering in my chest, making it ache.

That knife wasn't mine. It didn't belong in this kitchen. With a wariness I couldn't explain, I inched toward it, wonder and fear filling me. I began to shake, but I didn't know why. Familiarity pricked at me as I examined the blade. I knew I'd seen it—or one like it—before.

It was a steak knife, the kind found in restaurants. This one was super sharp, and I could imagine the blade slicing through a thick, juicy slab of meat like butter. *And the blood would bubble to the surface.*

I blinked. Where had the thought of blood come from? Although I didn't get steak that often, when I did, I liked mine well done. As I stared at the knife, my head began to throb. Why was that knife there? How had it gotten there?

Unbidden, I reached out and touched the handle, hand trembling.

A shudder shook my body as I jumped back, an image flashing in my mind. It was the river. A girl by the river.

I hit the wall behind me and stayed there a moment, pinned by some invisible force. What had I just seen? Memory? Daydream? Prophecy?

My cheeks were wet, and I realized I was crying. I missed her *so* much, and the pain threatened to overwhelm me. As I squeezed my eyes shut, I was right there in all the horror again.

With bated breath, I crept back toward the knife. Something told me I had to pick it up, even though I didn't want to. As my hand curled around the hilt, a scream echoed in my mind. For once, not mine. Someone else's, someone who—

What was that dried, rust-colored substance on the blade?

Realization flooded through me, and I dropped the knife like a hot coal. It clattered to the floor.

Blood.

I knew, instinctively.

Again, my thoughts flashed to a river. I had to go there.

❋

THE CLOSER I got to the river, the more I wanted to turn back. My heart began to race, adrenaline pumping through my veins. Although I'd left the knife behind in the kitchen sink after I'd washed it off, I now wished I'd brought it with me. I needed protection. Protection from what, I didn't know.

The image in my head had been on the sandy beach next to the river.

A girl.
Screaming.

Blood...so much blood.

As I neared the spot, my heart filled with dread. I couldn't escape the feeling that something terrible had happened and that, somehow, I had been a part of it. I didn't want to believe that, but fear and doubt gnawed at the edge of my mind.

Up ahead, birds circled something on the sand.

Vultures.

My chest tightened, and my feet were leaden as I propelled myself forward. Vultures meant dead things.

As I trudged nearer, my eyes blurred. I blinked several times, trying to clear them. Then the horror of the scene burst upon me.

A man and a woman were sprawled out on the sand, stark naked, with vultures picking at their faces.

I opened my mouth to scream, but no sound escaped. Turning from the heinous sight, I ran as far and as fast as I could. The sand grabbed at my feet as bloody images flashed through my mind.

They were dead. How had that happened? More screaming filled my mind, along with the sensation of warm blood running over my hand where I'd clutched a knife.

No! This wasn't happening. It couldn't be. I couldn't have had anything to do with this.

I ran for at least a mile before slowing. My knees shook, and I vomited into some bushes before sitting on the ground, stomach heaving, mind flailing around. What was going on? Was this real, or had I hallucinated an image of the bloody bodies?

After a moment, realization dawned on me that my cell phone was in my hand. I had to call somebody. Who was I supposed to call? I struggled to remember. I should know this.

9-1-1.

That was it. I dialed the three digits, my hand shaking so

hard I kept getting them wrong. Finally, the call went through.

"9-1-1. What's your emergency?" The young woman on the other end of the line spoke in a calm, clear voice, as though the entire world wasn't crashing down around her.

"There's some...something d-dead on the beach by the river. There are vultures everywhere. I think...I think it's a body...or bodies."

"Sir, take a deep breath. What's your name?"

I hung up and stared at my phone in horror. If I'd given her my name, the police would want to know why I had been at the river and how I had come to find the bodies. How could I tell them I saw the murder in a dream or a vision?

Or a memory.

My head threatened to explode. I grabbed it with both hands and rocked back and forth for a few minutes, trying to get ahold of myself. Why couldn't I remember coming home from the restaurant last night? It should've been a simple thing. At some point, I had gotten up and walked out. Why was it so out of focus when I tried to pull up those memories?

Sirens wailed in the distance, and I forced myself to my feet. I knew I shouldn't go back, but I couldn't bring myself to leave.

19

A myriad of emotions collided inside Matthew as they arrived at the river location Ruth had texted them. "I can't believe that...*principal*...would instruct the teachers to throw Jeremiah under the bus." He was fuming, and he didn't try to hide it. "What the hell does she think she's doing?"

"She probably thinks he's guilty. *You* think he's guilty." His partner was sitting in the passenger seat, being annoyingly calm. "Ruth too."

"Yeah, but I'm a detective. It's my job to think he's guilty until I find someone who looks more guilty."

Charli shot him a *you've lost your mind* look that he caught out of the corner of his eye. "You know how messed up that sounds, right?"

"Yeah, yeah, spare me the lecture. Besides, if we hadn't cut him loose last night, we might have a much better idea of whether or not he did it."

"What do you mean?"

Matthew rolled his eyes. *Come on, Charli. I'm surprised you haven't thought of this.* "Ruth said it was another dead couple that was found, right?"

"Yes, but we don't know how long they've been dead."

"We're heading to the beach by the river. Something tells me they couldn't have been dead that long. My guess is they were killed last night after we let our perp walk."

Charli fidgeted in her seat. "What reason would he have to go after any other couple?"

Matthew held up a finger, his other hand on the wheel. "One, we've learned that he wasn't a student well-liked by his peers. Maybe he had a grudge against some of them."

"We don't even know if the bodies belong to teenagers yet or if Jeremiah even has any links to these new victims."

He extended a second finger. "Two, he could be trying to cover his tracks by killing people he doesn't know."

Charli sighed and crossed her arms. "You honestly think the blubbering mess we were dealing with yesterday could think that coherently, to plan something like that out?"

"Which brings me to three." Matthew held up a third finger. "He's a tiger. He's got a taste for killing people, and now he can't let go."

"Excuse me?" Charli sounded bewildered.

"Sorry. Chelsea did a report on tigers one time. She told me that, apparently, once a tiger tastes human flesh, he won't eat anything else."

"That's a chilling thought."

"I know, right?"

"So you think Jeremiah Dunn is a tiger?" Skepticism laced Charli's voice.

"If not him, then someone."

"Meaning, if someone didn't kill one couple to cover their tracks, then there's someone out there who's gotten a taste for killing couples?"

"Bingo." Matthew snapped his fingers. "And just like that, we have another serial killer."

Matthew's words created a sudden, oppressive silence in

the car. There had been too much repetitious killing lately. First, a serial killer targeting young girls, then later, a guy murdering people he blamed for his troubles. The town was still on edge, and no one needed a repeat of either of those.

He glanced over at his partner. It wasn't just the town that was on edge. Matthew was, and he strongly suspected Charli was too. "It's been brutal lately."

"Yes, it has." Weariness dripped from her words.

He got it. He was right there with her. "I'm sorry for overstepping earlier. There's nothing I can do to help Chelsea, and you're all I've got in the way of family that I can do a damned thing for. I guess I got a bit overprotective."

Charli's eyes went wide.

"I'm not your daughter."

He groaned inwardly. "I never said you were my daughter." His tone came out angry, which was not his intention. *Good going. Real smooth.* "Look, you're like my sis...like my bossy, *older* sister."

Did his eyes deceive him, or did Matthew catch the barest hint of a smirk before she turned toward the window?

"That works, since you're definitely like my annoying little brother, even though you're practically old enough to be my grandpa."

"What?" His jaw dropped. "I'm not even old enough to be your dad. Not even close." Matthew glanced at Charli, and her hint of a smirk had turned into a face-splitting grin.

He heaved an inner sigh of relief.

❄

MATTHEW'S STOMACH cramped the closer they walked to the crime scene. He hated this part of his job so much.

"Oh, good, Officer Boy Band is here." Charli muttered the words under her breath. She hated when she couldn't remember names. She squinted at his badge as the young officer hurried over.

"Sir, ma'am." Officer Acosta's face was ashen, much to Matthew's surprise.

"The, uh, couple is naked and positioned like the one from the park. No clothes anywhere around. It's a little hard to make out features, because of the…" The young officer took a ragged breath and then forced himself to stand straighter. "The vultures beat us here."

Now that look on his face makes sense.

As a kid, Matthew had seen vultures tear apart a dead animal when he was playing near the woods. The sight had scarred him, and that had just been an animal. Watching buzzards pick apart a human body was not something anyone should have to see.

"They'd only just started, and we've chased them off, though."

"Thanks. That had to have been brutal." Matthew put a hand on the younger man's shoulder, steadying them both.

Charli pressed her hand to her stomach. "Who found the body?"

"A jogger." He indicated a woman sitting about thirty feet away. Her blond hair was pulled back into a long ponytail, and she wore a bright pink tank top with black bicycle shorts. Her head was down on her arms.

"Did she see anything suspicious before or after finding the bodies?"

The young officer cleared his throat. "She states that she saw a man running away from the area before she stumbled across the victims."

Charli pulled out her ever-present notebook. "Can she describe him?"

"No, but she was pretty sure it was a guy. As it turns out, there was a 9-1-1 call a couple of minutes after hers. It was a man who said he thought he saw a body. He hung up when the operator asked his name."

"Could be our runaway." Charli sighed. "Another jogger, maybe?"

"Well, let's go take a look."

"I'm going to text Janice and have her trace that 9-1-1 call. The caller may have been a random jogger, but you never know."

Matthew shrugged. "That's true. Good idea."

He let Charli forge ahead. The last crime scene had been upsetting. Matthew imagined, with the damage done to the bodies, that this one would be even worse. It was times like this that he thought Charli had ice water running through her veins. He didn't know how she could stay so cool. Maybe it had to do with everything that had happened to her as a kid.

Matthew could make out the bodies in the distance as he watched Charli stop and bend down to take a closer look. He glanced overhead. The vultures were still circling, agitated that they had been driven from their feast.

So not okay.

He shuddered, ambling forward and standing next to Charli, who was still crouched down. Both victims' eyes were gone, consumed by the birds who had started tearing at other parts of their flesh.

Each body was indeed posed as the other ones had been, hands on each other's genitals. The mess that had been made of their faces was going to make identification much more difficult, particularly without any ID cards as a starting point.

Matthew's stomach turned as he tried to take in what details he could. The couple looked young, perhaps another pair of teenagers. Or maybe they were in their twenties.

After a few moments, he couldn't take it anymore and

moved away, his stomach roiling. "Identification is going to be tricky."

Charli rose and moved back a couple of steps. "Maybe not. See the tattoo on the outside of her left thigh?"

"I saw it. A rose. Not like lots of girls don't get things like that tattooed on themselves these days."

"Yeah, but how many of those girls have gone missing around here in the last day or so?"

Matthew barely managed to swallow the bile that had risen into his mouth in time to answer. "Good point. Anything else of interest?"

Charli paced around the body, describing what she was seeing as he continued to focus anywhere but on the gruesome scene. He hadn't thrown up at the scene of a homicide since he was a rookie, and there was no way he was going to break that streak now.

"It looks like the ring finger on her left hand has been broken."

"She could have fought him." He tried hard not to envision that, but it made sense.

"Maybe." Charli didn't sound quite convinced.

He squeezed his eyes closed. "What are you thinking?"

"I don't know." She stepped away from the body so that she was in his line of sight. "I really don't like this."

"Who does?" He certainly didn't. Matthew was struggling against the vomit roiling in his belly. He'd seen more than his share of dead bodies, but something about the way these couples were stripped and posed was deeply upsetting. Add in the vulture mess, and he was so gone.

Every once in a while, he had a day where he hated his job. This was one of them.

"Never fear! Soames is here. Just your friendly neighborhood medical examiner."

Matthew whipped his head around as Soames

approached, a smile on his face. The guy was way too cheery, particularly for the situation.

Read the room, dude.

"Dr. Soames," Charli reached out and shook the man's hand, "you're awfully chipper today."

The M.E.'s grin was so wide it could split his face in two. "Well, as a matter of fact, I am." He took a step closer and dropped his voice to just above a whisper. "I met this woman…"

Matthew immediately tuned out the rest of the sentence. "I'm going to talk to our witness." He hadn't meant to sound like he was growling, but people would just have to cope. He wasn't feeling very upbeat, and he certainly didn't want to think about the M.E. bonking anyone.

He walked over to the witness. After a moment's hesitation, he sat beside her. "How are you doing?"

She looked up, her bright blue eyes red from crying, and took a shuddering breath. "Better than an hour ago."

He nodded his understanding. "Detective Matthew Church."

"Dr. Violet Walker."

She was green around the gills, and he could totally relate, but he thought it strange for a doctor. He forced himself to smile anyway. "What kind of medicine do you practice?"

"Grafting, cross-pollination, poisoning, pesticides."

Poisoning?

"Excuse me?"

Dr. Walker rubbed her eyes. "Sorry, reflex. I get asked that a lot. I'm a botanist."

That made more sense. "So what you're telling me is all your patients are vegetables?"

She burst out laughing. "That is the most inappropriate thing I've ever heard. But to answer your question, no, they're not. Some of them are total fruits."

Cute and funny.

Her laughter was contagious, and Matthew smiled. "Keep calm and carrot on."

She wiped away a tear. "Herb and Ivy are quite nice. If I had more impatiens like them, it would make my daisies."

Matthew kept up the wordplay. "What about Rose, though? I heard she can be a bit prickly."

"Nah, you just have to know how to handle her correctly, and then she's a real pussy...willow."

"I'd rather learn how to handle a violet." The words just sort of slipped out, stunning him.

A blush crept onto Dr. Walker's cheeks. "I'd like that."

I've done a lot of dumb things before, but did I just hit on a witness at a murder scene? If so, that has got to be the dumbest.

"I'm sorry. That was unprofessional of me." He struggled to find the right words to apologize.

At some point in his career, Matthew had studied vicarious trauma, and he realized he'd been using humor as a coping mechanism just now. *Maybe that's what Soames does too.*

The psychological response was common among first responders due to the disturbing scenes they witnessed.

She gave him a smile that made all the unpleasantness and awkwardness around them seem to slip away. "Actually, it was charmingly honest. I think the world could use more of that. And today, I certainly needed the laughs. You're a funny guy."

He grinned. "As much as I've enjoyed chatting, I do need to ask you some questions."

The smile faded, and disappointment surged through Matthew.

His discomfort must have shown on his face because she reached out and placed a hand on his arm. "It's okay. I know you're just doing your job. So ask away."

"Thank you." Slowly, the horror of the scene behind him settled back in. He sighed as the nausea returned. "Tell me what happened."

She grabbed her ponytail and pulled on the end of it. "I was out power walking."

"Power walking?"

She gave a self-conscious-sounding laugh. "I know, it's lame, but I'm doing this fitness challenge with my sister." She waved her hands in the air. "Not important. Anyway, I was out here trying to get some exercise. I kept seeing the vultures circling, and I thought it was probably some dead animal. When I got close enough to see what they were eating, well…I'm afraid when I close my eyes tonight and try to sleep, all I'm going to see are those poor people."

I can totally relate.

"May I suggest some light reading or a rom-com before bedtime just to get yourself relaxed?"

"Thanks. I'll try anything."

Matthew's heart went out to her. He always felt for families and witnesses, but there was something more here. He wanted to help ease her pain as much as he could.

Keep it together, idiot. Just ask her what happened.

"Once I could think, I called 9-1-1." Dr. Walker wrapped her arms around herself, shuddering.

"What else did you notice?" Matthew was used to Charli taking notes, so he'd become lazy about doing so himself. Now he wished his partner had walked over with him. Not only would she meticulously document every word said, but she would also keep him from making a bigger fool of himself.

Dr. Walker pointed down the beach. "Before I reached the bodies, I saw what looked like a guy running off that way."

Matthew glanced in the direction she was pointing. They

could check the area, but he doubted they'd find anything unusual or useful. "Can you describe him?"

Dr. Walker tapped her temple, as if the action would stimulate her memory. "Not really, I'm afraid. Dark pants, I couldn't even tell you what kind. Gray sweatshirt, I think. There weren't any logos on the back, that I could make out."

At least she did a good job noticing that. He was amazed at how many times witnesses couldn't even identify a suspect's clothing.

"Hair color?"

"I can't be sure." Dr. Walker fidgeted with her hands in her lap. "It was darker than the sweatshirt, but I know that's not much help."

He reassured her with a smile. "You're doing just fine. Any idea on height?"

She sighed as she shook her head. "I'm sorry. I wish I could tell you more."

"It's okay. Don't sweat it. Is there anything else you noticed in the area?"

"Bodies, buzzards, running man. That covers it."

Matthew couldn't help but smile again. "Very eloquent."

He spent the next few minutes asking additional questions, hoping to jog anything from her memory, but to no avail. When he was finished, he reluctantly stood.

Matthew handed her one of his business cards. "Here, please call me if you think of anything else, Dr. Walker."

"I will, Detective Church." The smile Dr. Walker gave him could have lit up the darkest day.

As he headed back to his partner, Matthew knew he was grinning like an idiot.

Charli raised her eyebrows. "You okay?"

"I'm fine. How's it going over here?"

Soames stood from where he had been crouched over the bodies, furrowing his brow. "The victims appear to be in their early twenties. It looks like their throats were slit like the other couple. With the damage done by the vultures, though, I can't be certain until I get them back to the lab. There is one thing that I can tell you that distinguishes this crime scene from the earlier one."

The medical examiner eased the woman onto her side. There, carved into her back were the words "Song of Solomon," followed by some smaller cut marks. It was hard to make them out because of their size and jaggedness compared to the larger letters. And everything was coated in bloody sand, which didn't help.

Charli glanced at Matthew. "Song of Solomon. That's a book in the Bible."

Matthew rolled his eyes. "I'm not totally ignorant."

"It looks like the killer tried to carve some numbers for a particular verse but ran out of room or time or both. Anyway, so far, that's all I got right now." Soames gently lowered the victim back onto the ground.

Matthew nodded, not surprised. Anytime there were environmental factors at play, it made things messy for all of them, but particularly Soames.

I wouldn't want his job for anything.

※

ON THE FAR side of the river, I found myself crouched in the bushes as the police examined the crime scene. I didn't want to watch, but I couldn't help myself. When two familiar faces showed up, I was even more riveted.

I still struggled to understand what was happening. Was it possible I had hurt those people? The blood in my shower. It was the second time this week. The first time...

I froze.

No, it can't be.

My mind didn't want to go there, but I had no power to stop it. What if I were somehow responsible for Mason Ballinger and Nicole Schott? What if I'd hurt them?

Bile rose in my throat, and I huddled in the bushes, vomiting again, as the detectives tried to figure out exactly what had happened. My sobs echoed through the air, but they didn't hear me.

I had to let them know what I suspected, but another part of me hesitated.

Not until I knew what I'd done.

20

Charli's brain was in overdrive as Matthew pulled into the parking lot at the precinct. Although they'd made a quick stop at Jeremiah's apartment, neither he nor his father appeared to be at home.

Where was the damn officer who'd been stationed to watch their house? They had radioed in and asked for an officer to swing by the house and wait until Jeremiah returned to bring him back in for questioning. There'd be hell to pay for that one.

Logic told her, though, that Jeremiah wasn't their killer, no matter what Matthew's gut or Ruth's stalker-turned-murderer profiling said. Even if he was, at least they knew where he lived and could run him to ground if they needed to.

What really worried her was the very real possibility that they were dealing with another serial killer. The press was already demanding answers, and Charli wouldn't be surprised if the story went national soon. Dead naked lovers in the park would make a hell of a headline, and she could practically hear the *Romeo and Juliet* sound bites.

The carving on the back of the new female victim could represent a refinement in the serial killer's pattern. Or it could be a copycat who was inspired by the original killing. Given how tightly they'd kept the details of that under wraps, the possible copycat pool was small enough to make it extremely unlikely.

She glanced at Matthew, who had seemed distant on the drive back. "You okay?"

He sighed. "Just wondering if we have a religious serial killer on our hands. You know, with the whole Song of Solomon thing."

"Yeah, me too."

"Why that book, though?" His voice was puzzled. "Why not Revelation or Proverbs or something?"

Charli pushed a short lock of hair behind her ear. "In a way, it's actually quite appropriate given that our victims are dead naked couples."

Matthew raised his eyebrows. "How so?"

"So you know enough to know that it's a book in the Bible, but not enough to know what it is?"

"Fine," he grouched. "I must have skipped Sunday School that day. Just tell me already."

"They probably just skipped all eight chapters of it in Sunday School."

"What? Why?"

"It's a series of letters between Solomon and his lover. It's erotic poetry about love, romance, and sex."

Matthew's eyes were huge. "No way. Seriously?"

His incredulity made Charli laugh all the harder. "It sure is."

"I don't believe it."

"In fifth grade, Joey McDonald was always very fond of quoting a section in chapter seven, where Solomon discusses how his lover's breasts are like fruit, and he plans to climb her like a tree and take hold of it."

"Dear heavens!"

Charli howled. "That's what she said."

After a few moments, the laughter faded. It had been a much-needed respite, but the cold, hard reality of the crime scene they had just visited reasserted itself. Charli turned to stare out the window, lost in her thoughts.

When they walked across the parking lot and hurried to their office, Charli suspected that Matthew wasn't in the mood to interact with anyone else either.

She set down her messenger bag. "I'll check missing persons reports."

Matthew grunted in response as he sat at his computer.

❄

CHARLI WHIRLED around in her desk chair. "I think I got her."

"Yeah?" Matthew stood and came around the desk to look at her computer screen.

"Anna Miller, twenty-two. Reported missing by her roommate this morning."

"That was fast."

"Yeah. Nothing on the guy yet."

In real life, there was no waiting period for reporting a missing person like TV made it out to be. Anna's roommate had absolutely done the right thing. *Unfortunately, it didn't change the outcome.*

"Right height, weight, race, hair color. Plus, the roommate mentions the rose tattoo." Charli poked her finger at the screen, as though Matthew couldn't read it on his own.

"I see it."

"Roommate said she last saw Anna and her boyfriend,

Parker Foster, yesterday evening before they went out to dinner."

Matthew kept reading over her shoulder. "Looks like Parker's coloring and build matches what we could see of the guy's body."

Charli dialed the number the roommate left. Moments later, it went to voicemail.

"Hi, you've reached Lauren Jensen. I'm probably in class or studying. Leave a message, and I'll get back to you ASAP. Toodles!"

"Hi, Miss Jensen. This is Detective Cross from the Savannah Police Department. I'm calling regarding the missing persons report you filed about your roommate, Anna Miller. It's urgent that you call me back as soon as you get this message."

Charli ended the call, drumming her fingers on the desk as she studied the picture on her computer monitor.

"Anna, why you? Why Parker?"

Matthew coughed. "You know she can't hear you, right?"

Charli shot him the middle finger. "Shut up."

"Hopefully, she calls back soon. I've been checking Jeremiah's social media, which has basically provided me with nothing since the kid rarely uses it. He has very few friends or followers, or people he's following, for that matter. Let me just check for any links between Jeremiah and the victims."

Charli tried to concentrate on her own work, as the *click-clack* of keys from Matthew's keyboard seemed deafening. Finally, Matthew peered around his monitor. "As far as I can see, Jeremiah doesn't have any obvious ties to Anna or Parker. Still, I'm going to call IT and alert them to look for those names on his computer."

While Matthew called downstairs, Charli rolled back to her computer. Neither Anna nor Parker had any brushes with the law. Parker had been fingerprinted in order to be a student and teacher assistant at Savannah State University, which was where Anna was going to school.

A rap at their door caused Charli to glance up. A uniform was standing there. "They've got Jeremiah Dunn in interrogation B."

Charli jumped up, tripping over her chair in her haste. "Thanks. We'll be right down."

Matthew hung up the phone, having just finished talking to IT, and followed her out of the room.

Downstairs in the interrogation room, Jeremiah was calm —a stark contrast to the last time they'd seen him.

He raised his head when they came in and gave a long, low sigh. "I should have known it was you two. Why can't you leave me alone?"

Charli sat across from him, a smile in place. "We'd love to. We just need to get a few things straightened out first."

"Look, I talked to one of those public defender guys. He advised me not to say anything to you about anything, but I don't care. I didn't kill Nicole. If asking me questions helps you find her killer, then go for it."

Matthew eyed Jeremiah as he sat next to Charli. "That's very open-minded of you." He provided the time, date, and names of the room for the video camera before asking, "Just to be clear, you don't want an attorney with you now?"

"No. I'm not here for you guys. I'm doing it for her. Don't you get it?" Jeremiah's face was earnest as he glanced between the detectives. "I loved her with everything I am. Whoever killed her…well, they might as well have killed me too." Jeremiah's voice cracked at the end.

Charli didn't have to fake the sympathy oozing from her. "At least you'll get to see her again in heaven. That has to be some consolation."

"Are you kidding me right now?" Jeremiah eyed her like

she was crazy. "There's no such place. And there is no God. If there were, He would have spared her. Or taken me too."

Charli had dropped the Bible reference just to see how he'd react. "You sure you didn't quote any Song of Solomon to her in your letters?"

"Song of what? Wait, is that about the dude who threatened to cut a baby in half or something? Why on earth would I talk about some awful dead guy?"

Matthew leaned forward. "Okay, how about you tell me about Anna Miller and Parker Foster?"

"Who?" Jeremiah let out another long sigh. "Do they have something to do with Nicole's murder?"

Are you really ignorant or just really good at playing people?

"You know, *Anna* and *Parker*." Charli tried to prompt his memory, making it sound like he should know who they were.

"They're not in any of my classes." Jeremiah squinted, contorting his face while he took a minute to think. "Are they freshmen?"

"Please." Charli rolled her eyes. "You know, Parker and Anna."

Jeremiah shook his head. "I don't get it. Are they singers or something? I don't listen to pop music. I'm into classical."

Charli sighed. "No. I can't believe you don't know who they are. After all, they know about you."

Jeremiah's face clouded. "Okay, I get it. Do they go to that church Mason kept dragging Nicole to? I told her it was a waste of time. I know she missed her dad and all, but he's in the ground, just like my mom, and now..." Jeremiah's lips began to quiver. "Now she's about to be too."

Charli scribbled in her notebook. "You think Anna and Parker went to church with Nicole?"

"It's possible. I mean, they're not in our class at school.

And besides hanging out with Mason, that church is the only place Nicole could have met anyone or made friends."

"I take it you didn't approve?" Matthew's voice was sympathetic.

"She was just wasting her time there. Just like she was wasting her time with Mason." Jeremiah deflated. He slumped and looked like he was on the verge of another crying fit.

Matthew turned to Charli. "Refresh my memory. What's the name of that church?"

Charli pulled out her notebook and pretended to flip through it, looking for the name. "It's in here somewhere."

Jeremiah spoke up. "Sunrise Church. The one downtown with that huge spire. You can see it for miles."

"Yeah, that's it." Matthew focused on Jeremiah. "You ever step foot inside there?"

"Religion is a joke." Jeremiah sniffed, wiping his nose on his shirtsleeve. "Why would I waste my time?"

Charli glanced down at her notes. "You followed Nicole everywhere else."

"Yes, I did." Defiance blazed in Jeremiah's eyes. "But not in there. *Never* in there."

Charli drummed her fingers on the table. "Why not?"

"Because."

She raised an eyebrow.

Tears flooded Jeremiah's eyes. "Because the last time I was in a church, it was my mom's funeral." Tears began to roll down his cheeks.

Charli sat back in her chair and glanced at Matthew, who was staring at her. He shook his head.

"Where were you between six last night and six this morning?" Charli didn't know the time of death, so she was tossing her net wide.

"Why?"

Matthew growled deep in his throat. "Just answer the question."

Jeremiah narrowed his eyes. "I was home on house arrest by my dad, thank you very much. I stayed in my room and worked on some code. I had to even use my dad's old computer from his office, because you all still have my laptop." He scoffed. "You gonna take that, too?"

Matthew's face turned menacing. "We might. How about we take every device you've ever laid a finger on?"

Charli jumped in. "Okay, Jeremiah. If we have any more questions, we'll be in touch. If you think of anything that might help us bring Nicole's killer to justice, please reach out." She handed him another card.

"That's it?" Jeremiah's confusion was evident as he wiped at his cheeks.

"Yes." Charli snapped her notebook shut and studied the young man, waiting for him to move. "You're free to go for now."

He nodded and rose to his feet, heading for the door. After he opened it, he hesitated on the threshold, and then turned. "Whoever did this is a monster and needs to be stopped. You need to find him and stop him."

"We'll do our best." Charli wished she could promise him more, but she knew from painful experience that she couldn't.

Jeremiah disappeared out the door.

Matthew raised his hands, palms up. "Well, I've got good news for you. I'm thinking you might be right, and Jeremiah isn't our guy."

"The bad news is that brings us back to square one." Charli dropped her gaze to the table, frustration welling inside.

"Let's check out the church. See if, by any chance, Anna or Parker did go there and maybe knew Nicole and Mason."

She sighed. "It's worth a shot."

Her phone rang, and she fished it out of her pocket. "This is Detective Cross."

"Hi, this is Lauren Jensen. I'm returning your call."

"Thank you for calling, Ms. Jensen. Do you mind if we come see you and ask you some questions about Anna?"

"Yes, please. Is she okay? Did you find her?"

"I'll answer all your questions when we meet. Where are you now?"

"I'm at our apartment. I'll text you the address."

Charli didn't bother pointing out that they already had it. "Thank you. We'll be right there."

Matthew stood. "That's good."

Before they could leave, Janice entered the room. "I see you let the Dunn kid go." She swaggered toward Matthew and sat on the edge of the table next to him.

"Yup." Charli plastered a stiff smile on her face. "We're heading out to another interview. Could you check ViCAP to see if there are any similar crimes or victims in the database?"

Janice nodded and flashed Charli a small smile before turning to Matthew.

Wow. That's the first time she's ever smiled at me. And I got a nod. What's going on?

"Anything I can do for you?" Janice batted her fake eyelashes at him.

"Checking ViCAP is all I can think of." Matthew glanced uneasily at Charli, his brow furrowed.

Janice leaned toward him, invading his space. "Sure. If you take me to lunch."

A perverse sense of joy spread through Charli when Matthew's face and neck turned a crimson red.

"Um, well, okay, I guess. I have to go interview the latest victim's roommate first."

"I prefer a late lunch. It helps facilitate a late dinner." Janice sashayed out of the room, hips swaying.

Matthew faced Charli, slack-jawed.

She couldn't help but think of Rebecca, who seemed more than a little interested in her partner.

Watch out, Janice. You've got competition.

21

"Oh, come on!" Charli gathered the deck of cards and tossed them back in the glove compartment. "I really don't want to deliver this news."

She and Matthew had a custom of playing a hand of blackjack whenever neither—or both—of them wanted to do a task. Often, it was telling someone's friend or loved one that they had passed away. Something they'd picked up their first year working together as partners.

"I know it sucks." Matthew opened the door of his truck. "You ready to do this?"

"As I'll ever be."

When Charli knocked on the door of Anna's apartment, a young woman with red, flyaway hair, green eyes, and a healthy smattering of freckles across her pale skin opened it. She did so within a second, as though she'd been at the door, waiting.

"Lauren Jensen?"

"Yes. Are you the detectives?"

Charli nodded and went through the introductions.

Lauren held the door open wide. "Come in."

They walked inside, past a small kitchen and into a living room filled with secondhand furniture from the seventies forward. Charli perched on what looked to be an ancient futon. After a moment's hesitation, Matthew sat in a formal dining chair.

Lauren followed them in and sat on the edge of an ottoman, glancing from one to the other and hunching her shoulders. "Something happened to Anna, didn't it?"

Charli searched the young woman's face. "What makes you say that?"

"The officer who took the report kept saying she was probably just with her boyfriend. Then two detectives show up," she gestured to them, "and you both have grim faces."

Charli leaned forward, doing her best to ignore the groaning of the futon beneath her. "Tell us about yesterday, about the last time you saw Anna."

Lauren licked her lips. "She was wearing her red dress. It was Parker's favorite. It was their one-year anniversary of dating, and they were going out to dinner."

Charli pulled out her notebook and began jotting the information down. "Where?"

"Angelo's." Lauren gave a small smile. "It's where they had their first date. Parker is always super good at remembering stuff like that. It's one of the things Anna loves about him."

Weird that we were just there.

"Did he pick her up, or did they meet there?"

"He picked her up around six thirty. He was wearing a suit, and he brought her roses. They're over there." Lauren pointed to a fresh bouquet in a vase on the kitchen counter.

Charli glanced at them. Fire-and-ice roses, white petals stained bloodred at the tips. Ironic. She turned back to Lauren.

"Please, something's happened." Lauren twisted a rose

gold bangle around on her left wrist. "I can tell. Where is she? Is she hurt?"

This is always the worst part, the pronouncement. Hope is lost.

"This morning, a man and a woman were found by the river. From her description, I'm afraid the victims are Anna and Parker. We'll need a positive identification, but we believe it's them. I'm so sorry."

Charli hated this part of the job with a passion. She witnessed the comprehension dawn on Lauren's face.

"I-I don't understand." Lauren's lower lip quivered. "How? What happened?"

Matthew cleared his throat and leaned forward, his voice gentle as he answered. "I'm afraid she and Parker were murdered."

Lauren blinked several times, her mouth set in a hard line.

Charli nodded, letting the young woman know it was true.

Pupils dilating, Lauren stared at them. "You…you have to be joking. I mean, who gets murdered? That doesn't happen."

Matthew grimaced. "Unfortunately, it does."

"No." Lauren was in full-on denial. "Not to people I know, not to Anna. Not to Parker."

Charli's heart went out to the girl. "We're so very sorry for your loss."

Lauren slid off the ottoman and onto the floor, where she pulled her knees up against her chest and wrapped her arms around them. "Why? Who would do such a thing?" Her voice was just above a whisper now.

Charli got down on the floor next to her, touching the young woman's shoulder. There was a slight tremor beneath her hand.

"We were hoping you could help us with that."

Lauren began to rock back and forth, still hugging her

knees. "I-I don't know. Anna was nice to everyone. I mean, she didn't interact with many people. She was always so focused on her classwork. Anna just started grad school this year. She was going to be a psychologist. I always told her she was going to be an amazing one and help so many people." Lauren paused to wipe her eyes. "She cared deeply and always had these amazing insights. Every time I had a weird dream, she could tell me exactly what my subconscious was trying to work out."

Charli kept her voice low and even. "What about Parker?"

"He was in grad school too. Second year, studying to be a dentist. Applied for a TA position. He was just a really good, decent guy. He was as focused on school as Anna was." Lauren wiped her eyes again, this time with her sleeve. "They both were on scholarships, and they worked so hard. The only free time they had, they spent with each other. They were perfectly matched, you know?"

"It sounds like it."

Lauren was shaking harder. Charli caught Matthew's eye and pointed to a throw blanket on one of the chairs. He grabbed it and handed it to her.

Gingerly, she wrapped the blanket around Lauren, who hardly seemed to notice. "Ms. Jensen, would you like some tea?"

The young woman nodded, her head jerking up and down. "I'm cold."

"You've been through quite a shock, but it's going to be okay." Charli spoke in slow, soothing tones to make sure Lauren was tracking what she said. "Do you want to get comfortable on the couch while Detective Church makes some tea?"

Lauren tried to get up, but she seemed unable to stand on her own. Ultimately, it took both Charli and Matthew to maneuver her up off the floor and onto the couch. Once there, Charli again wrapped the young woman in the blanket and elevated her feet.

While Matthew rummaged in the kitchen, Charli pulled a chair close to Lauren and held her hand. Though not her thing, she was aware the young woman needed physical contact. Plus, Charli was keeping a finger on her pulse to make sure it didn't become erratic, signaling that her health was in jeopardy.

"We got randomly matched together in the dorm freshman year. We've been roommates ever since. Did you know that?"

Charli flashed a gentle smile. "No, I didn't know that."

Everyone reacted differently to the grief and sudden shock of losing a loved one. Somehow, it always seemed amplified when the death was violent and unnatural.

"Parker was going to propose to her last night." Lauren sniffed, pulling the blanket tighter around her. "He told me. I was so excited for them."

The image of Anna's broken ring finger on her left hand leapt into Charli's mind. Had Parker already proposed? And if so, had the killer taken the ring off her finger by force?

Was this a theft case gone wrong? No. There were too many similarities to Nicole and Mason for that to be true.

Her thoughts quickened. Anna and Parker were celebrating an anniversary. According to Mason's father, Mason and Nicole were about to celebrate one, and Mason had bought the Claddagh ring in anticipation of it. Could that be just a coincidence?

"What were you doing last night, Ms. Jensen?"

Charli needed to get her alibi, even though she found it extremely unlikely that Lauren had anything to do with the murders.

"I had study group for Astrophysics. Everyone came over at seven and was here until midnight. I figured that's why

Anna was staying out so late. All the cars out front. Then I ended up going to bed and didn't notice she hadn't come home 'til…" A fresh wave of tears rolled down Lauren's cheeks. "I didn't mind if Parker came over at night. He did, sometimes. He still lived with his mom, so they couldn't go to his place for any private time. Sometimes, I know they'd go down by the river. Anna used to say it was so peaceful there. I told her that she didn't have to." Lauren's face crumpled, and she swiped several times at her tears. "I shouldn't have had the study group over. I should have made everyone meet at the library."

"It's okay." Charli rubbed the distraught woman's back. "It's not your fault."

Matthew emerged from the kitchen with a cup of hot tea. He handed it to Lauren, and she was able to take small sips.

Charli continued the questioning. "Did Parker have any enemies?"

"Gosh, no. He was as nice and as busy as Anna. I can't imagine anyone wanting to hurt either of them."

Matthew leaned forward. "You mentioned in the police report that Anna had a tattoo. Can you describe it?"

"Yes, it was a rose on her thigh." Lauren took another sip of her tea. "She got it our sophomore year when we were on spring break."

"Do you happen to have a picture?" Charli figured it was a long shot, but it could help them positively identify Anna's body.

"I don't…actually, yes. There's a Halloween picture that she and Parker took last year. He was a magician, and she was his assistant. It's framed in her room, and you can see the tattoo."

Tears were flowing freely down Lauren's cheeks, but she was holding up like a trooper. Charli had no doubt, though, that a storm was brewing inside.

"I'll get it." Matthew peered toward the hallway. "Which room is hers?"

"The first one."

He stood. "Mind if I take a look around while I'm in there?"

"No. I guess she won't mind either." Lauren let out a little sniffle.

"Why don't you stay here, and the two of you can talk some more?" Matthew looked probingly at Charli, who nodded.

※

Twenty minutes later, Matthew returned from Anna's room with a laptop and a framed picture. He handed the latter to Charli, who studied the girl in the photo. The tattoo on Anna's leg in the picture was identical to the one she'd seen just a couple of hours before.

Charli peered at Lauren. "Do you mind if we take the picture and the laptop? We can return them."

"No, I don't mind." She rested her mug on her knee. "They aren't mine."

Charli took Lauren's empty cup from her and put it on the table. "Do you have contact information for Anna and Parker's parents?"

"I have Anna's folk's cell phones, but they're on a cruise right now, so I'm not sure you'll be able to reach them. Anna complained that her dad was too cheap to get the international data plan, so they were always out of contact when they'd travel anywhere."

"Do you know which cruise line they took?"

Lauren shook her head. "No, but Mrs. Miller has several sisters who'd probably know. I don't have their contact information, though."

Charli jotted all the information down. "Do you have contact information for Parker's parents?"

Lauren gave a mechanical nod. "They're divorced, and I don't have his dad's number, but his mom still has a house phone. I have that number and the address. I've dropped Anna off there a few times."

"Thank you. That would be incredibly helpful."

Lauren shuddered and pulled the blanket tighter once again. "I just can't believe they're gone."

Matthew went to refill Lauren's cup, craning his head around the doorframe in the kitchen. "Do you have someone who can come stay with you?"

"My dad lives in Atlanta." Lauren clutched the blanket like it was her lifeline. "I'm going to call him."

"Okay." Matthew walked back into the room and handed her another cup of tea. "Is there someone nearby who can wait with you while he drives here?"

Lauren glanced at the apartment door. "I have a friend who lives across the hall."

"Why don't you get us those numbers for Anna and Parker's parents?" Charli smiled gently. "Then we'll sit here while you call your dad and neighbor."

22

Charli and Matthew waited until the neighbor from across the hall came over before heading out.

While Matthew drove, Charli tried calling Anna's parents, but both cell phones went to voicemail. She left messages to call her or Matthew back.

Matthew shot her a glare after she'd hung up. "Thanks a lot."

A grin spread across Charli's face. *Someone's grumpy today.* "You know they'll probably call me back, since it's easier to just call the number that comes up."

"Still, I don't like taking my chances." Matthew fumbled with the AC vent. "You know I hate those calls even more than you do."

"I wouldn't be so sure about that."

He glanced at her again. "Are you calling Parker's mom next?"

Charli tapped her phone with her index finger. "No. Let's drive over there. Maybe we can catch her at home."

"You're the boss."

Charli chuckled. "If only you'd remember that more often."

"Yeah, yeah. Just give me the address."

❋

As they walked up to Parker's house, the door flew open. A woman in nurse's scrubs stood in the doorway.

"Are you the detectives?"

Had Lauren already called her?

Matthew exchanged a glance with Charli, who gave a slight shrug. "Yes, ma'am. I'm Detective Church, and this is my partner, Detective Cross."

"I'm Margo Foster." The woman fixed the detectives with an unblinking stare. "Is it true that my boy is dead?"

Matthew's brow furrowed as he answered. "Let's go inside so we can talk."

Margo stomped her foot, but less from anger than extreme distress. "No. We can talk right here. Tell me…is my son dead?"

Although Charli had been the one to break the news to Lauren, she readied herself to take another one for the team. "We believe so."

Margo slumped against the doorframe, and Matthew hurried forward to catch her in case she fell.

"Let's go inside."

This time, Margo didn't argue. The house was neat and somewhat spartan. The older woman sank down onto a couch in the family room, and Charli and Matthew took positions in flanking chairs.

She looked at them with hollow eyes. "I got the call while I was at work. I don't want to believe it, but in my heart, I know it's true. Do you understand?"

Charli nodded. "A little."

Margo leaned forward so far as to make Charli uncomfortable, focusing a laser-like stare on her. "Are you a mother?"

Charli was taken aback. "No."

"Then you can't understand. When you're a mother, you know your child. You feel their pain. Your gut tells you when something is wrong with them, and it tears at you. I woke last night from a terrible dream, and I knew something was desperately wrong." She raised a hand to her chest. "I felt it in my soul. Parker wasn't in his room. I know he stays at his girlfriend's every now and again, so I tried calling, but he didn't answer. *He didn't answer!*"

"I'm so sorry for your loss." The words were empty and shallow, but they were the only ones she had. "I'm not a mother, but I know what it's like to lose someone close to me."

"You don't ever recover from something like this."

"No, you don't." Charli could at least affirm what the other woman already knew.

Matthew cleared his throat. "Do you know anyone who would want to hurt your son or Anna?"

Margo shook her head. "Not a soul in this world. They were both kind and gentle. They wanted nothing more than to help people."

He pressed on. "There's no one who might have borne a grudge or been jealous of them in some way?"

She glared at Matthew, as if offended by the question. "I can't imagine anyone who would bear ill will toward either of those kids." The woman shifted to look at Charli, fire in her gaze. "They were perfect angels."

And now they're with the angels...at least, I'd like to think so.

"Tell us what you know about their whereabouts yesterday evening."

Margo told a tale similar to Lauren's, sharing how it was

their anniversary and they'd planned to eat at Angelo's to celebrate.

"Did you know that Parker planned to propose to Anna?"

Margo crumpled in on herself, her face seeming older, beyond her years. "I-I did. We had a good long talk about it. I know that might sound funny, a boy talking to his mama about wanting to propose to his girl. But he was a thoughtful person, and he wanted to do things right. We had us a hard conversation."

"About what, exactly?" Charli had gotten out her notebook and was waiting for something she could write down.

"About why his daddy and I split up. Parker never wanted something like that to happen to him and Anna. I told him he didn't need to worry. As long as they were honest with each other and held fast to each other, then they'd get through whatever life threw at them."

Great life advice. Too bad Parker wouldn't get a chance to take it. "I presume things weren't that way between you and Parker's father?"

Margo scoffed. "Lord have mercy, no. That man hadn't an honest bone in his body. He was a traveling salesman, through and through. And it wasn't until we'd been married ten years and had Parker that I realized he'd been selling me that whole time, pretending to be something he wasn't, making promises he couldn't keep."

Parker's mother had a lot of fire in her, which was making for an interesting interview. Charli couldn't tell from moment to moment if the woman was going to cry or lash out. Still, she pressed on.

"How would you characterize the relationship between Parker and his father?"

"Detective Cross, you're barking up the wrong tree. Darryl might be a cheater and a compulsive liar, but he loved that boy and never would have hurt a hair on his head, not on purpose. Besides, he's out of town on vacation. I've called him, though, and he's taking the next flight back." Tears flooded the woman's eyes. "No way he'd miss our boy's funeral."

They spent another twenty minutes talking about friends and families, as well as any churches Parker might have attended. Establishing Margo's alibi for the previous night consumed another ten minutes. When all that was done, Matthew leaned forward and handed her a business card. "We'd appreciate you letting us know when he's back in town so we could talk to him as well."

Margo sniffled but managed to hold herself together. "All right, but he won't be able to tell you anything I haven't already. I can give you his number."

"That would be immensely helpful."

She rattled off the number, and Charli wrote it down. "Thank you for that. Now, would you mind if we took a look around Parker's room?"

"Please, go ahead. I doubt you'll find anything, but if there's even the slightest chance that something you find in there will help you catch the person who did this to my boy, then you're more than welcome."

They headed upstairs to the room she indicated.

Moments later, they were standing in Parker's room.

Matthew nodded with satisfaction. "Yup, this one's a grad student. Not a teenager, not a college boy."

Looks like a guy's room to me.

"How can you tell? I mean, there are no clothes thrown around, but between the papers, pens, and books, there's still a lot of clutter."

He smiled. "Yes, but take a deep breath."

Charli complied. "I don't smell anything."

Matthew held up an index finger. "Exactly! No old socks,

no rotting pieces of pizza. This is a man's room. And he's doing real work in it."

Charli rolled her eyes. "Well, let's split up the room. Which half do you want?"

※

AN HOUR LATER, they were leaving Parker's house empty-handed, except for his laptop, which his mother had sent with her blessing.

Matthew slid behind the wheel. "Well, now what?"

Charli got in and buckled up. "I think we should check out the church Jeremiah told us about. Notice anything interesting about it?"

"You mean it's the same church that the old geezer with the sign was telling us we should attend?" Matthew narrowed his eyes. "Yeah, I noticed."

"Then I think that's where we should go. Given the verse carved into Anna's back, I think we might be looking at a religious killer."

"And given that Mason was religious and helping Nicole find a little of that old-time religion, too, you think there's a connection?"

"Could be." Charli rolled her shoulders, trying to stretch out a kink. "While you were checking Anna's room, I asked Lauren if Anna was a churchgoer. She said no, but believed Parker attended on occasion."

"We should have asked his mother which church." Matthew hesitated. "We could go back in there now."

Charli shook her head. "We can always call and ask her later. Right now, I'm getting hungry."

Matthew glanced at the clock. "I guess it is getting near that time."

Charli's phone pinged, and she checked it. A text from Preston.

Heard about the new victims. You need anything?

She smiled and texted back.

A good hamburger. I'm starving.

Actually, I could use the same. I haven't eaten yet.

Me neither. Policing is hard work.

But you make it look so easy.

She smiled at the compliment.

Flatterer.

You know what they say. Flattery will get you everywhere.

A slight rush of heat rose to Charli's cheeks.

Will it, now?

Tell you what, why don't we meet at Wild West Burgers?

That was one of Charli's favorite places. She was curious if he knew that, or if it was one of his favorites too.

Love that place.

I thought you might.

Sounds like a winner. Meet you there in thirty?

You bet.

Matthew broke in. "Come on, Charli, don't leave me in suspense. Who is it?"

"It's Preston." Charli tore herself away from the phone and put it back in her pocket.

Matthew smirked. "Oh."

"He's suggesting lunch at Wild West Burgers."

He raised an eyebrow. "The man has good taste in burgers."

"You want to join us?"

"So much. Unfortunately, I don't think I can." Matthew turned bright red.

"Oh, that's right." Charli snickered. "I totally forgot you have that big date with Janice."

"It's not a date."

Charli nodded. "Uh-huh, sure. Keep telling yourself that."

Part of Charli felt guilty at how amused she was by the whole situation. But if being a detective had taught her anything, it was that she needed to accept the small joys in life when she could, no matter how ill-timed they were. And that included giving Matthew a little hell over a woman who was crushing on him.

Matthew growled, a vein popping in his neck. "It's not funny."

Charli chuckled. "Oh, I beg to differ. It's *hilarious*."

He threw her an exasperated glance. "I have no interest in her that way."

Charli patted him on the shoulder. "Good luck telling her that. She doesn't seem like the type who'll take 'no' for an answer."

Matthew's mouth set in a hard line. "And how's it going for you, telling lover boy you have no interest in him?"

For just a second, Charli's defenses rose, but she forced herself to stay calm. "We're not talking about me right now. This is your time. You and Janice. I'm telling you, love is in the air. Birds are singing."

Matthew stomped on the brakes hard, and the truck squealed to a halt. "All right, that's it. Get out."

Had she really offended Matthew that much? "You can't be serious."

"I'm deadly serious."

Charli blinked. "You'd honestly kick me out of the truck?"

"One hundred percent." He was glowering at her in a way that surprised her.

"Right here. Right now?"

"No better place, in my estimation."

Shock surged through Charli. She knew that she might have pushed the teasing a little bit too far, but she never would have guessed he'd get this bent out of shape. For a moment, she debated what to do. Apologizing was probably the most forthright.

But the more he glared at her, the more she didn't want to. If Matthew was going to be an ass, then why should she back down?

"I'm serious, Charli. Get out of this vehicle."

She raised her chin in defiance. "Give me one good reason."

"Because your car's right there, and our lunch dates are on opposite sides of town from each other."

Charli whipped her head around and found that they were in the parking lot of the bar from the night before. There, ten feet from them, was indeed her car.

Next to her, Matthew threw his head back and roared with laughter. "Got you."

Relief flooded through her. "I'm not gonna lie. You scared me."

"Good. You deserved it, after teasing me about Janice. And by the way, you never told me what you were doing with Preston. Were you on a date?"

Charli threw up her hands in surrender. *I'm so not answering that.* "Okay, I get it. I've got to go, so I'm not late to meet him."

With a grin, she got out of the truck.

Matthew nodded. "See you at the precinct after lunch."

Was it her imagination, or did her partner sound just a little trepidatious?

23

As Charli drove toward Wild West Burgers, she admitted to herself that she was looking forward to seeing Preston. It had been so good to bounce ideas off him the night before that she was excited for more of the same. And doing so over the best burgers in town? What could be better?

When she reached the restaurant, she walked inside to find Preston already seated. He waved her over, and she slipped into the booth across the table from him. The handsome GBI agent smiled at her in his easy way, and a frisson of excitement danced up her spine.

We're here to work, not fraternize.

Still, there was part of her that kept thinking it might be nice to do both.

"You have no right to look so fresh and lovely on as little sleep as you had."

She smiled at Preston's greeting. "What can I say? I'm the queen of the power nap."

Charli knew it was lame once she'd said it, but Preston smiled anyway.

He picked up the menu and perused it. "Which one's your favorite?"

"The smothered burger. Onions, mushrooms, and provolone." Charli started to salivate just thinking about it.

"Ah, nice choice. I like the cheddar blue. You can't really go wrong with meat and double cheese."

A minute later, they had given their server their order, and Charli found herself settling back into the overstuffed seat with a sigh.

Preston's gaze was filled with sympathy. "Long morning?"

"You have no idea."

"I can guess." He leaned his elbows on the table. "So is it true the second couple was found in the same manner?"

"Yes, with one interesting twist. The killer carved Song of Solomon into the woman's back."

"You're kidding."

"Not at all. It looks like he tried to carve a chapter and verse, too, but we've not been able to make it out."

Preston gave a long, low whistle. "That's some heavy stuff."

"We're on the same page there." Charli brushed her hair back from her face.

"Any connection between the two couples?"

"None that we've been able to establish so far, although we'll keep digging. We did interrogate Jeremiah Dunn and eventually let him go." Charli reached up and smoothed her hair. "He was released yesterday in plenty of time to have committed the second murders, but his interview didn't raise any red flags. And it seems like he is decidedly nonreligious."

Preston cocked his head to the side. "Well, it wouldn't be the first time nonbelievers still quoted scripture at police, either as a message or to be ironic or even to throw them off the trail."

She shook her head. "I don't buy that it's Jeremiah."

"Okay, that's good enough for me. Let's take him off the table for now." Preston made a wiping motion across the table, symbolically removing the young man.

That was easy. And so nice.

She couldn't help but wish that things were that smooth with Matthew sometimes. Charli picked up a glass of ice water and took a long swig. "Sounds good."

"So if not Jeremiah Dunn, who are we looking at?"

"That's just the problem. There isn't a real, viable suspect." She began to drum her fingers on the table.

Preston met her gaze, a quizzical smile forming on his lips. "But there's something you're thinking about super hard."

"I think there might be a religious angle."

He nodded. "I get that. Because of the Bible reference."

"It's not just because of that. There was a mentally unstable older gentleman at the first crime scene, a religious zealot who apparently feels burdened to warn people about the impending end of the world."

"I hear it's going to be a doozy of a show."

"Ha."

He waved his hands in the air. "Fire and brimstone. Seals. Horsemen. Oh, to have front-row tickets to that spectacle."

Charli rolled her eyes. "I'll pass, thank you very much."

The server arrived with a coke for Preston and a chocolate shake for her. It was the super thick kind that came in the glass with the extra ice cream in the old-fashioned metal cup on the side.

"That looks good. I think you ordered better than I did." Preston was practically drooling over her milkshake.

Charli pulled the spoon out and handed it across the table. She caught herself right before feeding it to him, handing him the spoon with an awkward jerk of her wrist while trying not to blush.

What is wrong with you? Get it together!

"Mmm, that's delicious." He handed her back the spoon, which she laid on the table. "Thank you for sharing."

"Just thought you'd like to know what you're missing out on."

Preston pinned her gaze with his. "Trust me, I do." His voice was soft, washing over her, making her feel warm inside.

She caught her breath and forced herself to look away, breaking the contact. "So, um, the old guy. He invited us to his church. Turns out it's the same one that Mason and Nicole attended."

Preston's smile slipped. "Ah, interesting. Now you've got religion at least loosely connecting everything. Any chance the new couple also went to that church?"

The server delivered their burgers, and Charli and Preston smiled their thanks.

"I don't think the woman did. We're not sure about the guy. It sounds like he might have been a churchgoer, but we're not sure if it was the same church." Charli really should have thought to ask his mom.

Preston took a bite of his burger. "Don't forget, people change churches too. Or visit a different one on occasion for an event or with a friend."

"Good point."

Charli took a long swig of the shake. It was so thick, she struggled to pull the liquid up through the straw, but the cold, delicious chocolate at the end made the effort worthwhile. Not to mention, it was the perfect pairing for a cheesy burger.

"So what's your move?"

Charli came up for air. "Well, I want to do some checking on our street preacher, Desmond Turner."

Preston nodded. "I wouldn't approach him directly,

though. I'd go to his church and ask around about him. Maybe get a list of the members."

"I agree. Plus, I don't think he could be the actual killer. His hands are too crippled to have used a knife that way, particularly if anyone was trying to fight back. And there's evidence both female victims did."

"Doesn't mean someone else at that church doesn't share his beliefs."

As they scarfed their burgers down, they chatted some more about the case. Finally, the last bite of burger was gone, and Charli's shake was empty.

"Thank you. That was satisfying. Both the food and the conversation." Charli flashed him a smile.

Preston smiled back. "Glad to be of service anytime."

She checked her phone and couldn't believe how fast the time had gone. "I really need to get back to work."

"I get it. Go. I'll grab the check."

She shot him a suspicious look. "Are you sure?"

He waved a dismissive hand. "I invited you, and I'm not on a pressing case at the moment."

A niggling feeling of guilt came over Charli for not having asked Preston what he was working on. Oh well, she'd have to make it up to him at some point.

"Thank you again." She gave him a fleeting smile before hurrying out to her car, calling Matthew as she walked.

"Hello?" His tone oozed misery.

"You ready to head to the church?"

"Yes, I can meet you there in ten minutes."

He hung up, and she chuckled to herself.

His lunch must be going really badly.

24

Charli watched Matthew as he climbed out of his truck. She'd beaten him to the church by about a minute.

As she left her vehicle and met up with him, she tried to summon up as innocent a voice as she could. "How'd your lunch go?" She couldn't, however, contain the smirk that twisted her lips.

He glowered at her and didn't dignify the question with an answer.

As they walked through the front doors into the lobby area, the sanctuary was in view. A sandy-haired man was walking down one of the pews, straightening hymnals and Bibles. They approached him.

"Excuse me. I'm Detective Cross and this is my partner, Detective Church. We're with the Savannah Police Department. We're looking for whoever is in charge."

The man looked young, late twenties or early thirties, but his blue eyes were bloodshot and dark circles indicated little sleep.

He offered them a half-hearted smile. "I guess that would be me. I'm Pastor Marshall Coleman."

Did pastors get as little sleep as police officers?

"Pastor?" That surprised Charli. She had pictured a much older person in the position. "Well, I'm glad we found you. We'd like to ask you a few questions."

He frowned. "About what?"

Charli pulled out her phone and showed him a picture of Nicole and Mason. "We wanted to ask you about two of your parishioners, Mason Ballinger and Nicole Schott."

Pastor Coleman took the phone and his face contorted in pain. He bit his lip before averting his gaze, shoving the phone back into her hands. "Yeah, they're good kids. Mason's family has been attending the church for years, since long before I moved in as pastor. Nicole is relatively new. Mason brought her. I heard about what happened…I've been trying to call Mason's parents…"

"Then you know they're dead." Matthew's manner was abrupt, surprising Charli.

The blood drained from the pastor's face. "That's what the news indicated. I was praying it wasn't true."

Charli gave Matthew a steely-eyed glare before turning back to the pastor. "I'm sorry for your loss."

Pastor Coleman sat down hard, as though his knees had given out, and he leaned his arm on the pew in front. He looked like he'd been punched in the gut and couldn't catch his breath.

Charli drew in her lower lip, struggling not to feel the pain that was etched on the man's face. "Are you okay?"

"It's just so terrible. I can't…I can't even get my head around it." He sucked in a deep breath. "Killed. They were both such nice young people. What's this world coming to?"

"What can you share about them?"

"Their poor families. I'm surprised I haven't heard from Mason's parents. There's a service to plan…" He rubbed the back of his neck.

Charli cleared her throat. "I suspect they'll be reaching out shortly."

The pastor nodded, heaving a sigh. "I can't even imagine what they're going through right now."

Matthew jumped in as Charli got out her notebook. "What can you tell us about Mason and Nicole?"

"Such good kids."

"Yes, you've said so, repeatedly." There was a touch of irritation in Matthew's voice.

"I'm sorry." The pastor ran a hand through his hair. "This is just such a shock."

Charli decided to try a different tack to detour the pastor's mind. "What can you tell us about a Desmond Turner?"

The pastor stiffened. "Desmond Turner? He's a parishioner. Why do you ask?"

"We encountered him at the crime scene, preaching about sin, sexual immorality, and the end of the world."

The pastor rolled his eyes. "That sounds about right. He's harmless, but he can deliver quite the impromptu sermon."

Charli sat in the pew in front of him and shifted so she could look him in the eye. "What makes you think he's harmless?"

A small smile tugged at the corner of Pastor Coleman's lips. "I've known him for several years, since back when I started as a pastoral intern. He talks a good story, but he's just a harmless old man. He's all bark and no bite."

Charli tapped her pen to the notebook on her lap. "How did he feel about Mason and Nicole?"

"I'm not sure he even knew them." He drummed his fingers on the pew. "This isn't a terribly large church, but not all the older members take the time to get to know the kids, which is a shame. After all, there is so much some of our old timers could teach this generation."

"Like what, exactly?" Matthew's tone had shifted to casual, friendly.

"Tradition, respect, fortitude, perseverance. Everything from how to catch a baseball to how to deal with life's curveballs." The pastor frowned. "Not all kids are blessed to be in a home with two parents. Sometimes, even those who are don't get the attention they need, because the parents are too busy providing for their family or living their own lives."

Charli tried to read between the lines. "So you think it's up to the church to pick up the slack?"

The pastor shrugged. "We always have. I guess I expect we always will." He closed his eyes for a moment, dabbing at them. "I'm sorry, I just keep thinking that I need to go over and see Mason's mother. I need to let the prayer chain know, and the bereavement team, so they can get meals flowing to the house."

Tears sprang unbidden to Charli's eyes. When her mom died, her father had lived for months off all the casseroles he'd gotten from their church. After the first three came in, he started putting them in the freezer. It had been the one comical spot in the whole horror of those days. He joked that he'd have to get a deep freezer if they kept coming.

Matthew interrupted her train of thought. "You were telling us about Mr. Turner."

With a long sigh, the pastor rubbed his face with his hands. "Right. Look, Desmond's harmless, like I said. He has dementia, and many of the members do what they can to help out, keep him company, and that sort of thing."

Dementia? Shit.

After Charli and Matthew continued to ask the pastor a few more questions, it ultimately seemed to lead nowhere. Frustration seeped through Charli as she handed Pastor Coleman her card.

"Please call if you can think of anything, even if it doesn't seem important. You never know when the slightest piece of information might create the biggest breakthrough."

Pastor Coleman pocketed her card and walked them to the door. "I certainly will. I hope you're able to find the person who did this terrible thing soon."

So did she.

Just before they stepped outside, Charli faced the pastor again. "Do you happen to know Parker Foster or Anna Miller?"

Lines appeared between Coleman's eyebrows as he considered her question. "I don't think so. Should I?"

"Would it be possible to get a copy of your church membership list?"

The lines deepened. "Why?"

"Standard procedure. Can we get a copy?"

"Sure." He glanced down at the card. "I can email it. Is this the best email address?"

She shot him a bright smile. "Sure is." She stepped outside. "Much appreciated."

"No problem." He let go of the door. "Let me know if you need anything else."

"What do you think?" Matthew sprung the question on Charli once they were in his truck.

"I'm not sure. I get kind of a weird vibe from him."

How do I even describe it?

Matthew twisted around in his seat to stare at her. "Okay, see now, I need to know something. How come you can vibe, but I'm not allowed to have hunches?"

Charli tilted her chin up. "Because my vibes are real, and your hunches aren't."

"Them's fighting words." Matthew started up the truck and gave her a mock scowl.

"Prove me wrong anytime."

Matthew waggled his eyebrows. "Oh, I will. For now, let's go visit our loon."

25

They'd been on the road for less than two minutes when Charli's phone rang.

"It's Soames." She put it on speaker. "Hey, Doc, we're listening."

"Always nice to be heard. If only the women I dated cared as much about what I have to say as you two do."

Charli couldn't help but grin. "Speaking of dating, tell us more about this special lady in your life."

Soames chuckled. "Well, there's not much to tell, except she's way out of my league."

Matthew guffawed, and Charli shot him a look. "You'll have to excuse Matthew. And I'm sure that's not true, because you're quite the catch." As much as Charli enjoyed the banter, they had to get down to business. "What do you have for us?"

"A mystery, as always. We found a partial bloody print at the base of Anna's head. Before you get your hopes up, we ran it, and there's no match in the system. No criminal record for our guy or gal, as the case may be."

Charli glanced at Matthew. "You don't seriously think our killer could be a woman, do you?"

"I always hate to underestimate women. After all, they can do anything a man can do, but also backward and in high heels, just like Ginger Rogers said. However, it would take an extraordinarily strong woman to overpower these young people. So unless the Olympics or the circus is in town, I'm leaning toward a man."

"Thank you for that elaborate explanation." Charli shook her head. Soames's sense of humor wasn't for everyone, but she always enjoyed it. "Anything else?"

"Same as the first couple, no signs of sexual assault, throats slit with a sharp object, likely a knife of some kind. Although, if I had to guess, I'd say it was a different knife. But we need more analyses to determine that with any kind of certainty. Similar instrument certainly, but these cuts seemed to indicate a serrated blade."

Matthew tapped his finger on the steering wheel. "So not a pocketknife or your average hunting knife? Maybe a fantasy knife?"

"Smaller ridges than that. More like a steak knife."

"Meat. It's what's for dinner," Matthew muttered under his breath.

Apparently, Soames heard him. "Okay, that's in extremely bad *taste*, even by my standards. You should *cut* that out."

Charli cleared her throat. "Gentlemen, can we get back to the topic at hand?"

"Okay, I'll *moo*ve on." Soames was really enjoying this. "I'd say from everything I've seen, this is the same killer."

"Great." Charli pushed her hair back away from her forehead, a twinge of anxiety flowing through her veins. "The last thing we need is another serial killer, this one going after couples."

"Yeah, there's always been that whole thing of safety in

numbers. Well, not this time." Soames's voice was actually serious.

And not when Madeline was kidnapped.

Charli wrestled her mind away from that one, pulling her attention back to the murders at hand. "What about the Song of Solomon carving?"

"Evolution of the killer's style or, perhaps, he didn't have time to carve it on the first girl."

"Could you make out the numbers?"

"No, the cuts weren't clean enough. I did mention that there was no sexual assault. However, unlike our first couple, these two were getting it on when they got killed."

Charli's mouth popped open. "They were having sex when they were killed?"

"That gives a whole other meaning to sex on the beach."

Charli smacked Matthew's hand. "C'mon."

"Just sayin'." He pointed to the right. "We're almost there, by the way."

"Anything else, Dr. Soames?"

"You'll be the first to know."

"Thanks. And hey, I'm happy for you." Charli ended the call and looked at her partner. "Serial killer. Basically, what we were already afraid of."

"Wouldn't it be nice just once to have it not be? Wouldn't that be a wonderful surprise?"

She snorted. "We need to find a way to grab our senile preacher's fingerprints."

"I thought we didn't like Desmond Turner for these murders because of the arthritic hands?"

Charli had been thinking about that. It seemed unlikely, but crazy people could show unprecedented strength from time to time. Plus, they needed to follow every lead. "I'm not ready to rule him or anyone else out just yet, male or female."

Matthew pulled over to the curb, his brow furrowing. "Interesting."

"What?"

"We're here. At Desmond's."

Shady Pines Care Center. That is *interesting.* "Well, at least he's already under medical care."

※

TEN MINUTES LATER, they were sitting in the director's office. Renee Gosling was a woman in her forties with short, wavy brown hair, shot through with streaks of gray.

Once pleasantries were exchanged, Renee got right down to business. "How can I help you, Detectives?"

Charli already had her trusty notebook at the ready. "We wanted to ask you about one of your residents, Desmond Turner."

Renee shook her head with a rueful smile. "Ah, yes, the famous Mr. Turner. The board has been considering making some changes to our operating procedures, thanks to him."

Charli leaned forward. "How so?"

"Well, it turns out Mr. Turner is quite the escape artist."

Charli glanced at the window. "You don't have an alarm system?"

The director laughed. "Of course we do, but him escaping us isn't the problem. You see, he has a lot of friends, members of his church who come by to visit and check him out of the facility. They take him to church, take him to lunch, take him to volunteer at different events." Renee ran a hand through her loose waves. "Yet amazingly, he doesn't get checked back in as often as he's checked out. At least, not right away."

Matthew frowned and shifted his bulk in the tiny wooden chair he was sitting in. "Why not?"

"They claim he performs one of his famous disappearing

acts. Inevitably, a few hours later, we'll get a call to go pick him up at the park downtown, where he's been preaching fire and brimstone to anyone who will listen."

Charli made a note to check how many silver alerts had been placed on Mr. Turner. "Why the park?"

Renee folded her hands on her desk. "Heck if I know. Maybe he likes the smells from all the restaurants across the street. Maybe it has some special connection to his past. Maybe it's the only place in town he remembers how to get to on his own. Take your pick. There're more theories if you want to hear them."

"That's okay." Charli jotted down another note before continuing. "So he's never found anywhere else? By the river, for example?"

"No, never. Always the park, without fail. I've heard him say he needs to commune with nature, and that's where he feels closest to God."

Charli shared a glance with Matthew. Desmond really didn't seem to be their guy. Of course, it didn't mean he might not know something anyway. "Could you provide us with a list of everyone who's checked him out in the last couple of weeks, and also dates and times he was picked up at the park for the same period?"

Matthew leaned forward. "And can you tell us if he was in the facility all of Saturday night and last night as well?"

Renee picked up her phone. "Of course. Give me one moment." She relayed the instructions to her assistant.

While the director was busy, Matthew leaned close to Charli. "You think he saw something he's not telling us?"

Charli shrugged. "We can't afford to ignore the possibility. He saw the bodies. He might have seen a lot more."

Renee finished her call and turned back to them. "I'll have that list for you before you leave."

Charli flashed her a bright smile. "We appreciate it."

"Some of his friends know to find him there when he escapes. People are embarrassed to admit they couldn't keep track of one little old man for a couple of hours."

Which might make it hard for any of them to admit—if he'd gone wandering during the time of the murders.

It was something to keep in mind, at any rate.

Matthew smoothed out a wrinkle in his button-down. "Is there anything else you can tell us about Mr. Turner?"

"He runs hot and cold. He's a sweetheart one minute and aggressive and temperamental the next. He has a very low tolerance for anything he considers sin." The director leaned forward. "On more than one occasion, he's berated other residents or staff for what he considers inappropriate behavior. The man's obsessed with that, actually."

Charli frowned. "Do you think he could be violent?"

"Accidentally, but not intentionally."

What in the world does that mean? "Would you mind clarifying that?"

"Of course. He gets upset and excitable." Renee straightened a stack of papers on her desk. "In that state, he might accidentally hit someone while flailing his arms or his sign that goes everywhere with him. He grazed an orderly on the jaw once that way, but I don't believe he'd ever intentionally hurt someone."

Charli snapped her notebook closed. "Thank you for that insight."

"Unless you have more questions for me, would you like to see him while we're waiting for your paperwork?"

Matthew stood, clearly happy to be free of the tiny, uncomfortable chair. "Yes, please."

26

Charli knocked on Desmond Turner's door. A muffled sound came from inside, and she opened it with caution.

Mr. Turner was sitting at a tiny desk barren of everything except for a small silver lamp and a large-print Bible that he seemed to be reading with a magnifying glass. The only other bit of furniture in the room was a twin bed—neatly made with a worn purple comforter—and a nightstand with another silver lamp and a stack of letters, brown and faded with age. Propped up in the corner next to a closet was his sign, the one Matthew had helped make the correction on in the park.

The walls held several religious pictures and framed Bible verses. Charli started studying them, searching for Song of Solomon, when Mr. Turner raised his head.

He frowned before recognition lit up his face. "Pretty detective from the park."

She smiled. "I'm not sure about the pretty part, but the rest is true."

Mr. Turner chuckled. "Come on, gals always know when they're pretty, even if they don't like to admit it."

For all his ramblings and rantings, Charli didn't sense any real malice in him. Maybe that was because he reminded her somewhat of one of Madeline's great-grandfathers who had died when the girls were ten. The old man had dementia. He would scream and yell sometimes, which could be scary. But a minute later, he'd be offering them butterscotch candies and money to go to the movies, even if they were too young to get there on their own.

All bark and no bite.

Still, Charli had to know for certain that she wasn't letting a passing similarity to someone she once knew influence her opinion or keep her from being objective now.

Mr. Turner focused his one good eye on Matthew. "And you, young fella, I see you haven't gotten yourself saved yet."

Matthew shook his head but didn't engage. He walked farther into the room, glancing around. When his gaze landed on the stack of letters on the nightstand, Mr. Turner jerked forward.

"Young man, don't go touching those and mussing 'em up."

Matthew raised his hands to show they were nowhere near the letters. "Yes, sir. What are they?"

"Love letters from my missus." There was pride in the older man's voice as he said it.

Charli walked over to get a better look. She could make out a hint of beautiful, cursive handwriting on a piece of floral stationery on top of the stack. "I didn't know you were married."

"You never asked. That's the problem with young people today. Always assuming they know everything, even though they haven't asked anybody a single question."

"Okay." Charli leveled a stare at him. "Tell me."

Mr. Turner slapped his knee. "Direct. I knew I liked you from the first." His smile faded. "Vivian was my world. We were married right out of high school and were together forty-nine years. She was real sick with cancer the last couple. I kept telling her to hold on, that we'd make it to see fifty. She tried, but the Lord wanted her too bad. Truth was, I didn't blame Him. She was in so much pain. He took her home a week before our anniversary." Tears glistened in the elderly man's eyes.

Charli found herself rapidly blinking in response to the raw pain in his voice. "I'm so sorry for your loss."

He cleared his throat. "I'll see her again. You mark my words. And as for the here and now, why, I count myself lucky. I had forty-nine years with the most wonderful woman on the face of this earth. Most can't say that. Some don't even get down the aisle before their love is taken from them. It's tragic. My son knows."

Charli had been scanning the verses on the walls, but her head jerked around at that. "What does your son know?"

"Tragedy, plain and simple."

Charli sank into the only other chair in the room. "What's your son's name?"

"Milo. Milo Cain."

Charli would never understand why people named a child after the world's first murderer.

"What can you tell us about Milo's tragedy?"

Mr. Turner stroked his frazzled beard. "Six months ago, he lost the woman he was going to marry. They'd known each other since childhood but had lost touch over the years. Then a couple years ago, they ran into each other and started dating."

Charli knew that word could be interpreted in many ways. "What do you mean by lost?"

The older man squinted at her, his forehead puckering.

"Lost, as in died. What did you think I meant? The woman wasn't a set of keys or a watch. She was a living, breathing human who choked to death the very day he proposed. It was terrible."

As the old man spoke, Charli resumed her study of his wall. There! Song of Solomon.

"The ring. It…" Mr. Turner glanced over his shoulder. "What are you looking at?"

Charli blinked, realizing she'd tuned him out. "The verses on your walls. They all seem to be about love or sex or purity."

"The entire New Testament is about love, young lady. But if you're talking about sex and marriage and immorality and all that, well, there's a lot about all that in there too. It's one of the evils in society, you know. One of the ways the evil one tempts and controls us."

"How so?" Charli prompted.

Mr. Turner's eyes flashed as his voice rose. "Men and women selling their bodies, squandering their most precious gifts with one-night stands and meaningless sex. It's an abomination! The Lord sees, and He does not tolerate such atrocities. The union of man and woman is a sacred one, not to be flouted by this current generation, this nest of vipers."

Matthew turned back toward the older man. "So you don't believe in premarital sex, I'm guessing."

"It's the devil's own work!" Mr. Turner roared, slamming his feeble fist on the desk. "It leads to horrors you've never seen, and you should thank God you haven't! Young women sell themselves. And men…men have lost respect for women. They don't even view them as people, just as objects to abuse and discard, like our poor Vicky."

The broken old man seemed to collapse in on himself as he began to sob, tears rolling down his cheeks. Charli caught

Matthew's eye, who shrugged, clearly just as surprised as she was.

She leaned forward and lowered her voice. "Who's Vicky?"

Mr. Turner looked up at her, the light of fanaticism fading from his good eye. "Our niece. My sister's girl. She came to live with us when her parents were killed in a car crash. She was four. Vicky was just like our own. We were so proud of her. Then, when she was seventeen…they took her."

Matthew rubbed the back of his neck. "Who took her?"

Mr. Turner shuddered, struggling to get the next few words out. "Traffickers…they found her…they got a boy to invite her to a party, and they took her. The police searched. We spent everything we had on detectives. They finally found her two years later, dumped in an alley down in Miami like a piece of garbage. We brought her home, but she never came home, not really. We tried to help, doctors, therapists, everyone. She died anyway. She killed herself because she couldn't live with the memories of what had happened to her."

He began crying as Charli and Matthew watched him in horror. Charli had heard stories like that, but this was the closest she'd ever come to meeting a trafficking victim. She couldn't even imagine the trauma the poor girl had endured.

What if something like that happened to Madeline?

Charli struggled not to get sick.

Matthew's hand shook as he passed his palm over his face. "As one father to another, I am so, so sorry for what happened to you and your niece."

Mr. Turner sobbed into his gnarled hands. "Thank you."

"We're sorry to have disturbed you." Charli couldn't think of anything else to say. Nothing would bring his niece back or bring him peace. At least she understood more of what drove him. His tirade at the female jogger in the park—the one he kept shouting at to put on clothes—took on a different light. Perhaps in the man's addled brain, he was trying to save her from being seen, being found, being abused. Or maybe he just had a vendetta against anything sexual at this point.

They headed to the door.

"Sex isn't bad."

Charli turned, startled as Mr. Turner addressed her private thoughts. "No, it's not."

He shook his head. "It's a gift from God that gets perverted by man and the devil. Passion, love, sex. They are a beautiful creation, but they are also dangerous. I saw you looking at the verse from Song of Solomon on the wall."

"Yes, Song of Solomon 6:8."

He nodded. "You won't find a better example in the Bible of love and the bond between man and woman, both its sanctity…and its savagery."

Before Charli could ask him what the verse was, the man shuddered, put his head in his hands, and began sobbing again.

Charli had been hollowed out inside. "Thank you for your time, Mr. Turner."

They left the room, running into Renee Gosling near the exit. She handed them the list of people who'd checked Desmond Turner out over the last two months.

Charli thanked her, exited, and they made their way swiftly to Matthew's truck. Once there, Charli leaned her head against the seat and perused the list.

Matthew swiped at his eyes. "Well, that was lots of fun."

"That poor old man." Her heart cracked for him.

"I can't even imagine."

Charli forced herself to look at Matthew. "What say we call it a night? You can drop me off so I can get my car."

"I was about to suggest the same thing. I think I need to

go home and scream into my pillow for about an hour, then call Chelsea's mom and discuss putting a tracking chip into her."

Charli blinked, trying to process what he'd just said. "You want to chip your daughter like she's a dog?"

"Or a cat. They chip cats, too, and I know girls have all that feline energy."

The idea was so absurd that Charli burst out laughing. "You honestly think Chelsea is going to let you chip her?"

"A father can try."

"And a father can fail. Epically."

27

Bright and early, Charli and Matthew arrived back at Midtown High School to discover a memorial program for Mason and Nicole was in progress in the gym. They stood in the back for a few minutes as the vice principal struggled to get through a few sentiments. Large pictures of each teen stood on easels, flanking the podium. A cacophony of sniffling and sobs rose from the gathering of students and teachers. One girl with long, red hair sat in the back close to where Charli was standing. The girl was weeping, her pain palpable.

I remember being her, but our school never held a memorial service. By the time they found Madeline's body, it was the next school year, and everyone had moved on. Everyone but me.

All Madeline had gotten was a couple of candlelight vigils, and Charli hadn't even been able to attend the first one. Her parents had kept her close to home after the ordeal.

She perused the gymnasium. In a way, these kids were lucky. They wouldn't have to wait for closure. There'd be no endless agonizing over what had happened. Everyone here knew what had occurred, even if none of them, including Charli, knew why.

Hopefully, some of Mason and Nicole's friends could help shed some light on that.

A young man with dark hair sitting next to the crying redhead kept glancing back at Charli and Matthew. Finally, he stood and walked their way.

"Excuse me. Are you the cops that were here asking about Mason and Nicole?"

Word travels fast. Then again, it was a high school. There was nowhere else like it for gossip.

"Yes." Charli spoke in a whisper to avoid interrupting the proceedings.

The young man nodded. "I'm Rogan Ortega. I went to church with them. My mom said the police were looking for me."

This was the kid who'd gone hiking. Or said he had.

"Yes, we have been looking for you." Charli used a nonthreatening tone. "Where have you been?"

He ducked his head. "On the toilet."

"Excuse me."

He pressed a hand to his stomach. "I got sick and ended up in the bathroom the past two days."

The kid did look green around the gills but was that from an upset tummy or a guilty conscience?

"At your house?"

If so, his parents had some explaining to do.

"Yeah. I did go to the urgent care center too. They gave me some medicine that helped."

She made a note to follow up on this later. Right now, she had some other things she wanted to know. "We're hoping you can answer some questions."

Matthew placed his hand on Rogan's shoulder. "Yes. It might help."

Rogan nodded, his face eager. "Anything I can do. My girlfriend, Lacey Freedman, is even more upset. It makes me feel so helpless. I can't bring them back, but if I can help get justice, I will."

Charli smiled. "We really appreciate that. Thank you. Let's step out into the hall."

They let Rogan lead the way. He walked until they could no longer make out what the vice principal was saying over the microphone. Then Rogan stopped and leaned back against a wall, his face a mask of sadness and exhaustion.

Charli pulled her notebook and pen out of her jacket as Matthew began questioning the boy, starting with details about the hike he said he took. They peppered him with questions regarding who'd gone with him and how long he'd planned the excursion.

"Was Mason supposed to go with you?" Charli asked.

"No. Hiking isn't really his thing, so he was going to spend the night and then head home for church." The young man's face reddened. "I was going to skip."

"You attended the same church?"

"Yeah. I've known Mason since, like, preschool." Rogan rubbed his eyes. "I didn't really know Nicole until they started going out several months ago. She started coming to church with him. I thought she was really good for him."

Matthew nodded. "So you thought they were a good couple?"

"They were amazing. An inspiration, you know?" Rogan ran a hand through his dark, wavy hair. "They always had each other's backs. He told me early on that he knew she was the one. I got it. I feel the same way about Lacey. Anyway, their six-month anniversary was coming up. He bought her a promise ring. I was so excited for Mason. It actually inspired me. I'm planning on giving a ring my grandmother left me to Lacey for Christmas."

Matthew raised an eyebrow. "Isn't that a big step?"

A sheepish grin spread across Rogan's face as he shrugged. "It's a ruby, so it's not technically an engagement ring."

"Still…" Matthew's expression said exactly what he thought about that, and Charli knew he was thinking of his daughter. He'd probably go bonkers if some teenager gave Chelsea a ring. "What else can you tell us about Mason and Nicole? Did anyone have grudges against them? Anyone you can think of that didn't like them or was jealous?"

Rogan gave a forceful shake of his head. "Not that I know of. They were both such nice people."

Charli bit her lip. Rogan seemed sincere. His information was limited, but she still appreciated his willingness to help. She wondered if he knew about Nicole's stalker.

"What about Jeremiah Dunn?"

Rogan wrinkled his nose. "That freak? What about him?"

Charli sighed. It was clear Rogan didn't think Jeremiah was a threat, but she and Matthew spent the next few minutes peppering the young man with questions anyway. In a nutshell, Rogan thought that Mason would've kicked Jeremiah's ass if he'd gotten within ten feet of Nicole.

As they were wrapping up, Lacey came out into the hallway looking for Rogan. She basically parroted what her boyfriend had to say about Mason and Nicole, but to be on the safe side, they provided her with business cards as well.

Once the detectives were back in Matthew's truck, he smiled at Charli. "Cute couple."

"Yeah. I hope it doesn't get them killed." A knot was forming in the pit of her stomach even as the words left her mouth.

Matthew frowned as he stroked the steering wheel with his thumb. "You think they're in trouble?"

Charli sighed, frustration welling up inside her. "I think they might be."

"There's got to be dozens of young couples in that school. Hundreds, thousands even, in the city." Matthew's tone conveyed his doubt.

"Yeah, but they were obvious friends of the first murdered couple, which might put them in the killer's crosshairs, particularly if the killer has a connection to the church."

"Okay. I see your point." Matthew adjusted the AC vent. "What do you want to do about it?"

"Let's call Ruth and the parents and see if we can't get a cruiser parked outside each of their houses for the next couple of nights. Just to be on the safe side."

It's probably a long shot, but better safe than sorry.

"Make the call."

Charli already had her phone out and was dialing their sergeant.

"Give me good news, Detective Cross."

Charli grimaced. "None yet, but we did meet a young couple from Mason and Nicole's church and school that could be on the killer's radar."

"Okay."

"I'd like to put cars outside each of their houses." It was a lot, given how little they had to go on, but maybe Ruth would go for it.

A long pause ensued before the sergeant responded. "It's thin, but if it's all we got, I'll make it happen. Text me the names and addresses, and I'll contact the parents. Meanwhile, get back here. We're going to have a full briefing in thirty."

If only we had something more that we could bring to that briefing.

"On our way, Sergeant."

Charli disconnected the call and turned to Matthew. "Well, you heard the lady. Let's get out of here."

28

Charli and Matthew walked into the precinct in record time. They hadn't even gotten to the stairs when Janice intercepted them. The woman nodded at Charli before flashing a sly, sexy smile at Matthew.

Wow, she's been cordial to me two days in a row. This is a record.

She winked at Matthew. "I missed you."

Heat crept up his neck. "I, uh…"

Janice threw a playful punch at Matthew's arm. "Don't worry, I know you're a man of few words."

With you.

Charli struggled to control the expression on her face. Janice was a good detective, but one thing was certain. She sucked at reading Matthew.

Janice turned to Charli. "Briefing's in the conference room."

"We're on our way. Oh, and by the way, did you have a chance to trace that 9-1-1 call?"

Heat infused Janice's cheeks. "I, uh…I'll get that to you as soon as I can." She led the march up the stairs, hips swaying from side to side.

Of course she didn't trace the call yet. She was too busy fraternizing with Matthew over lunch.

Charli winced at the thought, glad that Preston hadn't taken any of her initial hints. She didn't see Matthew caving to Janice, but that woman seemed determined to wear him down.

At the top of the stairs, they turned down a hall. And moments later, they arrived at the room that was serving as the command center for their latest murders.

I've spent entirely too much time in this room the last few weeks. Same table, same chairs, most of the same people. Only the faces on the murder board are different.

As the sergeant updated the board, Charli and Matthew took their seats.

"Now that we're all here, we can begin." Ruth tapped the end of a marker on pictures of each of their four victims before turning to face the assembled detectives. "Connections?"

There was a moment of strained silence.

The sergeant rolled her eyes. "The church?"

Charli shook her head. "Anna and Parker didn't go there."

"How about school? I realize that Anna and Parker were in college, but did they go to the same high school as Nicole and Mason?"

Charli flushed. *I have no idea.* Perhaps a teacher or administrator knew both couples. She shared a quick glance with Matthew.

Matthew met her eyes, grimacing. "We'll check on that."

"Please do," Ruth's tone was icy, "before we have another couple get their throats slit."

"Rings." The word popped out of Charli's mouth before she had time to process what she was about to say.

The sergeant raised an eyebrow as everyone in the room swiveled toward Charli, relief etched on several of the faces. If Charli had to guess, she'd bet they'd come up with nothing and were desperately hoping that she had a lead.

Ruth pinned her with her signature *I mean business* stare. "Explain."

Charli cleared her throat. "Parker had just proposed to Anna at the restaurant immediately before their murder. He gave her an engagement ring. Mason had recently bought a Claddagh ring to give to Nicole as a promise ring, something that was known to others."

"What others?"

"His father and his friend Rogan that we know of so far. And Lacey, Rogan's girlfriend. And Rogan and Lacey went to the same church as Mason and Nicole."

Ruth raised a hand to her temple and massaged in slow circles. "And that's the same church your street preacher attends?"

"Yes." Charli had an almost uncontrollable urge to start squirming in her seat.

Is it getting hotter?

Ruth narrowed her eyes. "The same church Jeremiah told you to check out?"

"Yes." Charli shifted in her chair.

Hold it together. You're a good detective. Don't let her intimidate you.

Ruth tapped the board with one of the markers. "Please tell me you've been there already."

Matthew cleared his throat. "Yes, but we only talked with the pastor. From what we understand, there are hundreds of members. We're waiting on a list."

"And how many of those members, besides Rogan and Lacey, knew about the Claddagh ring?"

"Well," Matthew shrugged, "we don't know."

Ruth jammed a hand on her hip. Then she turned back to the board and wrote *RINGS?* before facing the detectives again. "So were any of the parishioners friends with Anna and Parker?"

Charli's mind was working in overdrive. "I'm not sure if that's relevant, as most people don't know in advance when a guy is going to propose, so as to keep the secret."

A slow grin spread across Matthew's face. "Especially in case he gets turned down."

"Right. So maybe someone at the restaurant witnessed the proposal or knew about it in advance. Mason could have given them a heads-up so a special dessert or champagne could be prepared." Charli drummed her fingers on the table, her digits moving faster with each thought. "Then our killer, who could have been at the restaurant, followed the couple to the river."

Are we actually looking for a killer who has it in for couples in general and not just these two particular ones? What kind of mental illness, sick obsession, or trauma would trigger that?

"Detective Cross?"

Charli jumped out of her skin. How long had she been in la-la land? And why was the sergeant glaring like she was about to blow a fuse? "Yes, ma'am?"

"I said, have you questioned the staff at the restaurant?"

"Not yet, ma'am."

"Then I suggest you and your partner get on that. And obtain a list of employees." Ruth pinned her with a stare for another second before sweeping the room. "Everyone else, I want a list of church members, and I want to start combing through it."

Janice flipped her hair over her shoulder. "And if the church doesn't give it up willingly?"

Charli sucked in her lower lip. She was about to say that

the pastor had promised to send the list when Ruth barked, "Then we'll get a warrant, Detective."

Charli had planned to run a background check on anyone who'd signed Desmond Turner out of the care facility most recently. Milo Cain Turner, Desmond Turner's son, for starters. But that would have to wait, unless she could convince Janice to take care of it for her.

"All right, everyone, let's get moving. Find me some suspects, or at least some connection between these couples. Detective Jacobson, follow up with the high school and see if you can learn anything more. Detective Hill, get on the church member directory. Detective Cumming, see if you can find out if Mason and Parker bought their rings at the same store. Look at everything. Did they frequent the same parks, same restaurants, same service stations for their oil changes? Look at it all. Find our link."

Charli was impressed. While the rings had popped into her mind, she had yet to think about the store where they'd been purchased. Ruth was on fire—not that she was surprised. Her boss was damn good at her job.

Janice leaned forward. "What do you want me to do?"

"Back up Matthew and Charli. If they don't need anything, start scouring social media sites looking for a connection."

Janice rolled her eyes but held her tongue, and Charli really couldn't blame her. Checking social media was one of her least favorite activities too.

Ruth commanded the room with an iron stare. "All right, people, we have a partial fingerprint. Find the person it belongs to. Go, go, go!"

As everyone scrambled, Charli and Matthew piled out into the hall with the rest.

Janice followed them. "What do you need?"

"Can you run down someone named Milo Cain Turner?" Charli scribbled on a clean piece of paper in her notebook, tore it out, and handed it to Janice. "Here's his phone number."

Janice snatched the paper out of Charli's hands. "And Milo Cain is who?"

"Desmond Turner's son, and the man who's checked out Mr. Turner from the nursing home the most. It's a long shot, but—"

"I got it." Janice rose on her tiptoes and flashed Matthew a brilliant smile. "Be safe out there."

Is she about to kiss Matt? No way.

Apparently, her partner was afraid of that, too, because he took a hasty step backward. "Thanks."

Matthew led the charge downstairs with Charli close on his heels. Maybe one of the servers at the restaurant would remember someone with an unusual interest in Anna and Parker. Of course, elevated interest would be hard to catch, since everyone always stopped and watched when a proposal happened. It had to be one of the most commonplace acts of voyeurism. The question was, had anyone seemed unhappy? Unusually interested? Pissed?

They were almost out the door when her musing was interrupted by a commotion at the front desk. Jeremiah Dunn stood there waving his arms around, his face a blotchy red and his voice raised.

Charli slowed her pace.

Jeremiah spun on his heels. "Detective Cross!" He approached her with a stack of papers in his hand.

"What is it?"

"I've been trying to get someone to listen to me. I've compiled a list of suspects."

Matthew leaned against the desk. "What do you mean?"

Jeremiah's face was a mixture of pale and red, the exhaustion on his features plain. *Poor kid probably hasn't slept since this whole ordeal began.*

"Suspects. Potential killers. People who could have… hurt…Nicole." His bottom lip started to quiver, but he pulled himself up straight and held it together.

Charli wasn't sure what to say as Jeremiah tried to thrust the papers at her.

Matthew straightened, still resting his hand against the front desk. "What makes you think they're suspects?"

"I spent all night going over her social media accounts. Mason's too. I also checked on those other two, the ones you told me about last time I was here. I have names, posts, comments, everyone who's ever said something suspicious about any of the four of them."

Charli peeked at the stack of papers, intrigued. "Any links?"

Jeremiah exhaled, puffing out his cheeks. "No."

Disappointment swept through Charli, but she was careful not to show it.

"But these people should be questioned anyway." The young man gazed at Charli and then at Matthew. "They might have been blocked from some of the accounts, so they couldn't comment."

Matthew scratched his chin. "He's not wrong."

Jeremiah lit up at that. "Yes, thank you. I'm happy to go over it with you, point out the most suspicious activity."

Charli remembered first meeting the kid and how he'd been so caught up trying to hack Mason's TikTok that he hadn't even known about the murders. Or so he said.

"Any luck getting into Mason's TikTok account?"

Jeremiah's face fell. "Yeah, but the videos I was searching for weren't there. He probably deleted them."

Or there was nothing there to begin with. But Charli didn't mention that.

She twisted around, resting her palms on the front desk. "Larry!"

The officer at the desk raised his head.

"Please call Janice and tell her to sit with Jeremiah and go over his information."

"Of course, Detective."

Jeremiah beamed, his eyes sad and desperate despite the smile on his face. "Thank you, Detective Cross."

Charli gave him a stern look. "Tell her everything that's relevant. Don't leave anything out."

The young man danced from foot to foot. "I will."

"Don't waste her time, but make sure you're thorough."

"Yes, yes, I will."

Charli nodded. "Okay. We have to go now, but thank you for bringing this information to our attention."

Jeremiah gave her a grateful look that nearly broke her heart. "Thank you for listening."

Charli hurried out of the building with Matthew one step behind. "I'll drive this time."

When they got into her car, he turned toward her. "Janice is going to love you for that." His voice oozed sarcasm.

"She should. I just potentially saved her hours of slogging through that stuff on her own."

Matthew clicked his seat belt. "I still feel a little sorry for her."

"That's all right. I feel sorry for Jeremiah."

Mostly because he reminds me of me, back in the days after Madeline was kidnapped.

29

Charli and Matthew arrived at Angelo's right at the beginning of the dinner crowd. The smell of the food was tantalizing, but Charli gave herself a stern reminder that she was there for work, no matter how good the cheesy garlic bread was.

While questioning everyone as the place filled up would take longer, they'd likely have access to the same set of servers who had been there the night Parker had proposed.

The manager, Anton—a tall, slender Italian man with a jovial smile—grew serious when they explained the situation.

He bobbed his head up and down, a lock of wavy, black hair falling into his face. "Of course you may question anyone you need to."

Charli perused the restaurant. "Is there anyone not here today who was present on Monday?"

"Only Peter. He's called in sick."

She pulled out her notebook, suspicion pricking her. "Can you give me his last name and his contact information so we can reach out to him?"

"Of course. I will get you that in a moment. First, let me

introduce you to my *maître d'*, Clarice. Nothing goes on here without her knowledge."

Matthew shook the manager's extended hand. "Thank you, we appreciate the help."

A genuine look of grief flashed across Anton's face. "Anything we can do. It is a terrible tragedy, what has befallen this community."

"Is there somewhere private we can speak with your staff?" Charli glanced around the room, noting that it was filling up fast.

"Yes, my office." The manager gestured in front of him. "Let me show you."

As they followed him into the back, the smells wafted in the air from the kitchen, and Charli's stomach rumbled.

Anton smiled. "I will also send Emile with some pasta." He led them into a small but comfortable office with leather furniture and a worn but sturdy desk.

Charli was about to decline, but Matthew spoke up first. "That would be greatly appreciated."

As soon as Anton bowed and left, Charli glared at her partner.

He raised an eyebrow. "What? We gotta eat."

"Yeah, but that's just you and me. We don't eat while interviewing potential witnesses."

"Or suspects." Matthew shrugged. "Don't forget one of these people could be a killer. What better way to put them at ease than to talk over a good Italian meal?"

"I'm not sure everyone would agree with you." Charli's mind had flown to the mafia, who were notorious for mixing good Italian food with business, sometimes to deadly effect.

"You need to relax more. Besides, can you smell that?" Matthew inhaled and closed his eyes. "I mean, do you think you can sit here for a few hours and *not* faint from hunger?"

He had a point, but Charli refused to give him the satisfaction of admitting so. Instead, she just sighed and sat in the manager's chair, leaving one of the two chairs on the opposite side of the desk for Matthew. That was fine. If he wanted to put those they'd be questioning at ease, he could sit with them.

A moment later, a young woman in her twenties with sleek, blond hair and dark brown eyes popped her head into the office. "Hi, I'm Clarice. You wanted to see me?"

Charli smiled and nodded. "Yes, please have a seat."

The young woman sat next to Matthew, eyeing them both with open curiosity.

"I'm Detective Cross, and this is my partner, Detective Church, with the Savannah Police Department. We wanted to talk to you about the couple who got engaged here this week."

Clarice smiled. "You're going to have to be more specific. We get engagements here all the time. We got on some list online for romantic dining in Savannah."

Charli had her notebook open on the desk and her pen at the ready. "That's fortunate for the restaurant." Clarice looked so proud of herself that it gave Charli pause. "Or maybe it wasn't fortune?"

The woman gave a small shrug. "I promised a popular blogger front-of-the-line privileges for a year. It worked. He wrote the restaurant up, and the list ended up getting picked up by a lot of review services."

Matthew gaped at her. "That's pretty ambitious for a hostess."

"*Maître d'*." Clarice tucked a lock of shiny, blond hair behind one ear. "And I don't plan on being one forever."

Charli smiled. Clarice had a positive, bouncy energy that one didn't usually associate with a managerial position in fine dining.

The cheerleader of cheesy bread.

"That's commendable." Charli struggled to put the image out of her mind as she pulled up a picture of Anna and Parker on her phone. "This, however, is the couple we're specifically interested in."

The young woman nodded. "He booked a reservation two weeks in advance. I'm telling you, he was nervous as a cat when they came in. I could tell by the way she looked at him, though, that he had nothing to be worried about."

Anton was right. Clarice was highly observant. Charli made a note of that.

Her stomach rumbled, and she tried to ignore it and carry on. "Did you know either of them?"

Clarice shook her head. "No, but they seemed really nice. She leaned forward and lowered her voice, giving the impression that she was about to say something confidential. "It's the magic of that list. I have it on good authority we get more proposals than anywhere else in town. In fact, we've got another one tonight."

Charli stopped writing. "Tonight? It's Wednesday. Do you always have so many proposals on a weekday?"

Clarice smiled. "It does seem strange, doesn't it? But yes, we do. Anniversaries and other special dates don't always fall on a weekend."

Charli jotted that down. "What about the one tonight?"

"They're coming in at eight. The guy is real traditional. He wants the ring in a champagne glass. I tried to discourage him, but he's emphatic." Clarice rolled her eyes.

Matthew frowned, his eyes narrowing. "Why did you try to discourage him?"

Clarice's face scrunched up, and her perma-smile disappeared. "My cousin's friend died that way."

Charli bit her lower lip, trying to puzzle that out in her head. "What do you mean?"

"It was horrible, actually. Her boyfriend cooked this big meal and put the ring in the champagne. Someone came to the door, and he went to answer it." Clarice shuddered and wrapped her arms around herself. "She didn't see the ring and swallowed it. When he got back from answering the door...which ended up just being a solicitor...she was choking to death." Clarice's gaze fell to her lap. "Apparently, he tried everything, but he couldn't dislodge it. He called 9-1-1, and the operator tried to talk him through doing a tracheotomy, but ultimately, she died anyway."

Charli glanced at Matthew, whose face seemed to be contorted in horror and intrigue in equal measures. That was how she felt. This story was too strange to have happened twice. Two very different people telling them this tale of heartbreak. *What are the chances?*

Something inside Charli drove her next question. "Do you know the name of the guy?"

Clarice scrunched up her nose in thought. "No, sorry. My cousin just kept calling him 'the guy' when she told me the story."

"What about her friend, the woman who died?"

"Her name was Hazel. I only know this because my mom's name is Hazel and I thought it was a little old fashioned for someone around my age. I met her a couple of times. She seemed real nice."

Charli itched to pound the desk in frustration. "How long ago was this?"

"It happened earlier this year."

So the trauma is still fairly fresh.

Charli took a deep breath. "Does your cousin live here in town?"

"Yes." Clarice's face was puzzled. "Why are you so interested?"

Charli dug deep for patience. "Part of our job is to be

interested in everything. Can you give us your cousin's contact information?"

Clarice pulled out her phone, pulled up the name, and handed it over to Charli, who copied everything down in her notebook.

"Thanks." Charli handed the phone back.

As Matthew asked the maître d' a few more standard questions, Charli half listened. Her thoughts wandered to the poor guy who had to slit open his girlfriend's throat to try to help her breathe after accidentally swallowing his engagement ring. That would really mess someone up.

She pulled up a picture of Mason and Nicole on her phone. In a break in the questioning, she handed it to Clarice. "Have you ever seen them?"

Clarice nodded and handed the phone back. "That's the couple who was killed in the park, right?"

Charli nodded.

"Yeah, they came in here once a month just about. It's terrible what happened to them. You want to hear the weird part?"

Charli most certainly did. "Absolutely."

Clarice frowned. "He was in here the day they were killed."

Matthew leaned forward, clearly unable to hide his excitement. "Mason Ballinger? What was he doing?"

"He was making a reservation for next week. He requested our best table. Apparently, their six-month anniversary was coming up, and he had something special planned. He even asked us to bake one of our specialty cakes for the occasion. I had to cancel the order this afternoon. It's just so tragic." Clarice grabbed a tissue from the box on the desk and dabbed her eyes.

A surge of impatience zinged through Charli. She was ready to climb the walls. The solution was just out of her reach, making her want to pound her fists on the desk and scream in frustration.

Despite her inner turmoil, she forced herself to smile and continue the polite line of questioning, even though every second that passed was a second lost. "Did he say anything else?"

Clarice tilted her head to the side and tapped her chin. "Ummm…let's see. We talked about the cake. Anniversary. Special plans. Blah, blah, blah. No, that's it. The only other thing was that he was late meeting her at the park. He ran out of here fast after he'd finished ordering everything."

Adrenaline surged through Charli, and she jumped to her feet so fast that Matthew jerked, spun in his chair, and reached for his gun. "He was here."

"What! Where?"

Charli sank back into the chair, knowing she needed to be calm. "This restaurant."

Her partner's mouth gaped, a look of consternation on his face. "The killer's here?"

"No!" Her gaze bored into Matthew. *How thick can you be?* "He *was* here when Mason was here."

He scanned the room again. "Are you sure?"

"Yes!" She stood again and paced the room. "He must have followed Mason from here. He heard all about the ring and the plans for the big night."

Charli turned to Clarice, who had paled.

She tried to calm herself, but everything was crystal clear to her. Maybe Charli was overworked. Maybe she was tired of being harassed with terrible letters about her late friend. Maybe she just needed a vacation, but she was convinced that she wasn't paranoid or jumping to conclusions.

Charli leaned over the desk toward the maître d'. The woman shied away. *She probably thinks I've lost my mind.*

"Clarice, think. This is important. Did anyone else seem interested in Mason? Maybe leave right after he did?"

Clarice chewed her bottom lip. "I honestly don't know. I swear—"

Right then, the office door slammed open, hitting the wall with a loud *thunk*.

Matthew leaped out of his chair. "Shit!"

Charli had been ready to attack, too, but blew out a breath as a server carrying a tray of food rushed in. He must have kicked the door open with his foot.

"Sorry. The door opened faster than I'd expected. We're getting slammed! Anyway, this is yours."

Charli was about to tell him to take the food away when Matthew held up his hands, offering an easy smile. "Thank you."

She shook her head. Only Matthew would interrupt her breakthrough with concern for something so mundane.

The server's hands shook as he put the food down on the table. Charli tapped her toe on the floor, impatient for him to finish and get out of the way. He sloshed some water onto the desk and yelped in despair.

Clarice scrambled to her feet. "Let me get a towel." She practically flew through the open door, the server scurrying after her.

Once they were gone, Matthew glared at Charli, eyes narrowed. "Okay, what the hell is wrong with you?"

Charli picked up a letter opener on the desk and twirled it in her fingers. "We're close! Can't you sense it?"

Matthew kept his distance but eased around the room, a wary look on his face. "No, what I sense is that my partner has decided to play bad cop without provocation in entirely inappropriate circumstances and is brandishing a weapon at me."

"What weapon? I'm just holding a…" Charli set the letter opener down.

Once she had, Matthew snatched the little blade away and put it over on a bookcase, heaving a sigh of relief. Charli couldn't tell if it was real or for effect, but she guessed the latter.

He gave her his most serious face. "Now, do I need to take your gun as well?"

She rolled her eyes. "We're wasting time."

"No," Matthew shook his head, "I'm doing my job, and you're terrorizing innocent people with all your obnoxious crime-solving energy. People who might be able to give us information, if they're not too scared to think."

"The clock's ticking, and I'm not terrorizing anyone. I'm just ready to find our murderer."

Matthew ran a hand through his hair. "But we're never going to get there if you don't calm down. Take a walk around the building. Go splash some water on your face. Do what it takes and get my partner back. Then, after this is over, you and I are going to have a very serious conversation about what's stressing you out."

His last words propelled Charli to her feet. She was a live wire. She could hit something. Anything. Even Matthew made a tempting target. Instead, she stormed out of the room. She took a right toward the restrooms and, moments later, bent over the sink, splashing cool water on her face.

When Charli straightened, she studied herself in the mirror. The reflection was one she barely recognized—eyes filled with anger, mouth twisted and scowling, skin flushed.

Maybe Matthew was right. She sighed.

Oh, well.

She'd deal with that later. Right now, she had a killer to stop. Charli left the restroom and marched back into the office. Clarice had returned, and the pool of water on the desk had disappeared. Matthew was smiling and chatting with the maître d' about food as he devoured a plate of spaghetti.

Charli's stomach rumbled again, and Matthew glanced up, searching her face.

She gave a curt nod to let him know she was fine. He could make of that what he would.

Matthew turned back to Clarice, a disarming grin on his face. "You have to excuse my partner. When she gets hangry, it's not a pretty sight."

Clarice glanced at Charli, her face cautious. "No worries. I understand." Her voice was little more than a squeak.

Charli plopped down in the chair she had occupied earlier and glanced at the plate of spaghetti in front of her. As hungry as she was, she was certain that food wasn't her problem. Still, she obliged Matthew by taking a big bite of the pasta. Both he and Clarice visibly relaxed, their shoulders lowering, and the tendons in their arms retreating back beneath their skins.

Charli struggled to force two more bites down before addressing Clarice. "Sorry about earlier. It's been a long day. This is very good."

The maître d' smiled, although Charli was pretty certain it was forced. "Like I said, no worries."

Charli took another bite of the steaming pasta. "Did you see anyone leave the restaurant right after Anna and Parker?"

Clarice winced as she shook her head. "I'm sorry. Really, truly I am. That was a crazy night. Five tables all left at the same time, and I was busy taking names on the wait list. I'm sorry, I wish I could be more helpful."

"You're doing great." Matthew smiled at the woman.

Charli ran several possible scenarios through her head. "Do you get a lot of single diners?"

It made sense. If someone followed the couple from the

restaurant and killed them, he was likely alone or, at least, had parted ways with the person he was dining with, either right before or after leaving the restaurant.

Clarice tucked her legs underneath her on the chair. "Actually, more than you would expect."

Charli nodded, struggling to hide her frustration at that news. "Do you keep your reservation lists?"

The maître d' shook her head. "They're deleted off the computer every night. However, if you're interested in our single diners, most of them don't bother making reservations. It's more of an impulse."

Charli forced a smile, which probably looked more like she was baring her teeth. Whatever. It was time to move on. "Can we get a list of future reservations?"

"Of course. I can print them off or email them, whichever works best."

Charli circled the email address on her card. "Please send it here. What about security cameras?"

"We don't have any. The owner hates them; feels like they would invade our customer's privacy."

Crap.

"Thank you for your time, Clarice. We appreciate your help. We need to speak with the servers who were working the night Anna and Parker were engaged."

"I'll give you a couple of minutes before I send in Jonathan." Clarice wasted no time scrambling out of the chair. "You're in for a treat. Chef Emile's spaghetti is famous, but he'll be sending in some tiramisu, which is to die for."

After three more bites of food, Charli's stomach was settling down. *How long are we going to have to wait on the next potential witness?* She put down her fork and picked up her phone, dialing Janice.

"Yes." The woman seemed more tired than snippy.

Charli took a deep breath. "Can you search for obituaries

or hospital reports from the past year where a young woman died from asphyxiation caused by swallowing an engagement ring? Her name may or may not be Hazel."

There was a pause on the other end of the phone. "Are you serious?"

Charli curled her free hand into a fist. "As the grave."

"Okay. By the way, thanks for sending the kid my way."

Charli blinked. There was no animosity or sarcasm detectable in Janice's voice. Somehow, that seemed to upset the natural order of things. The urge to say something mean bubbled up in Charli, but she forced herself to swallow the impulse. "You're welcome."

"You did me a favor. I...appreciate it." Janice sounded constipated, as though she had to strain to get the words out. "I know everyone's said some pretty negative stuff about that kid, but he really did love Nicole. I feel bad for him." Janice cleared her throat. "Anyway, watch out. If he keeps up the good work, he's coming for all our jobs."

Sometimes, history repeated itself. Charli just wished it was the nicer parts and not the tragic ones. "Good to know."

Janice coughed hard, her voice weak when she continued. "All right. I'll check on the ring thing after I try to find Milo Cain."

Charli drummed her fingers on the desk. Why was this call taking so long? "If you could do the ring first, I'd be grateful."

There was a burst of noise in the background. *Is that Ruth?* Janice was tense when she answered. "Sure. Gotta go."

Matthew glanced up at Charli, his face full of concern. "What's wrong?"

"Janice. She was actually...not hostile. Almost pleasant." Charli shook her head.

Matthew chuckled. "Isn't this the part where you say hell just froze over?"

30

I was edgy, moody, like my whole body was overtaken by a fever. My skin was cool, though, so the fire was on the inside. The presence of the blood and the steak knife in my house had bothered me more than I cared to admit. And now, seeing those detectives earlier had triggered something.

Whenever I blinked, terrible images flashed behind my eyelids. Blood. Gaping throats. Diamond rings. They all kept playing themselves over and over. Some images were old and familiar. Others were new and foreign. Yet somehow, I sensed I wasn't imagining them.

What had happened Monday night?

That was the question that had been plaguing me these past two days, and it was morphing into a new question.

What had I done?

A steady sense of dread was filling me, and I'd been sleeping less and less. Now, after speaking with the police, a horrible suspicion overtook me. One I couldn't shake. The majority of me was sick—I wanted to throw up until there was nothing left of me but skin. There was a tiny part, deep inside, though, that felt...different.

And that scared me senseless.

But I had to know. I had to put the taunting images and menacing thoughts to rest, one way or another. I'd gone to Angelo's Monday night. The receipt I'd found in my pocket was proof enough of that. That must have been where the knife was from. I replayed as much as I could remember in my head.

I'd been sitting at a small table in the corner, where I often did when I was lonely and thinking of my princess.

Whenever that deep ache of loneliness gripped me, I'd close my eyes and remember her laugh, her smile, her light. I preferred to remember her that way instead of dead on the floor. If only I'd brought her here instead of making dinner myself, someone could have helped, and maybe she'd still be alive.

Going to the restaurant was a sort of remembrance and penance.

But not this time. Tonight, I was here to figure out what happened on Monday night. The maître d' welcomed me. She was always such a nice girl.

I sat there, eating, trying to recall my last visit, but it wasn't working.

Why couldn't I remember what had happened that night? And why were my thoughts so hazy? All I could recall was the last time I was here with my princess.

I gazed around the room, which was surprisingly full for a Wednesday evening. There were large, boisterous families at a few tables, a couple of business meetings happening over good food and wine, and several tables where couples were gazing at each other the way my princess and I used to.

Jealousy stirred in me, accompanied by anger and resentment. The feelings washed over me, and my hands shook as I sliced into my steak.

At a table fifteen feet away, a young man was laughing, his

nervousness palpable. It was the kind of apprehension that meant he was on a first date, was about to break up with his girlfriend, or was about to propose. Given the way the woman was looking at him, it was unlikely a first date. That meant a breakup or a proposal.

My stomach tightened into a thousand knots.

What's the difference? Either way ends in tragedy.

The voice in my head was foreign, dark, and so very angry. It frightened me. Could anyone around me hear that voice, or was I the only one? Fat drops of sweat broke out on my skin, the fire inside bursting outward. Everything around me began to fade—the sounds, the lights, the smells. My eyes became laser-focused on the couple.

A server approached their table with a tray. Two glasses of champagne.

No, you fool!

The ring was at the bottom of the glass, surrounded by tiny air bubbles.

Ring.

Air.

My hand curled around the steak knife.

Bloodcurdling screams erupted in my head as the man got down on one knee. Terror flooded me. More images came. Another man proposing, then dying.

I started up from my table as my senses began to leave me.

"*Wait until they leave.*" The angry, vicious voice whispered in my ear, telling me things I didn't want to hear.

I took one step toward the exit, looking away from the woman as she jumped up from the table with a shriek of joy. Before I could even take a second step, a familiar face appeared on the other side of a potted tree.

It was the female detective. Somehow, she was there and

congratulating the couple. She was also looking around, her sharp eyes searching.

For me.

As if some other person was manipulating my body, I turned and sank back down at my table, choosing a chair that put my back to her. Forcing a smile on my face, even though she couldn't see it, I smacked my hands together, applauding along with the others in the restaurant. Sweat ran down my skin in heavy droplets, fear overcoming the anger as I waited for her hand to slam down onto my shoulder.

Why was I so innately afraid of being seen?

Oh, dear God in Heaven, what have I done?

31

Charli had left the office to scan the restaurant during the proposal, but no one was paying undue attention to the couple. There were several tables with solo diners—all men—but no one who stood out at first glance.

To be safe, Matthew had called in a request for a squad car to follow the happy couple home. They had just left a few minutes ago and, so far, the officers had nothing suspicious to report. Charli and Matthew retreated back to the office to finish interviewing staff.

A server, the last one they had to interview for the night, left the room. Charli was exhausted, and by the way he was slouching in his chair, so was Matthew.

She figured one of them should speak before they both fell asleep. "You okay?"

He grunted a noncommittal reply, and Charli fought to stifle a yawn.

Before Matthew could respond, his phone rang. "Hey, Janice. I've got you on speaker."

"Oh." Her voice was a bit flat, a note of disappointment in it.

Matthew slid even farther down in his chair, kicking his legs out. "How's the hunt going?"

"Slow. No obituaries with those details. Have to wait for the morning to get hospital administrators to sign off on releasing information. Then I tried looking for Milo Cain and came up with nothing."

Charli frowned. "Nothing?"

"Zip, nada, zilch."

A ghost wasn't signing Desmond Turner out of the facility, so who was? Charli scowled. "Did you try running variations on the name?"

There was a lengthy pause. Then Janice answered, her voice irritated. "I'm not an amateur."

Charli winced. Janice was always proficient at these kinds of things, and she hadn't meant to antagonize by implying otherwise. "I'm…sorry, that's not what I mean."

Janice let out an exaggerated sigh. "Milo, every spelling variation. I've searched for first, middle, and last names. Cain, every spelling variation and every freaking surname that starts with those letters. Did you know there's about fifty of those?"

Matthew's eyes were bulging. "Wow. That's way more thorough than I would have done."

"I know." Janice's voice thawed as she answered Matthew. "There are a number of Milo Cains, of course, but none that would work within the parameters of our suspect. And tell your…partner…that I checked state databases. And the phone's a burner, so no records there. Either your Milo Cain is from way, way out of town, or he doesn't exist."

Matthew tried and failed to suppress a yawn.

Charli forced a smile so it would transfer into her voice. "Thank you, Janice."

"That's not all. I can't find where Desmond Turner ever had a son."

That was curious.

"Thanks. I'll follow up on—"

"Whatever." Janice was frosty. "I'm going home to get some sleep."

Back to her old self again.

After Janice hung up, Matthew pocketed his phone. "So where does that leave us?"

"Wondering why someone would put down a false name when checking Mr. Turner out of the care facility." She rubbed her head, which was starting to hurt. "That's a problem for tomorrow. Or maybe for never, if the hospital records turn up something."

Matthew stood and stretched, arching his back. "I hear you. For once, I agree totally with Janice. It's time to go home and get some sleep."

"Hey, wait. I just realized Janice never told us who called 9-1-1 when they discovered Anna and Parker's bodies."

"Crap. I'll send her a text."

❈

CHARLI DROPPED onto the couch in her living room. The temptation to just fall over and sleep there was overwhelming. She'd been pushing hard for a very long time, and even though it was the last thing she wanted to do, she forced herself to get up and check her messages.

Marcia Ferguson—Madeline's mother—had called early in the evening.

"Charli, it's me. I need to talk to you. It's not too late. We can find my baby's killer. Justice. That's what you do, right? It's been long enough. Call me as soon as you can. Please don't let me down."

The woman sobbed for several seconds before hanging up. Charli's heart hurt at how erratic and upset the woman was. She glanced at the time and promised herself she'd call Marcia tomorrow.

When the message was over and quiet once again reigned, Charli could feel the pulse in her ears. The sensation and the silence were too much.

She walked around the house, double-checking doors and windows.

I used to feel so safe here, but now...

Charli was determined not to let some harassing notes bother her. What did it matter if thugs tried to scare her?

She headed upstairs and got ready for bed. But when the time came to actually lie down, she was jittery. After wandering back downstairs and rechecking all the windows, Charli grabbed her notebook, bypassing the sitting room and Priscilla, that wretched mauve- and cream-colored sofa of her grandmother's. When Charli was younger, the piece of furniture had collapsed on her, and she swore up and down Priscilla had it out for her.

Instead, she curled up on the couch in the living room, reading back through all her notes as her brain fiddled with the problem.

Charli stopped when she came to Milo Cain. Although it could very well be an alias, why would someone use it in this situation? Because they didn't want to be officially connected to Desmond Turner? Then why check him out in the first place?

Everyone knew that the older man loved the park. Clearly, whoever checked him out and let him go was aware he'd go there. Maybe they allowed him to slip away, because a crazy old fanatic like him would make a good scapegoat for the murder of a young couple in the park.

Thoughts swirling through her mind like a tornado, Charli sat up.

Milo Cain. Most people chose aliases that would be easy

for them to remember, a name that had some meaning to them, or at least…

The same initials.

Milo Cain.

M.C.

She blinked, her heart beginning to race. There was only one person she'd talked to that week with those initials.

Pastor Marshall Coleman.

Charli flipped to the notes from their most recent conversation with Mr. Turner. The old man had told them that his "son" had lost his fiancée a few months prior under tragic circumstances. She double-checked the scribble, a tingling sensation crawling down her spine. The street preacher had dementia. Could he be confused? Yes, the "son's" fiancée had died on the night he proposed. What if he was "the guy" who had proposed to Clarice's cousin's friend, Hazel?

Maybe there was a connection to the church after all. Or at least, to its pastor.

She called Matthew, but it went to voicemail. *Come on, Matt. Pick up.* He was probably already asleep or talking to Chelsea. She gave it ten minutes, then called again.

Voicemail. Again.

She left a message. "Matt, I'm thinking that Milo Cain might actually be Marshall Coleman." Charli forced herself to slow down so her partner would be able to understand her message later. "It's a long shot, but I'm going to head to the church and see if I can find anything. I know it's late, but…" There was no way she was going to admit to having a hunch. "I don't want to wait until morning. I think Hazel might have been his fiancée, that he was the guy who had to do a tracheotomy and failed."

Charli got dressed as fast as she could. She was about to leave her bedroom when she paused and turned back. The small jewelry box on her dresser caught her attention, and inspiration struck. A second later, she tucked one of her most treasured pieces of jewelry in her pocket before leaving the room.

The drive to the church didn't take long at that time of night. She pulled up in the parking lot, noting another car there. She left Matthew another voicemail, letting him know where she was. As soon as she hung up, she worried her bottom lip before calling Preston.

Preston sounded half asleep when he answered. "Hey."

"I'm at Sunrise Church, the one Mason and Nicole went to. I think the pastor might be our killer. I might be off base, but there's some information that fits."

"Is Matthew with you?" By the sound of his voice, Preston was wide awake now.

Charli sighed, not wanting to admit that was why she was calling. "No, I haven't been able to reach him."

There was rustling on the other end of the line. "Text me the address. I'll be there in ten minutes. Don't go in without me."

Charli eyed the empty-looking church. "Okay."

She hung up and texted him the address. As soon as she had, Charli got out and walked over to the other car. It was empty, and when she peered through the windows, there was nothing suspicious. From there, it was several more feet to the front door, which she crossed in a few quick strides.

Glancing around, Charli peeked through the glass. Beyond the darkness, a dim light came from the direction of the altar.

"No!"

Ice ran down Charli's spine as the anguished cry came through the door. Male or female, she couldn't tell. But one thing was certain, someone was in trouble.

Wrapping her fingers around the handle, Charli eased the

door open with bated breath. She knew she should wait for backup, but someone needed her. She couldn't just stand out here and do nothing.

Just a quick peak.

Please don't squeak. Please don't squeak. Please don't squeak.

She let out a breath. The door hadn't made a sound.

She checked her phone. There were no new messages, but Preston was coming, and he knew where she was. Charli pulled the door open and walked inside. In the antechamber, all the doors were open into the sanctuary, where a soft light burned at the front.

"Hello, Pastor Coleman? It's Detective Cross." Her voice echoed through the darkness, but there was no response. "Are you okay?"

With her hand on her gun, Charli eased forward, her gaze swiveling in every direction. Had someone lit a candle and forgotten about it? But why was the door unlocked?

She frowned, having a hard time believing the pastor or staff would have left the church unlocked if no one was going to be around.

Charli took another step forward. "Hello? I saw the car outside. Is anyone here?"

A whisper hovered in the air around her. "Only us sinners."

32

Charli froze. She was alone, and she had no idea where the voice had come from. The hair on the back of her neck lifted, an overwhelming sense of dread that she was in danger coming over her. She bit her lower lip, forcing herself to stay calm.

Her phone chimed, and she glanced down. It was a text from Matthew.

On the way. Stay put.

She took a deep breath. Backup was coming.

Another message came through. This time from Janice.

The 9-1-1 call was from Marshall Coleman.

Oh boy. If the pastor wasn't their murderer, she'd be shocked.

"I'm Detective Cross. Does the other sinner have a name?" Her voice rang out loud and clear.

In the first pew on the left, a figure darted around in the shadows, and Charli thumbed open the snap of her holster.

She went into hyper focus as the seconds ticked by.

One.

Charli took a step to the side, her training causing her to turn her body to provide a smaller target.

Two.

She glanced around to make sure no one was sneaking up from behind.

Three.

A figure unfolded itself, emerging from the darkness. Creeping out of the shadows, he took a few steps forward and stared into her eyes.

Just the man I was looking for.

Charli released the breath she'd been holding for what seemed to be an eternity.

"Pastor Coleman?" She forced herself to remain calm. "Is everything okay?"

"Good evening, Detective." His voice was hoarse, like he'd been screaming.

She peered into his face—red, blotchy patches covered his cheeks and neck. *Or maybe he was crying.*

"I was driving by, saw the car, and thought I'd stop in."

His eyes narrowed to slits, and his voice deepened. "Is that so?"

She nodded. "What are you doing here so late?"

He held his arms out wide and spun in a slow circle, getting a little closer to her with each step. "Isn't it obvious? Talking to God."

Something was definitely wrong. This was not the same man she'd spoken with before. She took a deep breath and moved to maintain a six-foot distance. "Talking or confessing?"

Hollow laughter rang out, echoing off the walls. "A bit of both, I guess."

Where the hell is Preston?

Charli didn't like any of this, but she'd come here to ask some questions, and she was going to do just that. "Why do you check Desmond Turner out of the care facility under the name Milo Cain?"

The pastor shuddered, his body convulsing. This man seemed wearier, older. He heaved a sigh and sank onto a pew. "I guess there's no use denying it. I feel sorry for him, and I like him. But not everyone feels the same way. I didn't want the church to be the focus of their ire."

Charli risked a quick glance back toward the main entrance. *Keep him talking. Calm him down.*

A mounting sense of dread filled her heart. "You agree with Desmond about all the fire and brimstone stuff?"

Pastor Coleman gave a half-shrug, like a weight was dragging him down and he couldn't put any more effort into the gesture. "I can't say I don't."

Charli took a few slow steps, keeping the distance between him but trying to angle herself so she could watch him and the entrance at the same time. "And having him out there, yelling at people in the park. It makes a nice cover, doesn't it?"

His brow furrowed, confusion written all over his face. "Cover for what?"

"For what you did Saturday night."

The color leeched from the pastor's face, his entire body trembling as he leaned against the pew in front of him. The Bibles and hymnals in the rack rattled against the wood. "What did I do?"

There was no way she was going to make an accusation without Preston or Matthew there. The whole situation could turn explosive in a second. Instead, Charli changed her line of questioning. "Why don't you tell me about Hazel?"

The pastor jerked, like she'd slapped him hard across the face. "What do you know about my princess?"

A thrill shot through Charli. She was right. "I know that she died from choking on an engagement ring."

Pastor Coleman lurched to his feet and began pacing like a caged animal. Charli took a couple of steps back.

"It was supposed to be the best night of our lives! I was at the door for only a minute! Why didn't she wait to drink the champagne? I mean, we never had champagne. Most people see champagne and think, *Oh, maybe we're going to toast something.* Why didn't she see the ring?" He turned to Charli, eyes blazing. "Why?"

Charli held her ground, hand once more on the butt of her gun. "I don't know."

The pastor smacked his fist into his other hand. "Why did the 9-1-1 operator try to walk me through that procedure when she was on the floor and hadn't breathed in over five minutes and the ambulance was stuck in traffic?"

Just keep him talking.

"She was trying to help. It was a brave thing you did. It's not your fault it didn't work, but I know it must be painful."

His face twisted as anger clawed its way out of him. He smacked himself across the face, blood and spittle flecking his lips. "Why. Did. God. Let. Her. Die?!" He roared like a wounded animal, all his inner pain and rage bubbling to the surface.

He was spinning out of control, and Charli had only moments to reach him. She shouted the first thing that came to her. "It's not fair!"

The pastor spun to face her. "No, it's not!"

She nodded. "I know. You should have gotten to grow old together. I understand. God let my best friend be kidnapped, molested, and brutally murdered. Yet he left me alive to deal with the loss and the pain and the grief."

All Charli's anguish poured out of her. In trying to stop this crazed, wounded man from escalating, she'd joined him in his rage and impotence. Tears sprang from her eyes, running down her cheeks.

The pastor leapt forward, closing the distance between them. He clamped down on her wrists, pinning them to her sides and rendering her unable to grip her gun. At least, that's what Charli let him think.

He gazed deep into her eyes, and she forced herself to return his stare.

Charli shuddered, her skin writhing under his touch. She searched his face, but there was no order, no reason. Just pure, unadulterated grief that had spawned something dark of its own, something irrational and horrible.

Inhuman.

"You know what the worst part is?" He was no longer shouting. His voice was a desperate, anguished whisper. "No one understands. *No one!*"

She took a deep breath as his madness seemed to fill not only him, but also her. "I understand."

Tears streaked down the pastor's cheeks. "I know you do. I see it."

Charli didn't try to pull away from the crazed man's grip —although she knew she could. Not yet.

Keep him talking. See what else he reveals.

"And I bet you've asked yourself the same question I have over and over."

"What's that?"

The pastor's face hardened. Charli watched as the grief in his eyes morphed into hatred and madness. A slow, evil grin spread across his face. "With her dead, why should anyone else get to live?"

A chill ran down Charli's spine and, too late, she realized her mistake.

"Everyone must die." The voice that emanated from the pastor was different now. Low, guttural.

A crash made both of them jump. "You killed her, you bastard!" The shout came from the back of the church.

Wasting no time, Charli wrenched free of the crazed man's grasp, dancing back before turning to glance at the newcomer.

Sprinting toward them with a murderous gleam in his eyes was none other than Jeremiah Dunn.

33

Jeremiah charged down the aisle like a bull with one thing on his mind. *Revenge.*

Although the kid was much smaller than the pastor, he had a running start and nothing to lose.

Boom!

With reckless abandon, Jeremiah tackled the pastor, pummeling him with arms that spun like windmills.

Charli couldn't believe her eyes. "Jeremiah! Get off him!"

"Never! He killed Nicole." *Thwack.* Jeremiah punctuated his sentence with a well-aimed punch. "That woman I helped earlier at the precinct was right." *Thwack.* "She told me today that if anyone could find Nicole's killer, it was you." *Thwack.* "I staked out your house tonight and followed you here." *Thwack.* "You found him, and now I'm going to kill him."

He really means it.

"No, you're not! That'll just make it worse." Charli started forward, prepared to pull Jeremiah off the pastor.

"It would be justice."

Justice. That's what Marcia says she wants for Madeline. Is she looking for revenge instead?

"No, it would be murder." Charli had to find a way to reach him. "And you would go to jail. That would be adding one tragedy to another."

A figure appeared from the darkness. Before Charli could blink or respond, Desmond Turner brought his *The End of the World Is Nigh!* sign down on the young man's head and shoulders. How the hell had those gnarled, arthritic hands managed to swing so hard? The fury on Mr. Turner's face told that story. Adrenaline equaled superpowers.

The boy screamed in pain, but he kept hitting the pastor. As much as Marshall Coleman struggled, he couldn't buck Jeremiah off.

"Get off him!" Mr. Turner roared, taking another swing. The metal pole connected hard with Jeremiah's head, knocking the boy sideways.

Seizing his opportunity, Pastor Coleman threw him off and started to his feet as Jeremiah scrambled away from the barrage, arms up to deflect more blows to his head and face.

The situation was spiraling out of control, and Charli needed to get everyone in order fast. "Stop!"

But her command fell on deaf ears, the men attacking each other like rabid wolves.

"You killed Nicole!" Jeremiah shouted, finally back up on his feet.

The pastor leapt forward, knocking Jeremiah to the floor. "You're a liar!" He kicked him hard in the head, then again in the side.

"Enough!" Charli shouted at the top of her lungs.

They didn't listen.

Shit.

Short of pulling out her gun and shooting into the jumble of bodies, she wouldn't get any of their attention without physical contact.

I'm going in.

First things first, she needed the flailing sign out of the way. As much as she hated to do it, she yanked it from Mr. Turner's gnarled hands, then shoved the old man into a sitting position on the floor as gently but firmly as she could.

With one threat out of the way, she turned back to the fighting men just as Pastor Coleman brandished a knife from a sheath at his ankle. Lunging forward, she grabbed the pastor's arm before he could sink the blade into the younger man's flesh.

Possessing power beyond what she thought could be possible for a man his size, Coleman drove her backward and was on top of her before her back hit the floor. Charli went for her gun but had to abandon the idea as the knife glinted in the light. Grabbing his wrist, she stopped him a split second before he could cut her throat.

"You don't deserve to live." Spittle flew in her face as Coleman shifted position to give himself better leverage.

She couldn't outmuscle him, and the gleaming blade was edging closer to her throat. She had to outsmart him.

"I have an engagement ring in my pocket."

His dark obsession triggered, and his weight shifted just enough to give her an advantage. Charli let go of the pastor's wrist with her right hand, driving her fingers into his Adam's apple. He jerked back, gagging and choking.

In one swift motion, Charli twisted his wrist, and the knife clattered to the floor. She rammed her knee upward into the pastor's groin, and he grunted and fell backward.

Charli pulled her gun and sprang to her feet, kicking the knife out of his reach. "Stay down!" She kept her focus on Coleman but was relieved when Jeremiah and Mr. Turner didn't move.

A *smack* echoed through the church as the doors were thrown open, Matthew and Preston racing through.

She was out of breath and panting, but she managed to

get the most important words out. "Marshall Coleman, you're under arrest."

Matthew was the first to reach her side. "Are you okay?"

She grinned. "Just fine."

Matthew raised an eyebrow at the fallen pastor. "Why is he choking?"

"I hit him in the Adam's apple, but not hard enough to kill him."

Matthew glowered at the man on the floor. "You should have."

"It's okay." Her partner clearly needed reassurance. "I'm okay. Nothing broken."

Preston stepped between Desmond and Jeremiah, who was getting to his feet. "Everyone settle down. It's over." His voice was stern, commanding authority. "Understood?"

Both men nodded, too out of breath to respond.

I'm surprised Mr. Turner didn't have a heart attack. That was one hell of a boxing match.

Desmond Turner got to his feet and staggered to a pew. He collapsed, wheezing. "That boy attacked my son. I had no choice but to clobber him."

Son?

A puzzle piece fell into place. Desmond either thought of Pastor Coleman as a son, or in his demented mind, thought the pastor *was* his child.

Before she could ask Desmond about it, Preston said, "I told you not to go in without me." Frustration seethed from his voice.

Matthew snorted. "She doesn't listen to anyone, pal. I knew exactly where I'd find her. In the thick of it."

Charli put a hand on her hip. "Come on, would you have it any other way?"

"Yes!" they said in unison.

Well, there you have it—something they agree on.

She glanced at Matthew. "Read the pastor his rights." Charli turned to Preston. "Get Mr. Turner back to his nursing home." She spun around, her gaze settling on Jeremiah. "You and I are going to go for a walk outside so you can cool off."

34

The adrenaline had finally left Charli's body, and she was ready to drop. Once they'd gotten the pastor to the precinct, they'd officially booked him, getting his fingerprints in the process. They'd processed the knife and a burner phone. It'd take a couple days to access the device, but she wasn't overly worried about that right then.

She sat sipping a cup of coffee, taking advantage of the quiet as the pastor sweated in an interrogation room while she waited for the answer.

With a smile, she pulled her grandmother's engagement ring from her pocket. She hadn't had to use it to get a response from Coleman, but it had given her just enough of an advantage to take the maniac down.

"Thanks, Grandma."

Ruth finally came bustling down the hall, a massive coffee mug in one hand and a piece of paper in the other. Charli tucked the ring back into her pocket before her boss could see it.

A grin spread across Ruth's face as she waved the paper in triumph. "Print matches! Go get a confession."

Matthew returned from the restroom just in time to hear the sarge's proclamation. Charli nodded and dragged herself out of the chair she'd been sitting in for the last twenty minutes.

"You get Mr. Turner back to the nursing home okay?"

He nodded. "Yep. Surprise, surprise. Milo Cain checked him out earlier."

"Shocker."

Who would check him out now? Charli didn't have time to think about it before her partner drew himself up to his full height. "Get your game face on."

Charli pushed her shoulders back and smoothed down her hair. It rattled suspects when the interviewer looked good. She smiled like this was the beginning of her workday and not the end of an incredibly long one.

Together, they marched into the interrogation room and took seats across from the pastor. His face was bruised and bloodied.

They took their time adjusting their seats, placing their coffee and file folders on the table, and letting him fidget while they organized themselves.

"Can I get you some coffee or water, Pastor? Anything to eat?"

Marshall Coleman simply shook his head.

She gazed at the handcuffs encircling his wrists.

Fine. Time to get down to business.

After providing the time, date, and names of the participants in the interview for the video, Charli took a deep breath. She'd been thinking about what her first question should be and had decided to choose a startling one.

"So did you plan to kill Mason and Nicole, or was it on impulse?"

The pastor jolted like he'd been slapped. Here was the

man she'd met earlier that week, not the devil she'd tangled with earlier.

"I didn't kill them. I couldn't."

Charli tapped her file folder and kept her voice gentle. "Unfortunately, the facts say otherwise."

Of course, the facts didn't say anything of the sort, not where that couple was concerned, but he didn't know that. At least they had him dead to rights on the second couple.

He shook his head and grabbed fistfuls of his hair, his handcuffs clinking together. "I am not that person."

"Then tell me what happened." Charli let sympathy ooze into her tone. She wanted him to feel like he could confide in her. The man who'd been praying and admittedly confessing to God back at the church might just want to confess to her as well.

"I...I don't know." He banged his head on the table, then left his forehead resting there.

Charli leaned toward him, careful to keep her voice soft. "Okay, what do you *think* happened?"

The pastor didn't raise his head. He clenched his fists but otherwise remained still. "I woke up the next morning, and there was blood in my shower. I'd had disturbing dreams, but I had no idea how the blood got there."

Charli made a note to have the team that would be searching Marshall's house check the bathroom thoroughly for any blood residue.

"What do you remember about Angelo's a few days ago?"

"I went to eat there. I remember being downtown. I was just about at the restaurant when...when..."

Charli witnessed the man's struggle to recall what had happened. She'd seen a lot of liars in her time, but she could swear that his struggle was real.

"Someone stopped me to talk, and then...I woke up at

home." The pastor lifted his head and pounded his forehead with his fists, his grief and fear palpable.

Matthew glanced at her, and she gave him a little nod.

Charli leaned forward. "Now, I want you to think carefully. Was the person who stopped you Mason?"

"Mason…yes. He said something about Angelo's and Nicole…he bought her a ring that he showed me a couple of weeks ago. Then he walked off, and I…I…I don't know." Marshall buried his head in his hands and shuddered.

"And then you followed him to the park and killed him and Nicole."

"No!" The pastor shook his head violently, repudiating what she was saying.

"Yes, you did." She was clear and firm.

"I couldn't." His voice was cracking, breaking.

He's trying to convince himself at this point more than me.

Charli took a deep breath. "Pastor Coleman, look at me."

Slowly, he raised his head, his eyes haunted and bruised.

"What did you think when you realized Mason planned to give Nicole the promise ring? What was the first thought that came to your head?"

"It wasn't fair that my princess died, so now so would they. We'd kept our relationship pure, but they were fornicators. They didn't deserve to live." Realization crossed the pastor's face as his body shook. "I've been having nightmares…so much blood."

Charli wasn't about to stop pushing now. "What about the other couple from Angelo's, the ones who got engaged on Monday?"

"Why did they have to do that?" He rocked back and forth, tears streaming down his face. "I was just trying to eat dinner with my princess."

Charli glanced at Matthew, who shifted in his seat before

switching his attention to the pastor. "You were eating dinner with Hazel?"

"Yes. I mean, no, she wasn't actually there. It just seemed like she was. We used to eat there often. I should have proposed there." The pastor's sobs were louder now.

"But you didn't." Though Matthew's hands were clenched into fists in his lap, his words were as soothing as the expression on his face.

"No." The pastor shook his head. "And she died. Just like those kids. Just like that couple."

Charli cleared her throat. "That couple didn't just die. You followed them to the river and killed them."

The pastor screamed in anguish, his shrieks echoing off the walls. After several moments, he stopped, staring down at the table.

Charli was close. She just had to push him over the final edge. "When did you realize you killed them?"

Silence.

"Pastor Coleman, can you hear me?"

Taking his sweet time, the pastor lifted his head. "The next morning, I found a steak knife on my kitchen counter." Hollow eyes bored into Charli's. "It wasn't mine. I figured out last night it probably came from Angelo's because I also found a receipt in my pocket."

Charli didn't let her gaze waver. "Were you at Angelo's tonight?"

He nodded in response.

Adrenaline coursed through Charli. *We are so close to a confession.* "Did you see the couple get engaged?"

The pastor nodded again.

Charli forced herself to keep the excitement out of her voice. "And then what happened?"

"I grabbed the knife, I got up, but then…"

She leaned forward. "Then what?"

"Then I saw you, standing behind the potted tree, and something told me to hide."

"So you didn't kill that couple tonight, but you killed the couple from Monday night, and you also killed Mason and Nicole on Saturday?"

Pastor Coleman stopped shaking and exhaled a long breath. "Yes."

Charli leaned back in her chair, spent and satisfied. There was always catharsis when someone confessed.

"What did you carve into Anna Miller's back?"

She held her breath. For one, she was curious. And two, if he remembered, that would go a long way toward establishing his competency.

"Song of Solomon. Chapter Three, Verse Four."

"And what does that verse say?"

A small smile played on the pastor's lips. "'I found him whom my soul loves.' It was my princess's favorite verse."

Charli studied the shell of a man sitting across from her. Grief could make people do strange things, even terrible things. She had seen it many times before. Her thoughts went to Marcia Ferguson, and her worry for her late best friend's mom increased. She really needed to reach out to her. The message she'd left hours before had sounded like she was spinning out of control.

The pastor stared at them, tears streaming down his face, his features twisted with grief. "What happens now?"

Charli pushed a pen and a pad of paper across the table to him. "Now you're going to write it all down and sign it. And then we're going to get you some help."

35

An hour later, Charli and Matthew walked out of the interrogation room with a signed confession.

Charli handed it to a beaming Ruth. "He may not be competent for trial," she warned her boss.

"That will be up to his lawyer and the judge." The sarge tucked the paperwork under her arm. "Good work on this, both of you. Go home, get some rest. Take the next few days off."

Charli nodded, wishing she could ignore the exhaustion seeping into her bones. The way she felt, there was every possibility that she would sleep straight through until then. She and Matthew tromped down the stairs.

When they reached the lobby, Jeremiah was sitting in a chair. He'd clearly been waiting for them.

The young man had a massive bruise forming on his left cheekbone, a cut over his right eye, and a missing chunk of hair from his scalp. He looked like he'd been in the fight of his life.

Because he was.

He raised his head as Charli stopped in front of him. His

eyes were hollow, still bearing the grief of losing the girl he'd worshipped for so long.

A surge of pity swept over her. She was also a little jealous, because she was about to give him the news she'd long wished some cop would give to her. "He confessed."

Jeremiah blinked, clearly trying to wrap his head around what she'd just said. "He killed her…he admitted it?"

"Yes, although he doesn't really remember doing it." She hesitated, but Jeremiah needed closure even more desperately than she once had. "He's mentally ill."

Jeremiah nodded, taking that in. "That doesn't mean I have to forgive him."

"No, you don't. But you have to forgive yourself."

"For what?"

Charli was going to give him the advice she'd needed someone to give her, only no one had. "You need to forgive yourself for not being able to protect her, to save her. For not being there to stop her dying, or to at least hold her hand and sit with her."

Tears filled Jeremiah's eyes and began to flow down his face. "That's going to take a long time."

"I know, but you have to try."

He nodded his understanding. "Thank you."

"I'll see that you get all your stuff back. The pictures."

"There's no need." He put his hand over his heart. "The only picture I need of her is in here."

Tears stung Charli's eyes, but she blinked them away. Each recognized the grief the other carried with them, the scar that never faded.

"Take care of yourself, Jeremiah."

"You too, Detective."

Charli walked outside, where Matthew was waiting for her.

He glanced back toward the building. "You think the kid's going to be okay?"

Charli cleared her throat. "It will take time, but he'll get there."

Matthew put a hand on her arm. "What about you?"

She straightened her shoulders and forced a smile. "Me? I'm already there."

"That's crap, and you know it. You're just lucky I don't kick your ass for going in without backup."

She released a long, slow sigh. "It is what it is."

"I'm sorry if I overstepped with keeping an eye on you." Matthew scrubbed a hand across his face. "I won't do any more drive-bys of your place without permission."

"I appreciate that. Honestly, I overreacted. You were just trying to look out for me, be a good partner. And you can keep doing it because, honestly, I *am* concerned."

He grinned. "No yelling at me, then."

"No yelling."

"Great. Well, don't be surprised to see me driving by tomorrow. I expect to be checking up on you a lot."

She forced a wan smile on her face. "You have my permission."

"And now that I know what Powell's car looks like, I won't be worried when I see it parked there in the morning."

Obviously, he was fishing for information, but Charli was too tired to fend him off with any kind of finesse. "Preston is a great agent and a friend."

Matthew rolled his eyes. "Come on, calling him a great agent is almost as gross as you crushing on him."

"I'm not crushing on him!"

"Aha! Now I'm certain of it."

Charli considered punching him in the arm but was simply too tired. "Hush."

Matthew's grin turned serious. "You drive home safe and get some good sleep. You've earned it."

"So have you. I'll call you tomorrow if that will make you feel better."

"It actually would. Good night, Smalls."

She moved away before he could see her smile at the nickname. It had once been a source of irritation to her, but she now recognized it as affection.

"Night, Biggs."

Charli headed to her car. On the drive home, her thoughts shifted to Madeline, and she vowed she'd go over and visit Marcia as soon as she slept for a few hours and got some food in her. Not necessarily in that order. In the immediate future, Charli was looking forward to a hot shower before doing anything else.

After arriving home, she closed and locked the front door, then flipped on the light switch in the sitting room.

Charli stopped dead in her tracks for many seconds before rage sent her stumbling forward.

Had a hurricane gone through the house? The couch was flipped over, and the loveseat she'd hated for years was slashed in several places. Papers had been flung around the room with abandon, and on the mirror on the far side of the room, someone had left her a message in bold, red print.

You will die!

So much for getting some rest.

The End
To be continued...

Thank you for reading.
All of the *Charli Cross Series* books can be found on Amazon.

ACKNOWLEDGMENTS

How does one properly thank everyone involved in taking a dream and making it a reality? Here goes.

In addition to our families, whose unending support provided the foundation for us to find the time and energy to put these thoughts on paper, we want to thank the editors who polished our words and made them shine.

Many thanks to our publisher for risking taking on two newbies and giving us the confidence to become bona fide authors.

More than anyone, we want to thank you, our readers, for clicking on a couple of nobodies and sharing your most important asset, your time, with this book. We hope with all our hearts we made it worthwhile.

Much love,
Mary & Donna

ABOUT THE AUTHOR

Mary Stone

Mary Stone lives among the majestic Blue Ridge Mountains of East Tennessee with her two dogs, four cats, a couple of energetic boys, and a very patient husband.

As a young girl, she would go to bed every night, wondering what type of creature might be lurking underneath. It wasn't until she was older that she learned that the creatures she needed to most fear were human.

Today, she creates vivid stories with courageous, strong heroines and dastardly villains. She invites you to enter her world of serial killers, FBI agents but never damsels in distress. Her female characters can handle themselves, going toe-to-toe with any male character, protagonist or antagonist.

Discover more about Mary Stone on her website.
www.authormarystone.com

Donna Berdel

Raised as an Army brat, Donna has lived all over the world, but no place has given her as much peace as the home she lives in with her husband near Myrtle Beach. But while she now keeps her feet planted firmly in the sand, her mind goes back to those cities and the people she met and said goodbye to so many times.

With her two adopted cats fighting for lap space, she brings those she loved (and those she didn't) back as characters in her books. And yes, it's kind of fun to kill off anyone who was mean to her in the past. Mean clerk at the grocery store...beware!

Connect with Mary Online

- facebook.com/authormarystone
- twitter.com/MaryStoneAuthor
- goodreads.com/AuthorMaryStone
- bookbub.com/profile/3378576590
- pinterest.com/MaryStoneAuthor
- instagram.com/marystoneauthor
- tiktok.com/@authormarystone